KIELI

Long Night Beside a Deep Pool

Yukako Kabei

Illustrated by: Shunsuke Taue

D0988970

THE END OF AUTUMN

Owner of the live music bar Adolph Sax

That night, a customer wandered in right before closing. He was a tall, lean redhead with an air of being a little out of it—someone who struck you as lucky not to have fallen prey to the thieves loitering about the neighborhood.

"We're closing up shop for the day, sir," the owner said with a frown.

The man cast his eyes casually around the darkened hall and murmured, "Can I just stay for a little while? I'll go home soon."

" . . . Fine, as long as it's just a little." The man seemed like a traveler who'd come a long way, and he couldn't bring himself to refuse point-blank. "Want a drink?"

"No."

The guy sat down lightly on a chair at the bar, lit a cigarette, and looked at the shabby stage on the far end of the room.

The sign outside might proclaim that this was a "live music bar," but the truth was that ever since he'd been owner, there hadn't been a single actual live performance. Yet the man was gazing at the empty stage as if he saw something there, and straining his ears against the silence of the room as if he were listening to a band he couldn't possibly

It was a shock. The owner had never imagined being visited by another human being who could hear *that*.

"And you are . . . ?"

The man's gaze returned to the owner at this question, and his expression softened slightly. He said he'd come searching for an old friend. That friend had once been a regular at this place; he didn't come around anymore, but the owner could talk about the memories. The redheaded stranger listened to him in almost complete silence, continuing to smoke. He was a man of few words.

As the customer was on the verge of going home, the owner asked him his name. In response, he got a shake of the head and, "Never mind me, but if a girl should come here . . . take care of her." It wasn't as if there were only one girl in the world, but apparently that was the only way the man was capable of talking about her. The owner also wasn't sure what the fellow meant by "take care of her," but considering how unsociable the guy was, it was a pretty sincere thing to say.

"Sure." The owner nodded. "I'll remember that." The man dipped his head a little in reply.

After that night, the man never came around again.

Almost a year had passed by the time the girl arrived.

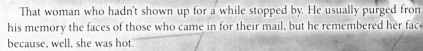

THE BEGINNING OF SUMMER

East South-hairo Port post office worker

That woman who hadn't shown up for a while stopped by. He usually purged from his memory the faces of those who came in for their mail, but he remembered her fac because, well, she was hot.

"Your letter's here."

She must've been waiting for a letter. He thought his words would make her smile, bu instead she gave a look of astonishment, as if that couldn't possibly be right. *Don't peopl usually come to the post office because they get a slip telling them they have mail?*

He took an envelope from the pile of mail whose wait time had elapsed and wa: about to be disposed of, and passed it to her. She opened the sealed envelope on th spot. Watching casually, he saw that it contained one memo and what looked like som old paper money. Perhaps there was an important message inside, because when th

woman looked down at the memo, she froze in place for a while.

"Hey, lady, you're backing up the line," said a put-out elderly woman behind her, elbowing to the front. However, the beautiful woman completely ignored her, as if her existence in this world didn't even register.

"When did this arrive?" she asked.

"If I remember, about two or three months ago . . . say, by the way—" But before he could continue with "Would you like to grab a coffee with me sometime?" she had shoved the letter in her pocket, turned on her heel, and walked away—and now the old woman had plopped herself in front of him, blocking his view.

"Hurry it up, will you?"

"Yes, ma'am." As he apathetically dealt with the mail she'd handed him, he looked out of the corner of his eye for the beautiful woman. She was exiting into the street in front of the building, and a girl who'd been waiting outside with her things was running up to her. She looked to be about fifteen or sixteen. She didn't seem to be the woman's little sister, so she must have been a friend or a maid or something. A mountain of random bulky boxes and bags of clothes, hats, and purses was piled up by the shoulder of the road. He could hear their exchange before the post office's glass door shut:

"Did you get something?"

"Nah. Come on, let's go."

"You still want to shop? Next come with *me* to get what *I* want to buy."

"Sure, but that's pretty unusual for you. What do you want?"

"A radio cord."

" . . . That's the best you can do?"

I hope she comes in here again. He resolved that next time he would screw up his courage and ask her out, but in the end he never saw either of them again.

AND AUTUMN ONCE MORE
Young siblings in the "Witch Hunt Town"

It was a bustling town. In the small country village where she and her little brother were born and raised, everybody would be back at home by this hour, sitting around the dinner table and praying. Did the people of this city not thank God for their daily bread before dinner? She marveled at the adults around her buying junk food at outdoor stalls and cramming it into their mouths on the spot as if that was normal.

"Hey. . ." She'd only taken her eyes off of him for a second, but when she looked to her side, the brother who had been standing there next to her just moments ago had disappeared. *Oh no, if we get split up in such a crowded place . . . !*

"Monica!"

As she turned ashen with fear and searched the crowd with her eyes, she heard a faint, very relaxed voice calling her from far away. Monica was relieved to spot her brother on the other side of the busy street thronging with people, but his next words made her heart flip in her chest.

"Yay, Monica, I caught a witch!"

Now she saw that he was bothering a stranger next to him by hanging on to the hem of her coat. "Stop that, Il!"

So the boy *still* hadn't let go of the idea of finding a witch and catching her. She'd told him so many times that there were no such things as witches!

Yet as Monica hurriedly cut through the crowd to run toward him, she couldn't help feeling that, come to think of it, the girl in her black outfit did look kind of like the "apprentice witches" you read about in fairy tales.

When she'd been her brother's age, she'd still believed, too. Not in the ghastly witches loathed in the Scriptures who had sold themselves to devils, but in the witch girls from fairy tales, who were clumsy and bad at magic and unsociable, but kind of cute when they smiled—she'd thought *they* were sure to exist.

She'd been much younger when she'd believed these innocent things, and naturally the woman standing there was not a witch. She wasn't a witch, but. . .

KIELI

Long Night Beside a Deep Pool

NEW YORK

KIELI: Long Night Beside a Deep Pool
YUKAKO KABEI

Translation: Sarah Alys Lindholm

This book is a work of fiction. Names, characters, places, and incidents are the product of the author's imagination or are used fictitiously. Any resemblance to actual events, locales, or persons, living or dead, is coincidental.

KIELI Vol. 4
© YUKAKO KABEI 2004
Edited by ASCII MEDIA WORKS
First published in Japan in 2004 by
KADOKAWA CORPORATION, Tokyo.
English translation rights arranged with
KADOKAWA CORPORATION, Tokyo,
through Tuttle-Mori Agency, Inc., Tokyo.

English translation © 2011 by Hachette Book Group, Inc.

All rights reserved. In accordance with the U.S. Copyright Act of 1976, the scanning, uploading, and electronic sharing of any part of this book without the permission of the publisher is unlawful piracy and theft of the author's intellectual property. If you would like to use material from the book (other than for review purposes), prior written permission must be obtained by contacting the publisher at permissions@hbgusa.com. Thank you for your support of the author's rights.

Yen On
Hachette Book Group
1290 Avenue of the Americas, New York, NY 10104

www.HachetteBookGroup.com
www.YenPress.com

Yen On is an imprint of Hachette Book Group, Inc. The Yen On name and logo are trademarks of Hachette Book Group, Inc.

First Yen On Edition: April 2011

Library of Congress Cataloging-in-Publication Data
Kabei, Yukako.
  Long night beside a deep pool / Yukako Kabei ; [illustrated by Shunsuke Taue ; translation by Sarah Alys Lindholm]. — 1st Yen Press ed.
    p. cm. — (Kieli ; [v. 4])
  ISBN 978-0-7595-2932-8
[1. Fantasy.]   I. Taue, Shunsuke, ill.   II. Lindholm, Sarah Alys.   III. Title.
  PZ7.K1142Lon 2011
  [Fic]—dc22

2010032696

10 9 8 7 6 5 4 3 2

OPM

Printed in the United States of America

THE STORY OF A CERTAIN CLEANER
AND CORPSE ON A WINTER MORNING

The cleaner found the corpse on a winter morning when the town's hazy air was frozen through. He was listening with one ear to the static-filled music coming from the portable radio on his belt, picking up the garbage along the town walls, and the first comment that popped into his head was the foolish thought that it was a very corpse-like corpse.

After squatting down and looking at it for a while, he took his stiff, cold hands from his cleaning implements and rummaged through the dead person's things. In addition to a few small bills more than half-dyed a brownish red, which were stuck into the pocket of his work pants, the man carried only a few solitary cigarettes and a cheap lighter. It was an impersonal corpse with nothing but a few coldly impersonal things.

"Boy, he was hard up!" the cleaner grumbled, tucking the bills into his own pocket.

But then, completely disregarding his own actions of just a second ago, he murmured, "Poor guy...this is just cruel." It wasn't hypocrisy or an attempt at vindication; the words tumbled out of his mouth straight from the heart, and at the sound of them, even he was surprised to find that he had such a conscience.

Hugging his knees and curling up against the cold, he looked anew at the corpse lying at his feet.

The body was so miserably beat up all over that the cleaner could hardly tell what kind of injuries could have reduced him to such a sorry state, or even where exactly he was wounded. If this had been nighttime, he would surely have mistaken the man for garbage and set about cleaning him away.

His face was a horrible sight, too — half crushed with a

wound that was sort of a bored hole, perhaps from a bullet. But the left side of it was still hanging on, if just barely, and peering at it, the cleaner thought the man seemed still young.

This foolish young punk had wasted the long life ahead of him on something stupid. He must've let someone tempt him into a shady line of work...Hmm, come to think of it, it was just about time for the early morning public broadcast. If this was part of a known incident, there might be a report on it.

When the cleaner turned the dial on the portable radio at his waist to check, he heard a hoarse voice so faint he almost mistook it for part of the static; but no, it had definitely made a claim on his hearing—

"Don't..."

The cleaner's hand froze.

Moving only his eyes, he nervously let his gaze slide from the radio to the corpse.

With his bloody right cheek still pressed to the ground, the corpse moved his thin lips slightly. No sound came out. After all, half his mouth was gone, and most likely his tongue and vocal cords weren't in any shape to be used.

And yet for some reason the cleaner thought he had heard him speak.

"Don't change it..."

His jaw dropping blankly, eyes still glued to the corpse, the cleaner half-unconsciously turned the dial back to the original channel with jerky, marionette-like movements.

The channel's sound quality was so bad that if you didn't know better, you'd only recognize it as noise. But if you listened closely, you could hear the comfortable, low-key sound of slightly distorted string instruments mingled in with the noise and the morning air.

This clandestine music program was broadcast daily from a guerrilla radio station located God only knew where. It was what they called "antiestablishment music," the kind regulated by the Church, and naturally if he'd listened to it in broad daylight in the middle of town, he'd have been surrounded by Church Soldiers before he could blink. Getting to play it as his background music without having to worry about being observed was the lone, secret perk of this cold, low-paying, humdrum early-morning job that otherwise inspired absolutely no will to work at all.

"You like this?" he asked experimentally. The man's single eye remained closed. His one good cheek assumed a sort of relieved expression, almost like that of a kid who'd fallen asleep listening to a "once-upon-a-time" story, and he fell still once more.

The cleaner was a little disappointed not to get an answer. Then, "Oh!" The startle reflex finally kicked in, and he sprang to his feet as if bitten. "W-Wait there! I'll go get you some water!"

Whether the man could drink the water in his current state, and more fundamentally why he was even breathing in said state, not to mention the fact that the cleaner had what little money the man had owned in his pocket and would therefore actually be better off if the man stayed dead — at the moment, all those thoughts were the furthest things from his mind. Spurred on by some impulse, he took off running so hurriedly he almost fell. There was running water at the toolhouse a few blocks away. Was there anything he could *put* the water in…?

That was when he heard the sounds of many metallic footsteps behind him.

Thief's instinct sent him diving reflexively into the shadow of a nearby building. When he gingerly stuck out his head to look, he saw five or six people in white clerical robes ooze out of the morning mist. The way they blended in almost perfectly with the milk-white town wall standing behind them made them seem hardly there at all, yet at the same time the group had an intimidating air.

Church Soldiers…

One of the men in clerical robes began to look as though he would turn his way, so the cleaner clung to the wall and stopped breathing. Noticing that sounds, however faint, were still coming from the radio at his waist, he switched off the power in a panic.

After waiting a while, he sneaked another look and saw that the group in clerical garb had surrounded the man curled up at the bottom of the wall and were all looking down at him so impassively that it was as if they wore identical masks. After some muttering in dull voices, one of them carelessly tossed the man over his shoulder like some not-very-important piece of luggage. From his white-robed shoulder, the back of the man's head hung down like that of a floppy doll, but as proof that he was no doll, large drops of black-red blood dripped down his hair.

As if all that had happened was that they now had one more thing to carry, the group in clerical garb unconcernedly re-formed their ranks and disappeared, melting into the morning mist. The cleaner watched them from the shadow of the wall, breathing silently, until they were completely out of sight.

The whole scene was such a milk-white haze that he could barely make out the details, and the farther away they got, the less real it all seemed. The rust-colored blood staining the man's hair was the one image that remained burned vividly into his vision to the last.

Looking back on it later, he was sure that must have been a procession of the dead heading for the other world.

Common sense said it was impossible for that corpse to have moved in the first place, and from then on the cleaner sincerely believed that he had accidentally witnessed the dead taking a new member of their ranks off into oblivion.

CHAPTER 1

"ONCE UPON A TIME, A WITCH WAS IN A TOWN."

Internally she heaved long, deep sighs, and quelled the periodic pounding of her heart. She mustn't let anything show on her face. This was that sort of game.

"Nobody's folding, are they?" asked the dealer, and she and the rest of the people surrounding the table shook their heads in silent agreement. "All right, let's see them, then."

Following the dealer's command, they showed their hands one by one. Everyone else seemed fairly confident, yet not quite calm. She quickly surveyed their cards. A federation army flush, three of a kind (weapons dealers), two pairs (bishop's staff and exile), and four of a kind (snipers). Sighs of dismay and victorious whistles filled the room.

"What about you, little lady?" asked the man to her right, the one who held four of a kind. If she held something worth less than four of a kind, he would win this hand.

She glanced at him out of the corner of her eye without betraying any expression on her face and then finally allowed herself to crack a small smile. As her opponents looked on doubtfully, she spread her own cards on the table.

One shepherd, then two...three...four...

...Five.

Their eyes widened in shock as they stared at the cards. "Impossible," breathed one of them. "Is she crazy?" breathed another.

The shepherd card was the weakest one in the deck, nothing better than a pain in the butt that weakened your hand further the more of them you had. However, when you collected five of them, it spelled revolution, and neatly flipped the value of all the cards in the game.

"I'll be taking this, then."

As she collected the money tossed in the center of the table, this time her internal sigh was one of relief.

Leaving the gambling parlor behind her, Kieli cut her way quickly through the crowd on the dark nighttime street without once looking back. When she turned at the first corner and entered a quiet little alley, she came to an abrupt stop. She took a big, slow breath and finally let herself sigh out loud without restraint, leaning against a cold concrete wall.

"I did it..."

She'd been nervous, imagining that maybe nobody would play with her because they'd all think she was just a kid, or that if she won, a bunch of scary-looking people would block her from going home, but fortunately, she'd managed to escape with her life and a decent amount of money.

Kieli heard an impressed male voice coming from below her chin. *"Wow, you sure surprised me. I never guessed you had a talent for cards."* When she looked down, the same little old radio as always was hanging from its cord around her neck.

"I've got a ways to go yet."

She wasn't being modest or anything; the person who'd greatly influenced Kieli in the realm of cards was much better at it, and had a much more perfect poker face...though every once in a very long while, he also chose the strangest moments to make silly mistakes.

...*I did it*, she told herself again, a little proudly. But then she almost immediately felt empty.

"Okay, let's meet up with Beatrix." Kieli forcibly shook off the mood and lightly pushed herself off the wall.

"Where is that woman, anyway?"

"She said she had some kind of 'preparations,'" the girl replied, heading back to the large street from which she'd come.

"Oh, there you are," came a voice from the corner, around which someone's face was peeking out.

Kieli gulped and stood still, wondering if he'd overheard her conversation with the radio.

"Ah, I'm glad I caught up with you."

She dimly remembered the face of the man casually walking into the alley toward her. He was young, apparently a traveler, and had been at the same table as her in the gambling parlor.

"I mean, I'd been wanting to talk to you, but you left so fast."

"Did you want something…?" she asked, looking up at him with her head down and taking half a step back. The man raised both arms above his head in a dramatic gesture of surrender.

"Hey, now, you don't have to look so scared. I just wondered if you'd go to dinner with me, that's —" Suddenly he broke off, eyes widening in surprise. "Wait, are you by any chance really young? How old are you?"

"…I'm sixteen," Kieli answered stiffly. *Boy, this guy's cheeky.*

"Sixteen?!" he screeched. "Hmm, sixteen…that's kind of borderline…" He covered his mouth with one hand and started mumbling to himself with a conflicted look on his face. "She looked a little older to me before, though...maybe because she made a strong impression..."

"Um, if you don't want anything with me, would you mind letting me through?" Kieli glared up at him, frowning (*What does he mean by "borderline"?*), and stepped forward again as if to chase him out of the alley. He took a step back, looking intimidated, so she was inwardly relieved; but then the very next moment hands grabbed her shoulders and held her in place.

"Wait, now. We might as well at least have dinner."

"Please let me go —"

"Lay off, jerk!" an angry voice cut in abruptly, and at the same time Kieli felt the air around the radio swelling up.

"No, Corporal, don't!" she shouted at once. He broke off his shock-wave attack at the last moment, and a little leftover burst of air leaked from the speaker.

Oh no...She quickly hugged the radio to her chest and shot a glance at the man in front of her.

He was looking around for the owner of the voice, one hand still on her shoulder. "What? Who was that?"

Stupid Corporal, you've got such a short temper, she grumbled inwardly. Just as she braced her foot against the asphalt and prepared to launch herself at the man, knock him aside, and run away, they both heard something rolling up to them from behind the man with a great clattering noise.

The man looked back over his shoulder and immediately let out a yelp, turning back toward her as if he was about to start running at her, so Kieli reflexively leapt aside to flatten herself against the wall of the nearest building. Just then, a giant rectangular object struck the man in the back right before her eyes, and he fell forward theatrically, planting his face square into the asphalt.

The thing that had come rolling toward them was a large trunk attached to a wheeled cart, and when it sent the man flying, it changed trajectory, listed violently, and then toppled over onto his back as if to finish him off.

Oh dear. Back still flattened to the wall, Kieli looked down on the man at her feet not unsympathetically.

"Ouch! What the hell…?" He crawled unsteadily out from under the trunk, holding a hand to his scraped face. With a hateful expression, he turned around and opened his mouth to say "You bastard! What are you —"

However, he cut off his complaint midsentence and stood gaping in shock.

Kieli raised her head and followed the direction of the man's gaze, then instinctively cowered back a little with equal shock.

The figure of a person stood haughtily between the tall concrete walls that formed the entrance to the alley, hands on hips. The streetlights on the main drag backlit the figure so that it stood out against the sky as a looming shadow, and in the middle of its face a pair of perfectly circular, opaque glasses gleamed grotesquely like the compound eyes of a huge insect.

"Haven't you ever heard that famous saying from the mother-planet philosopher that goes, 'Women hate obstinate men'?" came a woman's crisp voice from the spectacled shadow. "You can tell she's not into you. Hurry up and get lost."

"Hey, it's got nothing to do with you. You show up in that weird getup and —"

"What, couldn't you hear me?"

The spectacled figure advanced a step, the heel of her boot echoing loudly against the pavement, and the man swallowed his protest, intimidated.

"Can you understand the national language? Are your ears properly connected to your brain? If you want, I can crack open that thin-looking skull of yours and connect them for you. I've always wanted to try performing a surgery."

The shadow took another step forward, and the man scooted backward with an audible gulp, still sitting on his rear.

"I'll tell you one more time, since you obviously need me to. If you still can't hear me, I really will have to open up your head…" The low tones of the woman's voice echoed dangerously in the dim alley, and light reflected harshly off her opaque glasses.

"Hurry. Up. And. Get —"

"Shit!" Before she could finish, the man sprang to his feet and made a break for the exit on the other side of the alley before he had even fully regained his feet.

"Oh, you're done, just like that? If you're going to hit on someone, have more guts about it!" Her blatantly bored-sounding taunt chased after the man as he disappeared between the concrete buildings.

"What a wimp. All I did was threaten him a little." She snorted, her glasses directed toward the spot he'd just vacated.

The radio retorted in an exasperated voice, *"I got the feeling he actually ran away because of your outfit."*

Privately agreeing, Kieli left the shelter of the wall and took a second look at the outfit of the woman before her. Her trade-

mark long blond hair was completely hidden away under the scarf on her head, the collar of her detective-style trench coat reached her jawline, and to top it all off, half her face was obscured by round glasses thick as the bottoms of two milk bottles — no matter how you looked at it, this person was definitely suspicious. If Kieli didn't already know her, even she would want to have as little to do with her as possible.

"What's with that outfit?"

"Isn't it perfect?" the woman replied, for some reason puffing out her chest proudly.

"I'm not sure that's how I'd put it..."

This costume must have been what she'd meant by "preparations." Kieli could understand that it must be for hiding her face on the streets of the city, and in that sense it might really be perfect, but in another sense Kieli was not without doubts.

Unable to decide how to respond, she merely stared back blankly. Beatrix seemed to lose interest, and summarily ended the conversation with, "Well, whatever. Anyway, more importantly, I hope you made money."

"Yeah, I made some." Enough for them to pay for the inn tonight and the train fare to their destination, plus a little extra to live on. She'd left the gambling parlor after earning the absolute minimum needed to get them by for the time being. Her cardmaster (not that he'd ever concretely *taught* her anything) believed that there was no need to make a show of yourself by winning too much, but apparently the spectacled woman was completely unimpressed with this philosophy.

Pouting with displeasure, she said, "Why did you stop at

'some'? Win all you can! Honestly, you're so useless." She picked up her fallen trunk as she made this unreasonable complaint, and just as Kieli thought she was about to start walking with it, she pushed it over to Kieli as if that were only right. Kieli unthinkingly took the handle of the cart, and then sighed with mixed feelings. Her only luggage was a medium-sized sports bag that had been stuck onto the cart as an after-thought, and this trunk — which, large as it was to begin with, was bulging alarmingly on both sides and seemed as if its fastenings would pop off any second — was filled entirely with Beatrix's things (mostly clothes).

Thanks to Beatrix's copious impulse buying at the shopping district they'd stopped by in Westerbury, their travel money had run out before their destination. The last of it had been spent on this sorry trunk, and as a result they'd been kicked off the train at a station they'd had no intention of stopping at when the conductor discovered they had no paid tickets, and as a result of *that* Kieli had been forced to gamble in order for them to quickly escape their current state of such destitution that they couldn't even afford a place to sleep for the night.

"Let's go. We have to find a hotel right away, hole up in a room, and get the hell out of this town first thing in the morning. Honestly, this outfit is so annoying! This is why I said this town was the last place I ever wanted to stop! Why did we have to get kicked off the train *here*, of all places?!"

Still wailing, she took off walking at a brisk pace, and Kieli hurried after her dragging the cart. *Maybe the phrase "you reap what you sow" doesn't exist in Beatrix's vocabulary?*

"What does that woman think gives her the right to act so high and mighty all the time?"

"Beats me..."

"Sheesh, why is it that all Undyings have these uncorrectable personality flaws? I think there was some kind of basic problem with the reanimation technology."

Kieli didn't dare respond. Instead, she let her eyes play about the town's nighttime scenery as she dragged the clattering cart behind her.

It was a remote town far from the center of Westerbury parish, but its atmosphere was still heavily influenced by the commercial city of Westerbury, and it was open and friendly, and fairly lively even at night. For a city of its age, it had been rezoned in thoroughly modern style. All the buildings lining the streets were comparatively new, but the bell tower standing in the city square, which she could see in the distance on the other side of the houses' roofs, stood out as the sole aged oddity. Its outline blended against the blue-gray sky, faintly lit up by the city lights.

Perhaps Beatrix had aired all of her grievances to her satisfaction, because when Kieli glanced at the profile of the woman walking diagonally in front of her, she had fallen silent. She was staring fixedly at the top of the bell tower, with a meaningful expression that Kieli couldn't interpret in her blue eyes shielded by the thick glasses.

They were in the outlying Westerbury parish town of Toulouse.

People said that an Undying woman had once lived here, in

this town famous for a minor historical incident called the Witch Hunt or the Great Fire of Toulouse.

And today, decades later, she had unwillingly come back here for the first time.

At the entrance to the city square, bustling with the noise of the people illuminated by its twinkling decorative lights, Kieli and Beatrix stood dumbfounded for several moments.

Lit diagonally from below, the bell tower rose pallidly into the sky directly in front of them, and rows of souvenir shops stood on both sides of the path leading up to it, their signs displaying reliefs of what must have been scenes from the Witch Hunt. They had everything from textiles and jars with the same Witch Hunt designs, to witch pies and witch candies, to people performing readings of the witch's legend on the roadside with exaggerated gestures.

They'd just found a room at an inn near the station. Since it was still early, the innkeeper had recommended that they take a look at the bell tower while they were out having dinner. Beatrix hadn't seemed too thrilled at the idea, but Kieli had pointed out that they might as well since they were here, and so they had come back out into town. (After all, whatever Beatrix might say, Kieli could tell she had the bell tower on her mind.)

And now this was the sight that greeted them.

The church that had burned down in the Great Fire of Toulouse had been rebuilt in a different location, so this place didn't serve as a house of worship anymore. But rumor had spread that the witch's vengeful ghost haunted the bell tower that had miraculously escaped the fire, and opportunistic peddlers had gathered here to take advantage of this by opening sketchy businesses around it. Apparently this square was now developing into a tourist destination for those traveling between Westerbury and North-hairo.

This town might be remote, but it was still more or less a part of the Westerbury region. Perhaps this just meant the Westerbury entrepreneurial spirit had taken root even here.

"It's hard to believe a witch hunt could've happened in such a cheerful town, huh?"

... *Whoops.*

As they began to walk through the clamor created by the shouted solicitations of vendors, the sonorous voices of actors, and the buzzing of the crowd, Kieli must have let herself be swayed by the rosy atmosphere, because she'd let that slip without thinking. Immediately regretting it, she turned to gauge Beatrix's reaction.

"True," the spectacled woman next to her said, nodding. As her expressionless gaze roamed the area, she at least gave no outward sign that Kieli had hurt her feelings. Looking nowhere in particular, she continued in a flat voice, "Negative emotions like fear and suspicion can spread impressively fast. Sometimes a whole town can transform overnight, like they're under mass hypnosis."

"Beatrix...," Kieli began, trying to gloss over her mistake, but in the end she couldn't think of anything to finish that sentence with, and she sank into an uncomfortable silence.

She wasn't sure why she hadn't drawn the connection before, but now she remembered that she'd once been treated like a witch, too, back at the boarding school in Easterbury. She didn't know who'd started it. What began as childish teasing grew oddly concrete as it spread and developed into something that almost seemed real, and so in the first month of the new semester, Kieli's isolation from the other girls at her school became complete.

Now that she considered it, she hadn't thought of those times at all lately. It seemed like something so far in the past it might as well have been before she was born. And yet it had been only two years since she'd been taken away from there. No, perhaps she should say it had been two years *already*...

"Hey, hey, I just thought of something," Beatrix suddenly piped up next to her.

Kieli dragged her attention out of the internal world she'd begun sinking into and returned it to the outside. "Hmm? What?" she asked, a little anxiously.

Looking up at the vendors' signs through those opaque glasses, Beatrix answered, "Don't you think they ought to give me a cut of these profits?"

This ridiculous question was posed so seriously that Kieli's voice slipped into a falsetto squeak. "Huh?!"

"I mean, it's all thanks to the witch that these guys are making money. In other words, thanks to *me*. And yet *I* live such a life of poverty that it's a struggle paying for one night's lodging! What's with that? I should definitely have the right to bleed them for a cut of it."

Beatrix was actually clenching her fists as she insisted on her point. *Our life of poverty is because of her wasteful spending, and I'm the one who struggled to pay for the night's lodging, not her...* Kieli glared at her profile with narrowed eyes, and then looked away with a sigh, unable to summon the energy to respond. *Maybe it was stupid to worry about her feelings.*

Absently, she looked up at the bell tower in front of them.

Rising into the night sky lit diagonally from below with three interplaying lights, it seemed dreamlike, but from a certain point of view sort of eerie, too...

Huh?

Kieli thought she saw a person at the top of the tower, and was momentarily struck with terror.

She strained her eyes to look harder, but the only thing showing through the arched belfry window was the giant old bell hanging from its rope that would never be pulled again, and she didn't see anything particularly strange. Maybe the lights had cast the shadow of a pillar or something onto the bell.

She shrugged it off and turned to Beatrix, who was muttering to herself, undiscouraged, about the best way to bleed the vendors for a cut of their profits. "Beatrix, I'm hungry. I'm going to go buy something."

But just then, a voice suddenly cried out "It's a witch!" and something grabbed Kieli from behind. To a casual observer, Beatrix may have looked defenseless as she prattled on, but she immediately closed her mouth and assumed a ready stance. A moment later Kieli turned around as well, but all she saw behind her were the waves of tourists walking by —

"It's a witch!"

She heard the voice pipe up again from somewhere below her jaw, and looked down. A small boy was holding fast to the hem of her duffle coat. "Um…" Not sure how to respond, Kieli froze up. The boy looked up at her with shining eyes.

"You're a witch, right? Yay, Monica, I caught a witch!"

"Stop that, Il!" A second, strict voice sounded above the boy's excited one. A girl a little older than he was came running up to them from the other side of the crowd. She yanked the boy's hand away from Kieli's coat while Kieli stood there dumbfounded, and the girl forced his head down into a bow, bowing apologetically herself. "I-I'm so sorry my brother was so awfully rude!"

"But she looks exactly like a witch! I've seen 'em in pictures!"

"You dummy, I've told you before that you shouldn't use such terrible words lightly!"

Thus scolded, the boy fell silent. Kieli didn't think what he'd done to her was bad enough to be called *awfully* rude, so now she herself felt at a loss. "Um, no, that's —" She turned to Beatrix for help, but for some reason Beatrix's lips were pursed in displeasure as she readjusted the round glasses that had begun to slip down her nose.

"This just doesn't sit right with me somehow," Beatrix cut in. "Why are *you* the witch? Isn't the Witch of Toulouse supposed to be exquisitely beautiful? And she had a bigger chest than yours, too."

"...You don't have to rub it in." *That* didn't exactly sit right with Kieli. She glared at her strange, spectacled traveling companion. Beatrix seemed completely unruffled by this, uttering an exaggerated sigh and proclaiming, "Honestly, now I'm just tired. Doing this tourist stuff is starting to feel ridiculous, too. I'm going to head back. You can just grab yourself something to eat and come along when you're ready."

"Sheesh, Beatrix..." Watching the woman's back disappear into the crowd after this one-sided dismissal, Kieli saw her old roommate in the completely self-centered attitude and the blond hair that peeked out from under her headscarf. *Oh well,* she thought, and sighed resignedly.

She turned back to the still apologetically cringing girl and her brother, and stooped a little until she was level with them. "Um, you're kind of putting me on the spot...it's okay now, just please stop bowing."

"Okay!" said the boy, immediately brightening.

His sister chided him in a whisper, but finally raised her own head as well. Even so, with her eyes still downcast she apologized again. "Really, I'm very sorry." She cast a sidelong glare at her brother. "He saw how you were dressed, and so he..."

Kieli looked down at herself and let out a little cry of understanding. Long black hair and a black coat. In a corner of her mind, she called up the memory of the witch-ghost rumors the innkeeper had told them about as they'd left.

From what they'd heard, there were apparently multiple witnesses with accounts that corroborated each other. It was a woman with long black hair and a gruesome burn on her face, dressed all in black. From the top of the tower, she spread her arms wide and bitterly called out in a spine-chilling voice, "It's hot...it hurts...I hate them...I must avenge myself on the humans...forget not the follies of the past..." The description was way too specific, and the witch's dialogue was melodramatic and just unbelievable. But doubters who'd decided the "witch" must be a setup to attract customers had investigated the bell tower and found no tricks there, and apparently many found the explanation that it had been a real vengeful ghost after all most convincing.

To Kieli, who knew the Witch of Toulouse — in fact, not only knew her, but was traveling with her — it was naturally unthinkable that she had become a vengeful ghost, and moreover the "all in black" description didn't fit her at all. Just what *was* this "ghost of the witch"...?

"Il, if I've told you once, I've told you a thousand times. There's no witch anymore. She was burned to death a long time ago."

"But her *ghost* is here! Everyone says they've seen it."

"The people here are just exaggerating to get customers. Even though the witch was an evil being, God in His infinite mercy forgave her and brought her to heaven. Remember how we heard that story in church about how even the servant of the Devil was forgiven when he mended his ways?"

"..."

Maybe the girl had noticed Kieli's unconscious frown at her lecture to her brother, because she looked up at her, puzzled. Kieli schooled her expression. "Okay then, I'll be going now," she said, and left the young siblings. She found herself automatically walking quickly, and afraid they would notice, she didn't look back.

She bought a slice of "witch pie," then made her way to the corner of a square removed from the bustling crowd of sight-seers and sat down at the side of the road. When she put the radio next to her and turned it on, there was a brief burst of static, and then scratchy, fast-paced music began to quietly fill the air. It was a forbidden type of music she couldn't listen to in front of other people, but a little noise here should be fine.

"Corporal?" she asked, and after a pause a man's voice answered through the distorted sound of stringed instruments.

"Yeah."

She'd left his power off since entering the busy square earlier, because he'd said he didn't like the clamor. Come to think of it, the atmosphere of the crowd rife with noise and excited emotion was similar to the Colonization Days carnival she'd visited in Easterbury.

It was almost Colonization Days season again this year. *It's that time again, huh,* she thought to herself as she gazed at the streetlamps dotting the square and munched her pie. (Who knew what made it "witch pie"; it was a totally commonplace pie with onions and meat filling.)

It was now autumn, and the night breeze had started to feel chilly. Kieli hunched her shoulders a little inside her coat, pushing away the hair that had fallen annoyingly in her face. "Corporal, you've gotten kind of quiet lately, huh?"

"...Huh? I have?"

"Yeah. You don't complain much anymore."

"I haven't really changed, I don't think...it's probably just that the person I usually complain about is gone."

"Oh, right." Kieli's response was strangely hollow.

After that they both fell quiet. The silence was uncomfortable, so Kieli tried to think of some other topic of conversation. *"Anyway,"* the radio eventually piped up in a somewhat forced tone, perhaps thinking the same thing she was, *"I hope we find out something about your mother."*

She gave a flustered nod, startled to hear him broach the subject she'd just hit upon in her mind before she could voice it. "Oh, uh, yeah. I never guessed that Beatrix was secretly checking into her for me."

"...Well," began the radio, and then paused. *"She's definitely not very open about her feelings."*

It was a year and a half ago now since she'd lived in the town where she'd first met Beatrix—the mining town in West South-hairo with its view of the spaceship ruins. After a certain incident had made them leave, they'd lived bouncing between the towns of East South-hairo together. Beatrix said that even though the South-hairo continent housed a belligerent group called the Watch, the fact that it was not only a huge place but also had few Church Soldiers overall made it the second most convenient place for an Undying to hide, after the metropolis of Westerbury.

Maybe Beatrix had busily dragged Kieli around from place to place on purpose to keep her from getting depressed...but it was probably just that the woman got bored easily.

Their second spring living on the South-hairo continent had

passed, and they were entering its comparatively long summer when their life in East South-hairo came to an abrupt end. Beatrix, who'd shown no sign whatsoever that she was investigating any such thing, told Kieli out of the blue one day that she'd gotten a lead on Kieli's mother through her information network.

The place they needed to go was a town on the parish border between North-hairo and Westerbury. To get from East South-hairo to the North-hairo parish, you had to return to the main continent on a sand ship, then switch to the railroad and go north through Westerbury—even if you powered through the trip with the least amount of time loss by the shortest route, it took close to a month. On a normal journey with breaks incorporated, it could take two or three months.

Beatrix had left the decision to Kieli (though she'd seemed to be in kind of a bad mood for some reason): "Do you want to go? We don't have to if you're not interested. North-hairo is a long ways away." After a bit of hesitation, she'd opted to go. The truth was that at this point, she wasn't really dead set on finding out about her mother or her birth. But all the same, even though she'd adapted to their fairly uneventful daily life, she also felt a constant sense of unnaturalness about it. Plus, more importantly than anything else, their destination was North-hairo parish, which people called the domain of the capital, and Kieli thought that was probably her main reason for wanting to do this.

Spring a year and a half ago, the man who'd taught Kieli cards had left South-hairo for the capital. Or at least, she thought he had. That's what she'd been told.

She hadn't heard anything from him since.

A year and a half. Summer and fall and winter and spring and summer had passed, and now fall was half over again.

Before she knew it, her birthday had come around again and she'd turned sixteen, and the hair she hadn't cut had grown halfway down her back. She was two years older and somewhat taller than the fourteen-year-old girl she'd been the winter she left boarding school in Easterbury, but she thought that in some indefinable way she might've reverted to the girl she'd been then.

Also, she was back to wearing a black duffle coat just as she had then (though she still sure didn't feel like wearing a skirt, so now she was in shorts and boots).

One day she'd just looked down and noticed that she'd started dressing this way for some reason.

Maybe she was hoping against hope. Maybe she was thinking that just like that day at the end of her fourteenth autumn when she'd run into him at the Easterbury train station, he might...

...*I'm an idiot.*

Deciding not to dwell on it anymore, Kieli stuffed the rest of the pie in her mouth, picked up the radio, and stood up, opening her mouth to say "Let's go" in a pointlessly flustered voice, as if trying to talk her way out of something. However, it came out in a muffled "Lessngo" sort of a way.

As she brushed off the hem of her coat, she looked at her all-black outfit that seemed to wish to sink into the darkness of the surrounding night, and she remembered the siblings from earlier. She felt guilty for having run away from them like that, exasperated at herself for still being such a child.

But she was sure God had no intention of gently calling the souls of the Undying to heaven. Plus, if it were true that the souls of all those who believed in God were promptly carried off to heaven, then why were there ghosts bound to this earth even after their deaths, suffering?

It's hot....

Kieli quickly gulped down the food in her mouth. "What's wrong, Corporal?"

"What do you mean?"

"Well, just now, you —" Kieli began, then broke off and cast darting eyes around the area. There was some kind of commotion in the crowd on the street leading up to the tower. They'd been noisy for a while, of course, but now the commotion had become feverish and agitated.

When she jogged back there and stuck her head out into the street from between two souvenir stalls, it looked as if some kind of argument had broken out; there was a mass of people thronging in one corner of the road.

"Just now there was a black-haired woman in the tower, and she was glaring at me!" The man's insistent voice and the jeers of those who said "There's nothing there!" whizzed back and forth through the air.

Kieli came to a stop behind the ring of curious onlookers, watching the fight from a distance. Some of them were peering into the belfry, searching for something, and Kieli looked up at the top of the tower, too, over the heads of the crowd, but as one might expect, she saw no one there.

She saw no one, but...

"Corporal, there's *someone in that tower*, isn't there?" she murmured without taking her eyes off it.

"*Kieli,*" he warned her in a soft whisper.

Kieli frowned lightly. "I know. I won't poke my nose in," she replied, a little peevishly, and tore her eyes away from the tower. She wouldn't go poking her nose into things that might be dangerous just out of curiosity; the Corporal had admonished her about it very strictly—no, that wasn't the reason, it was because she wasn't a child anymore. Yes, that was it.

She turned her back on both the distant bell tower and the nearby crowd, but before she left, she half-turned toward them one more time.

She still didn't see a person in the belfry, but she was aware of someone's unwavering gaze piercing her in silent appeal. Its owner must have known that Kieli could see things.

Even after she'd spun around and started walking, she could still feel that gaze on her back. But its owner just observed her without trying to say anything.

...*I won't stick my nose in*, Kieli whispered in her heart. It was less a rejection of the being in the tower and more a perverse obstinacy directed at herself.

But if they have some business with me, they can just come to me.

She no longer had a sense of heat or a sense of pain; it was just uncomfortable how tight the skin of her cheek was, so she rubbed it, and the burned-raw skin peeled off and stuck to her palms.

The area was wreathed in flame and smoke and the night's darkness, and through the roaring of the wind fanning the fire, she could hear the people's screams and cries. Smoke filled her throat and she couldn't breathe, so she couldn't even call for help.

Somehow the feelings of suffering and fear seemed far away now, too.

Her consciousness fading, the girl looked down at the flame that leapt onto the hem of her black maid's uniform as if it had nothing to do with her, and began to think in tones of self-ridicule, *Why did things turn out this way?*

"The woman who's been living at Mr. Haller's estate is an Undying"—though she'd been the one to spark that rumor, she'd meant no harm at all; in fact, she'd actually been itching to brag, and ended up confessing everything to a friend in town even as she warned that it must be kept absolutely secret. "The lady I'm serving is actually a witch. So she'll stay that young and beautiful forever, without ever aging a day."

After that, things happened astonishingly quickly. The rumor spread in no time, as if the entire town had been infected in a mass outbreak of some bacteria, and the witch at Mr. Haller's estate was captured and thrown into a dungeon underneath the bell tower, sentenced to burn at the stake. But after the fire took the witch's beautiful golden hair, it spread with the same speed as the rumors, raging viciously all over the town.

I don't want to die yet...

She tried to stand up, but she no longer had the strength left even to lift her own head. The arms that she'd managed to move just moments ago wouldn't cooperate anymore either.

There was one last thing she absolutely had to do, but it looked as if that was going to be impossible. As she watched the fire spread over her skirt, a blurred darkness steadily encroached on her vision.

"...So..."

She wanted to at least say it here and now, so she summoned up what strength she had left to squeeze sound out of her throat, but she wasn't sure whether she'd managed to get out the whole sentence.

With her cheek on her pillow, Kieli lay in bed with her eyes open and stared at a fixed point in the dim blue-gray darkness of the room.

She was in a hotel bedroom. On the other side of the closed curtains was the night sky, a shade darker than the dimness of this room. A strong wind beat against the windowpane.

In front of the window stood an unmoving human form. Rather than blending into the night, the black maid-style apron dress she wore strangely emitted a hazy, dark light. Everything from her neck up disappeared into the darkness, so Kieli couldn't see her face, but she could tell the girl was staring right back at her.

Kieli spoke to her silently. *Well, look at that. You really did come to me.*

The form drew closer. Her footsteps made no sound, but for some reason there was a clear sense of something dragging across the floor.

"Hey! Kieli—" The radio's voice broke in from somewhere outside Kieli's field of vision. *"Kieli, run!"*

Lying unmoving on the bed as the girl's form approached, Kieli steadily returned the gaze she couldn't see in the darkness. Perhaps she actually couldn't move, but she hadn't tried to, so she didn't know.

"Kieli, come on! What are you doing?!"

She heard the Corporal's shock wave shoot off in the wrong direction and hit the wall. She remembered leaving the radio on the side table, but which way had it been facing? *I might have left it facing in a weird direction.*

The girl in the maid uniform was right in front of her now. She didn't stop walking, but she didn't bump into Kieli either; she slipped into a position overlapping Kieli's body, and then disappeared—

It felt as if her field of vision went mushy for an instant.

A few seconds later, Kieli slowly sat up in bed. The radio was still annoyingly crying out all kinds of things like *"No, hey, stop, snap out of it,"* but she ignored it as she picked up her coat and left the room.

"I know it was somewhere around here...ah, here we go."

Her murmured voice bounced off the walls of the spiral staircase, filling the air with unfamiliar echoes. Her fingertips had found a lamp as she trailed them along the wall; she lit it now, feeling impressed that it was even still there. A yellow light gradually flickered on, illuminating the old stone wall and a small area around itself.

She touched her hand to the cold stone and confirmed by touch the places here and there that had been burned.

The bell tower was closed to the public and could be viewed only from the outside. She'd waited until midnight to sneak in so that there would be no one around. It had miraculously survived the Great Fire, but that was all that could be said for it; it had become quite crumbly, and the building itself was old anyway, so it was pretty dangerous to be inside. She cautiously held onto the wall as she looked around her. Her vision was horribly distorted, and she realized that she was still wearing her soda-bottle glasses even though there was no danger of anyone seeing her in a place like this.

"... Well, excuse me. I'm not wearing this lame getup for the fun of it, you know," she grumbled to no one in particular, sliding the glasses off and putting them in the breast pocket of her trench coat. She left her scarf on, since it also protected her from the cold, and looked around once again.

It was a cramped, claustrophobic space. The only things there were the stone walls, a low ceiling, small doors with barred observation windows, marks showing where keys had once hung on the walls, and a narrow spiral staircase that vanished into the darkness of the floor above.

The concept of an underground dungeon beneath a church bell tower was a disquieting one, but as she understood it, these spaces had originally been not prison cells, but chambers where the devout had sequestered themselves to offer up deep prayers.

I feel surprisingly blasé about this…

She'd wondered how she'd feel when she returned here — would she feel nostalgic, or would her hatred deepen? — but to her relief, her conclusion was that no particular emotion welled up within her at the sight.

Taking the lamp from its slot on the wall, she tried holding it up to one of the barred windows so that she could look into the cell. Other than the simple washstand she could see in one corner of the small room, there was nothing left there, and the floor was covered in a thick layer of dust and ash. She was pretty sure that at the time there had also been a paltry little bed.

The sight of that hard, small, simple bed without the slightest bit of comfort to it, and of herself lying sulkily in it all those years ago, appeared hazily before her eyes like a lamp lit in the darkness. That other Beatrix grumbled and cursed at the wall ("And here I'd finally found a place where I didn't have to work, I could wear nice clothes, and I could live a good life…damn it, I want a bath, and a smoke…"). Then she flipped over in bed with a sigh, feeling empty-hearted. She raised her head when she sensed a presence approaching, and saw someone peeking in at her through the observation window in the door.

It was a raven-haired girl in a black maid's uniform. Beatrix felt as if she'd seen her before, but she was a plain girl, and there were lots of servants at Haller's estate, so frankly she'd never taken any notice of her as an individual.

"What do you want?" she spat curtly.

The girl ducked her head in surprise, and said, "Um, I brought you food…" She disappeared momentarily from the window, and then slid a tray of bread and stew under the door.

"…Who told you to bring this?" Who would bring food to someone about to be executed, anyway?

"No one."

Beatrix furrowed her brows at that. "No one?"

"That's right…um…" When her face appeared in the observation window again, she was cowering in such fear it was unnatural. "I…I…" The girl seemed to want to say something, but every time she started to, she just clammed right back up again, which had Beatrix irritated in no time. She no longer had the patience or the reason to be an adult about how she dealt with people in this town.

"I don't want it. And I would hate to find poison in it or anything. Just take it and go home."

"Poison?!"

"Listen, my mood is shot to hell right now. Would you please leave?"

Beatrix didn't suppose she'd die just from a little poison (she didn't really know since she'd never *been* poisoned; it might make her feel bad enough to wish she were dead); she simply used this as an excuse to chase the girl off. When she flipped over in the narrow bed and turned her back to her visitor, she could sense the tray on the floor being withdrawn after a short pause, and then hesitant footsteps echoed off the walls, disappearing up the stairs.

After that, there were no more visitors until the group of dopey-looking townsmen came to cart her off to the stake in the square.

The sight of herself sulking in bed facing the wall melted gradually into the darkness, and the scene returned to that of an empty cell with nothing but a broken washstand covered in ash and dust.

It wasn't as if this was a memory she was particularly attached to; she simply remembered that yes, she'd had a conversation like that in this cell toward the end. Yet when she thought about it, it was true that out of all the villagers who'd completely reversed their attitudes and started treating her like a monster as soon as they found out she was an Undying, that servant girl was the only one who'd come and spoken to her like a normal person at the end. (It was totally not normal to bring an Undying food! Was she stupid?) And that was after even the head of the Haller family, who'd sheltered her until then, had given up reasoning with all the townspeople lost to mass hysteria; when they pressed him, he'd turned her over without a fight.

After the Great Fire of Toulouse, he'd died in an epidemic or some such thing, and the Haller family no longer existed in this town. Half of Beatrix thought it served him right. The other half sympathetically thought that he'd been a very unlucky man. As for what had happened to the servants, she assumed that some had been caught up in the fire and that some were still living in the area, but either way she didn't have any particular memory of them.

She'd deliberately avoided Toulouse up until now, not just because her face was known here, but even more importantly because she'd been afraid that it would bring back painful memories. But as it turned out, the incident was no more to this place now than a piece of history to be used as a consumer attraction, and it felt no more significant to her either. To her surprise, the old wounds she'd thought would bring her fresh pain were completely healed over.

I have to admit, this is a letdown. I suppose I'm not the type to obsess over the past…

The face of a certain someone she wished would take a page from her book in that department floated into her mind. Thanks to his troublesome personality, she'd been forced to take on the baggage called "Kieli"…but, well, looking back on their time together now, it didn't seem too bad.

Having someone around who didn't reject her existence might actually be kind of nice.

Not that I'll ever tell her that.

Mentally sticking out her tongue, Beatrix broke off that train of thought and left the dungeon with its faint burnt smell and slight patina of memories.

She climbed the spiral staircase narrowly enclosed by stone walls, her footsteps echoing quietly. When she brandished her lamp at the top of the stairs, the iron door leading to the surface came into view framed by two gently curving walls. It was open just a sliver. A fierce wind raging on the other side made the heavy iron door tremble.

The moment she pushed the door open and stuck her head outside, the wind caught her scarf and set it flapping. "Whoa!"

In Toulouse, the winds were strong at night. Because an intricate network of high rock ledges stood to the west of the town, winds from the west beat against each other on their way through the cliffs and whipped themselves into fierce whirlwinds before they came into town. On the flipside, when morning came, gentle breezes blew in from the flat eastern wilderness to caress the roofs of the houses.

The Great Fire had happened on a night just like this one.

Fumbling a little in the wind and darkness, Beatrix snapped the bolt back into place. It wasn't as if she'd come here to do anything in particular, but as she stepped away from the door she felt as if the end result had been that she'd wasted time and effort on something pointless.

After a few steps she paused and looked up at the tower jutting up against the night sky, holding her scarf to keep it from blowing away.

Still, she did feel that coming here had made her feel better about things somehow. *I suppose it would be praising Kieli too much to say this is thanks to her. But then again, if I weren't traveling with her like this, I probably never would have come here again.*

"Time to go back," she murmured to herself, and pivoted lightly on her heel; then she paused questioningly.

There in the central square wrapped in the black of night, she saw a small figure flitting around. Quickly she blew out the lamp, hiding herself against the wall and relying on the faint light of the streetlamps as she peered into the darkness. First the figure crouched down and scrambled around the tower's front gate, and then it suddenly began to circle around to the back, still half stooped over and looking as if it was dragging something.

Because the black hair and black coat blended so seamlessly into the darkness, the whiteness of the person's skin stood out starkly, and Beatrix identified her immediately.

That's Kieli! What in the world is she doing…?

She'd gone to bed quickly after returning to the hotel, without talking much, and she'd seemed sound asleep when Beatrix had sneaked out of the room at midnight (the radio had annoyed her with questions about where she was going, so she'd turned it to face the wall, from which position it had bad-mouthed her with increasing vehemence).

"Ki—" Beatrix readily began to call out to her, but at that exact moment the girl lifted her head as if to look around. When Beatrix saw the face peeking out from between strands of that tousled black hair, she instinctively fell silent, flattened herself against the wall, and stilled her breath.

The girl looked back down again without incident and disappeared behind the tower, still stooping as she dragged something behind her.

Plastered against the wall, Beatrix followed her with her eyes and grimaced. *Blech. What's that?*

Who knew what trouble Kieli had gotten herself into now, but overlapping the girl's white face, she'd seen the slightly off-center face of someone else.

The face of a corpse charred almost beyond all recognition, its hideously burned skin half melted off.

Dragging the large tin can she'd punched a hole in with both hands, she walked around the wall from the front of the bell tower to the back. The side of the can made a harsh noise as it scraped against the ground, and a black liquid leaked out. The nauseating smell of stale oil filled the air.

The can was empty by the time she'd gone halfway around the tower, and when she casually let it go, it rolled along the ground at her feet with a cheap clatter. The remaining dregs of oil spilled out and spattered their stains across the ash-black ground.

She stood by the wall and took a lighter out of the pocket of the duffle coat, bringing it close to the end of the torch she'd wrapped with cloth. With a crackle, its flame flared up for an instant before her eyes, then immediately jumped to the cloth she'd stained with oil. The torch began to blaze with an amber glow in the dark square, and heat and tiny sparks rained down on the face of the girl as she looked on in silence.

Burn her to death!

She could hear someone's voice sounding in her ears. *Hurry and burn her to death! Burn her very bones to ash! Or else she'll come back to life!* Accompanying the provocative, half-crazed cries, she saw the scene of that day unfolding within the torch's flame. There were the townspeople surrounding the stake constructed in the central square, brandishing their fists and looking possessed. But the next moment, cries of distress rose up not from the person bound to the stake, but from the townsfolk. Fanned by the strong winds, the fire they had stoked to burn harder and fiercer leapt through the square, attacking the crowd in the blink of an eye and devouring them with tongues of flame.

She could see herself, too, darting this way and that, stuck smack-dab in the middle of the crowd frantically running about. Walls enveloped in black smoke crumbled in front of their eyes, blocking their escape, and flame jumped to the hem of her maid's uniform. She hurriedly tried to put it out, but beating it with her hands had no effect, and her arms and legs glowed bright red like heated iron; her skin peeled off; her bones melted —

The girl snapped back to her senses with a gasp and surveyed her body.

The duffle coat wasn't burning. Neither were the arms inside it, or the legs below it. Lively sparks popped up from the tip of the torch she still held, but that was all.

She sighed and lifted her eyes to gaze at the torch's flame again. It was still just a little fire now, but when she dropped it to the ground, it would be fanned by the wind and blaze throughout the town in no time, and then whirling tongues of flame would engulf everything.

Just like they did that day.

Tonight, she would recreate the Great Fire with her own hands. All these people who'd forgotten the tragedy their own foolishness had wrought back then, who actually *used* it to make merry in front of the tower ... Since simple threats hadn't sufficed, she needed to teach them a lesson with a real nightmare.

The hand that held the torch was trembling slightly. Her heartbeat quickened.

It's okay. You have to do this. The girl rallied her quailing emotions, forcibly reminding herself that she hadn't had hands or a heart in a very long time; this trembling and pounding belonged to the owner of this body, not to her.

She returned the lighter she'd been gripping to the pocket of the jacket and gripped the torch in both hands. Slowly, she lowered it to the oil-stained ground. When she let go, everything would begin, and then everything would very rapidly end —

"What are you doing?"

She whirled around, startled at the voice interrupting her thoughts. A person appeared out of the shadow of the bell tower.

"Who are you…?"

The girl stiffened, partly at the suspicious look of this woman wearing a scarf low over her eyes in the pitch-darkness, but mostly intimidated by her sharp air. Still, she thrust the torch in front of her and threatened for all she was worth. "D-Don't come any closer!"

"Get out of her body right now," the woman ordered menacingly, taking a step toward her. Still holding the torch high, the girl took an equal step backward.

"If you come near me, I'll light the fire for real! Th-This girl will get caught up in it and die, too. So stay away from —"

"Kieli." The woman raised her eyebrows crossly and called the *other* girl's name. "I know you can hear me."

"Wh-What are you —"

"You're still conscious, aren't you, Kieli?"

"What?" the girl squeaked, utterly surprised. "Y-You're lying!" Reflexively she raised the torch above her head and began to bring it down toward the ground, as if she were driving off something within her, but then someone else's will took over her muscles and stopped her arms. "No! Why...?" *How can she interfere with me?!* In her confusion, she swooped the torch around randomly but the other person's will got in her way and she could manage only stiff, awkward movements. "No! Don't come out!"

She resisted with all her might, and a spark flew from the torch she brandished to the cuff of her coat. A sensation that by rights she should have lost long ago shot along the back of her hand. "Hot!"

That instant, in the back of her mind she saw the skin of that hand peel off and the arm begin to melt, dripping like candy.

"No!" The girl waved her arms about wildly, though even she didn't know whether she was trying to put out the fire or shoo away the illusion. However, the burnt smell only spread, and her efforts failed to extinguish the flames.

"Idiot! What are you doing?"

"Stay away from me!" Seeing the woman run toward her and sensing she was about to be overpowered, her panic increased; when she struck the woman's face with the torch, she was appalled at her own actions. Her aggressor's scarf was consumed in seconds!

Unfazed, the woman merely ripped off the scarf and threw it onto a patch of ground unstained by oil. Then she grabbed the girl's sleeve and, with total disregard for her own burning palms, beat out the fire there bare-handed.

"Ah..."

As the woman ended her performance by putting out the

torch with the heel of her boot, the girl numbly collapsed to the ground. Sitting on her backside in a daze, she looked up at the woman standing before her.

The abandoned scarf revealed a pale profile that was beyond lovely despite the minor burns. Lit by the remaining flames at her feet, her hip-length golden hair shone with a burning radiance as it streamed in the winds of Toulouse.

There was no comparison between this woman and herself, who had played a fake. Hers were the very features of the Witch of Toulouse —

Sighing aloud, the girl cursed her own foolishness. *Why didn't I notice until now? I admired her so much; I can't believe I didn't realize she'd come back.*

"Kieli." Done extinguishing the fire, the witch cast her a harsh look from the corner of her eye. "Chase her out. I'm fully aware you can do it, Kieli."

At this, the girl's shoulders jumped. She tensed her whole body, refusing to turn it over. *I don't want to give it up yet. Please, just a little longer…*

Maybe the body's owner had heeded her wish; this time, she didn't interfere.

"What are you thinking, you idiot?" The witch's expression turned sharply severe, and she stepped forward with her boot as if to put pressure on her. "If you're not going to do it, *I'll* drive her out of there, by force if I have to."

"W-Wait, please, I…," the girl broke in, but then she hesitated and trailed off midsentence. *No, I have to say this now, since I've been given the time. Since I couldn't say it to her directly back then.*

Her mind made up, the girl threw herself to the ground before the witch's boots.

"It was my fault! It was me who told the townspeople about you! And because of that, horrible things…"

"What are you talking about?" came the witch's dubious voice from above her head. The girl continued, kneeling with her forehead practically touching the ground where the ashes of the scarf lay. "I've always wanted to apologize. They did such cruel things to you because of me…I'm sorry. I'm sorry. I'm sorry…" Guilt, and yet also relief that she'd finally been able to say it, filled her heart. Her sobbing echoed in the darkness. The tears steaming down her cheeks stained the ground in countless places with smaller, more transparent marks than the oil had made.

After a while the witch, who had been standing there silently, crouched down with the toes of her boots pointing toward the girl. "…I see, so you're the one who came to my cell that day."

The girl nodded wordlessly, blubbering.

"Did you burn to death in the fire?"

Nod.

There were a few seconds' pause before she heard the witch's voice again. "…What are you, stupid? Have you been unable to pass on this whole time because of *that*? Of course I knew one of the servants had let the secret slip. Even if you hadn't said anything, someone would have leaked it eventually. Where do you get off acting like some tragic heroine all by yourself?"

The girl looked up, somewhat embarrassed by this ruthless speech, only to find the witch squatting and hugging her knees like a child, peering into her face — wearing a characteristic slightly mischievous smile, like when she'd come to the estate for the first time, like when the girl had first seen her and thought she was adorable.

"As you can see, I'm doing fine. *You* had a much harder time of it. You died suffering, all burned like that, right?"

She cast her eyes downward and shook her head. "I...I don't mind! This is my punishment...!"

"I'm telling you, that's what's stupid," the witch replied bluntly. "Come on, it doesn't matter now. I'm not bothered by a little thing like that anymore. It's actually more of a burden to have you forever worrying about it...honestly, I don't know why so many of the people around me have such troublesome personalities."

There was an exasperated sigh, and a soft, gentle hand stroked her head.

A voice echoed in her mind.

It's all right now, isn't it? You suffered for a long time. I'm sure you must be tired... It's all right now...

"...Yes...."

She felt her consciousness slowly melting away, as if she were being enveloped in a soft light and purified.

Whispering her thanks to the other consciousness that spoke to her from within her mind, the girl returned the body to its rightful owner, as was only right.

The scenery filling the train window was an endless, boring, sand-colored sky and a gently sloping wilderness that carried the soft eastern winds to Toulouse. The train sped along the wilderness tracks, spouting a long stream of smoke the same color as the sky and painting the scenery an even more monotonous hue.

Once they exited the city of Toulouse, the tracks bent north-northeast and headed at last for the border between the Westerbury and North-hairo parishes.

"You're unbelievable — you're unbelievable — you're unbelievable — you're unbelievable —"

That same line was still being repeated over and over again. Kieli had already heard it thousands of times since this morning. She slouched in her seat and seriously wondered why human ears had no lids. Rebukes continued to pour from the speaker of the radio she'd placed by the window, which had no way of knowing how she was feeling. It seemed the radio had been raging around in its own radio way and fallen off the side table, because when she'd awoken in the morning it had been lying facedown on the floor spewing curses and static.

Apparently it'd been purely Kieli's imagination that he'd grown quiet lately.

"Why would you do something so reckless?!"

"I got this feeling it'd work out okay somehow…"

"Oh, I see, 'okay somehow'… It's not okay at all!"

At his loud cry of anger, Kieli hastily reached over to turn the volume down, but apparently the radio had realized its error, and it broke off in a fit of coughing. Kieli thought the lecture was over, but this naive expectation was promptly dispelled as it merely continued in a somewhat modulated voice.

"*You'd better never do that again. Got that? Swear it to me.*"

"Uh...uh-huh..."

"*What, you're not going to tell me you have some kind of problem with that?*"

"...No."

"*Listen, we're lucky that this time it just happened to be a ghost who meekly left by herself; if she'd been a normal spirit there's no TELLING what could've happened. Dead people want to drag others along with them. It's their nature. It doesn't matter whether the spirit wishes for that consciously or not; it's just the way things work...*"

She'd heard that hundreds of times already today, too.

Kieli did feel a certain guilt for having worried him, but even she was sick of this tirade, which seemed likely to go on until the next station if she was unlucky. She let it flow in one ear and out the other, glancing at the seat across from her own.

Beatrix was glaring unhappily at the scenery with one elbow propped against the window. Apparently the reason she'd been scowling as if she hated the whole world since this morning was not the burns on her face and hands, which had healed to the point where you'd notice them only if you looked for them, but rather the fact that a lock of her precious hair was burnt. The right cuff of Kieli's coat was rather charred, too, and there was a large adhesive bandage on the back of her hand that covered a slight burn.

"How could you tell?"

Without moving from her position, cheek leaning against her hand, Beatrix glanced her way and responded with a question. "Tell what?"

"That I was conscious."

Maybe the ghost's ego had been weak; though everything had been hazy as a dream, Kieli had technically been conscious even while possessed. The moment she'd been released she'd fainted, and when she'd opened her eyes, she'd been lying on her hotel bed and her burn had been treated.

"'How'? I can't believe you..." Beatrix said with a sigh, thoroughly disgruntled. "Because you put the lighter back in your pocket instead of tossing it away."

"Oh...!" Kieli found this convincing. She felt for the lighter through her coat. It was important to her, so after the girl had lit the torch, her will had automatically exerted itself to put it back in her pocket, and that had been how she'd noticed that she could interfere with the girl's ghost.

"Honestly, everybody just gives me trouble," Beatrix spat irritably, and returned her gaze to the scenery. Watching her face with its faint traces of the burns, Kieli abruptly realized something. She'd never once shown the lighter to Beatrix, and it had never come up in conversation — how long had Beatrix known?

She remembered the sensation of Beatrix's hand at the end, felt through the ghost of the girl. Maybe that hand clumsily stroking her hair even as the woman complained that she must be an idiot hadn't been meant just for the other girl, but also for her. It was just a "maybe," though.

The conversation died, and Kieli propped her own elbow against the window, casually directing her eyes outside.

The scenery barely changed at all even though they were going quite fast. On the other side of the long stream of sand-colored gas, the sky and the earth came together to form the hazy horizon line. Although they were still just faint, low shadows beyond the horizon at this point, at the far north end of the continent the contours of the rocky mountain range that sprawled from one end of the world to the other like a rampart were coming into view.

Again feeling a small but heartfelt guilt for worrying them, Kieli murmured "Sorry…" in a voice that both Beatrix and the radio could hear, but that didn't sound intended for either of them.

CHAPTER 2

THE STATION CHIEF AND THE DOG WAIT IN VAIN

She woke up from a dream.

Half-sitting up from her seat in alarm, she cast her eyes about. She was in a long, narrow train car that shook rhythmically. From the speaker of the radio placed by the window, she could hear up-tempo music playing at low volume, and outside the window, the vast, boring scenery of sand-colored afternoon sky and wilderness streamed gently by.

When she looked diagonally across from her spot in their set of facing seats, a young man with copper-colored hair and sloppily crossed legs was smoking and watching her suspiciously. "What's that for?"

He probably meant something like, *What's that weird behavior for?* but he'd completely abbreviated his sentence. It was his usual curt way of talking.

"Oh…I had a scary dream…" she began, and then choked up. Everything was like it always was, but for some reason she was horribly relieved, and the words stopped up in her throat came tumbling out all at once. "I woke up from a nap and our seats were full of people I didn't know, and the radio was gone, too. I thought that was weird, so I looked in the other seats around us and even in the other train cars, but I couldn't find anybody anywhere, so when I saw the conductor from behind I tried to ask him, but when he turned around he was a faceless white doll, and then I realized all the other passengers were smooth, featureless dolls, and they all stood up with jerky, creaking joints and swarmed off the train. They pressed me into the line, too, and I got herded off the train, but there was no platform there and I fell into a deep pool wrapped in cloudy white mist—"

He listened with a bored expression as Kieli explained as much of her dream as she could remember, and then he quirked the corner of his mouth with the cigarette still between his lips to give her an equally bored response. "Huh? What's with that?"

"Hey, I was scared!"

"Okay, okay." He obviously wasn't taking her seriously, and Kieli pouted. Recrossing his legs with a long-suffering look, he blew out his smoke in a different direction and mumbled grudgingly, "I'm right here, aren't I?"

She woke up from a dream.

Half-sitting up from her seat in alarm, she cast her eyes about. She was in a long, narrow train car, the radio was placed by the window, and outside the afternoon wilderness streamed by.

When she looked across from her spot in their set of facing seats, a beautiful woman with long, braided golden hair was watching her suspiciously. "What's that weird behavior for?"

"Oh...," Kieli began, and then cut herself off. "Ahaha, I was just daydreaming..." She plunked back down on her seat with a weak laugh. Beatrix blinked; she seemed to have been in the process of lighting a cigarette, but for some reason she abandoned the project.

A man's voice could be heard from the radio's speaker, blending in with the faint, staticky music. *"This was our first long trip in a while. We'll get there by tomorrow, right?"*

"Yeah," answered Beatrix unenthusiastically.

"What will we do when we get there?"

"We'll make contact with the informant. Everything else depends on what he says."

"You're sure a slapdash planner."

"Now that's just rude. I've thought this through plenty. The first thing I'm doing is selling you off to get money for the trip back."

Kieli had been leaning against the window letting their conversation wash over her, but she couldn't let that one pass. "You can't do that," she broke in, lifting her head.

"Why not?" Beatrix shot back, pouting. She ought to know very well why not, but apparently she'd been pretty serious. "You'd better make some more money at cards, then."

"There's no guarantee I can win every time, you know. Besides, weren't you the one who told me people should earn their keep themselves?" she argued with a scowl.

Beatrix puffed out her chest with bizarre self-importance. "That's not it; this is a legitimate information fee." The reply made no sense to Kieli.

"Information fee?"

"You found a clue about your mother thanks to me, right? So as repayment for the information, you'll bear my travel expenses. It's only natural that information be provided at a cost. Nothing in this world is free, you know. That's what the adult world is like. And you're fifteen now, so get used to it."

"I'm sixteen," Kieli corrected, deciding to let the first part of Beatrix's reasoning slide. The other woman looked startled, as if she was just now realizing this.

"When did you turn sixteen?"

That reaction was just too much. At a loss for words, she merely gazed back at her companion in silence.

My sixteenth birthday was half a year ago already... Kieli hadn't said anything about it at the time, and it wasn't as if she particularly wanted Beatrix to remember her birthday, but they'd met right after she'd turned fifteen and it had been more than a year since then, so even the slightest consideration should've told her that Kieli was a year older.

Then, gazing at this woman who looked exactly the same as she had a year and a half ago except for her ever-changing hairstyle, she thought maybe she shouldn't have expected anything else. To an Undying whose life was basically eternal, at the most a year and a half must seem the same as a month and a half seemed to Kieli.

"Kieliiii, are you mad at me?" Maybe Kieli's sudden silence had made Beatrix uncomfortable; now she was peering at Kieli and speaking in a cajoling voice, as if to gauge her mood. "Come on. I promise I'll celebrate your birthday next year, okay?"

"Whatever; I know you'll just forget."

"I won't forget this time! I swear! Do you want anything?"

"No, I don't want anything, so stop buying yourself stuff, too..."

If she had to pick, she'd actually rather Beatrix do something about her sense of finance than her sense of time. When she glaringly explained this, Beatrix responded in tones of wounded shock. "Why should I? I'm not causing you any trouble."

"You're causing her LOTS of trouble!" interjected the radio.

Silently agreeing, Kieli glanced overhead. A giant trunk that was probably seriously pushing its weight capacity had been forcibly stuffed onto the shelf there, causing it to creak along with the movements of the train.

And one trunk's worth of impulse buys was comparatively tame. There had been an occasion when she'd returned from work and found Beatrix at home for once, only to behold that their entire apartment had basically been turned into a walk-in closet. With scarcely a sidelong glance at Kieli's shock-frozen form in the doorway, Beatrix stood gaily holding up different outfits in front of herself in the mirror — but she always grew sick of clothes soon after she bought them and sent them off to a charity, saying she'd never wear them again; so maybe she was actually performing a useful service for society after all.

However, when she'd made this comment to Beatrix herself, Beatrix had flown into a rage and the whole thing had turned into a serious incident: she'd shipped off the radio along with the clothes, and Kieli'd had a devil of a time getting it back. Come to think of it, that had been right around her birthday.

Something occurred to Kieli. "Don't you have a birthday, Beatrix?"

"You just blithely ask the most unpleasant questions…" The woman had given her an earful about birthdays before, and sure enough, her cheek twitched in sudden irritation. "I have no idea. Maybe I did once, but it's long forgotten now."

"Then let's make it a day in the middle of summer," Kieli continued lightly, unruffled. Beatrix blinked dubiously.

"Why?"

"Just go with it. I'll celebrate your birthday next year, too." Even if she didn't visibly age, she could at least have a birthday.

And after all, Kieli's birthday wasn't an exact birth date, either.

Beatrix froze momentarily, cheek still slightly tense, and then jerked her gaze to the side. "Don't go deciding these things on your own. It's a nuisance."

"Oh ho, you're a little happy, aren't you?" the radio piped up teasingly. Beatrix glared.

"If you want an anniversary to celebrate, too, I'll make today that glorious day."

"What?"

"The anniversary of your death." At which point she grabbed the radio in one hand, stood up, and began to open the window with a clatter.

"Stop it, you idiot!"

"That's what a *radio* gets for talking all high and mighty to a *person*."

"Hey, I'm a person, too!"

Watching the horseplay of woman and machine from her detached position, Kieli let a wry little laugh slip out of her throat.

Next year, and the year after that, Beatrix was sure to be the same beautiful, impulsive, catlike woman. And the radio might be a little more beat up, but he'd still be the same short-tempered, nagging, rock-loving Corporal.

There was a part of her that simply accepted that on her next birthday, and the birthday after that, she'd probably still be living this same life with Beatrix and the radio as if it were the natural thing to do. She leaned her head against the window and let her gaze return outside, thinking perhaps that would be okay.

"…Huh?"

At some point the train had decelerated, and the scenery was flowing more gently. As Kieli cocked her head in confusion, it slowed down even more, to the point where someone walking could probably catch up with it. Eventually the train came to a slightly jerky halt right there in the middle of nowhere.

Kieli exchanged glances with Beatrix (who was dangling the radio like a punching bag and knocking it around). "We stopped. I wonder what's wrong?"

"Don't ask me."

She could hear commotion coming from the other seats in the car, too. But of course they couldn't very well get off the train, so they just sat there waiting. After a while the conductor appeared from the rear door of the car. Facing the passengers' suspicious gazes all alone, he flinched a little, and then apologized for the inconvenience and began explaining the situation.

"Is it okay if I go outside for a little while?"

After being emphatically warned not to miss the train's departure, Kieli obtained permission to go. She jumped lightly down from the step onto the track.

When she'd walked along the train a ways crunching the

rail bed gravel underfoot, she found a weather-beaten platform up ahead, on one corner of which she could see a shabby
station house. The train had come to a stop just past the tip of
the platform, and a little in front of the engine car the conductor and engineers in their railway uniforms, plus a few passengers who had come to help, were outside working to clear
rubble from the track.

It didn't look as if there was much she could do to help,
so watching them work out of the corner of her eye, she
scrambled up a pile of broken concrete onto the side of the
platform.

She'd heard that it had been a long time since this station fell
into disuse. There had once been a town behind it, but since it
was an inconvenient distance from the city centers of Westerbury and North-hairo and had no industry to speak of, it had
increasingly lost population, and apparently now there was no
one living there anymore. Because part of the crumbling platform had broken off onto the track and blocked their way, the
train was stopped temporarily while they worked to clear it.

The winds of the continent's interior wilderness blew past
the ruined platform, feeling frozen on skin used to the South-
hairo climate. Kieli shoved both hands into her coat and pat-
tered a little farther along its deserted surface.

Her fingers brushed the lighter, and she gripped it tightly
inside her pocket, as had become her constant habit. When
she'd awoken alone in the bed of the three-wheeled truck that
day a year and a half ago, she'd found it lying in a corner. It
certainly wasn't an expensive one; in fact, to be frank it was
totally cheap, the kind of thing he probably hadn't even cared

that he'd lost. But it had been waiting in Kieli's pocket ever since for the day it would be returned to its owner.

… *The day to return it might never come.*

Lately she'd started to think that way. She could easily imagine that just like the lighter, he'd soon stopped caring that she wasn't with him anymore either. To him a year and a half probably wasn't much, but to Kieli it had been more than enough time to begin having those thoughts.

A much stronger gust of wind sent her hair and the hem of her coat flapping. Her hair was annoying her these days, and she was thinking of cutting it once this business with her mother was over. It was about time to throw away the lighter, too. *After all, it's just a cheap thing,* she griped internally to no one in particular.

When she shook her head lightly to get the hair out of her eyes, she caught sight of something brownish standing stock-still at the edge of the gray-white platform. "Huh?"

At first it looked like something someone had left lying around, but no, it wasn't "lying" there; it was *sitting* there.

A medium-sized dog with a shaggy red-brown coat.

He was sitting next to the remains of the ticket gate and facing straight ahead at the tracks, but perhaps he noticed Kieli; he turned his head toward her and gave a single audible wag of his tail.

She was pleased at receiving what seemed to be a greeting, but then he immediately turned away and faced forward again with an uninterested expression.

"Sorry, he's not a very friendly dog. He's only affectionate with his master," a voice behind her said abruptly. When she turned to look, an old man was standing in the ticket gate. She had no idea how long he'd been there. His deep green coat and cap were the uniform of the Westerbury area railroad employees. Fitted on his right arm was an armband trimmed with gold. Though his age and the color of his uniform were different, somehow his air reminded Kieli of a certain conductor she'd met on an Easterbury train.

"Thank you for traveling with us today. I am the station manager here," he intoned, putting a hand to the brim of his cap. It was a rather formal greeting, but then he quickly adopted a casual attitude and continued with an embarrassed smile and a self-conscious slant to his white eyebrows, "Though really, I just became the station manager automatically because I'm the only employee."

"Nice to meet you…" Kieli responded without thinking. She stood there for a while without saying anything else before finally wandering over to the ticket gate, hands still in her pockets. "Is that your dog?"

"No, no. He just comes here every weekend to meet his owner, who works in the city during the week. Most people in this town go to work in the Westerbury commercial district."

"Oh, I see," Kieli answered vaguely, turning her gaze to the red-haired dog who sat small and quiet by the gate. The dog looked back at her for just an instant and gave another wag of its tail, then faced forward again. She drew up to it with a light smile and crouched down next to it, her back against the wall. Squatting like this with her arms around her knees, her eyes were almost on the same level as the dog's. She let her eyes wander around the station. Surely she was seeing the same scenery as he was.

There was the meager platform with its single railroad track. Beyond the rusty, broken-down iron-wire fence spread a wilderness dotted with the occasional shrub.

I wonder how long it's been since workers stopped coming back to this town.

The autumn wind began to sting, and she wrapped the hem of her coat around her legs where they were bare underneath her shorts, propping her chin on her folded knees. It looked as though it would be a while before they finished clearing the tracks.

Suddenly she heard the station manager's laugh above her. When she turned around to look at the ticket gate, he coughed uncomfortably and said, "I'm sorry, I hope you won't take offense. You see, it just looked as if there were *two* dogs there now."

Kieli blinked at this and turned to examine the dog's profile next to her. His dark brown eyes, half-hidden by his shaggy hair, were still trained on the platform as if nothing had happened. It was rude to think of him like this, but with his grubby red-brown hair and his thin frame, he was a very scruffy-looking dog — and yet his attitude was so strangely aloof that she couldn't help laughing a little.

This time, the dog flapped his tail twice against the ground as if in small protest.

"Sorry," she apologized seriously, stifling her laughter. Then, after thinking for a moment, she shifted her crouched body a half-step and leaned her side against him.

There was dust and sand and the stink of dog, and somehow she felt as if she could also feel the warmth of his red-brown fur through the sleeve of her coat. She found herself inexplicably growing a little warmer. Letting the sounds of the wind whistling across the deserted platform and the shouts of encouragement between the railroad workers wash over her, she closed her eyes for a little while.

In a corner of the hushed gray-white platform, a lone black-haired girl in a black coat sat all by herself hugging her knees. (Well, it wasn't that Beatrix couldn't see the scruffy redheaded dog sitting next to her, but she had no interest in getting involved with it, so she deliberately blocked it out — honestly, why did that girl meet some such thing every single place they went?)

Beatrix had been gazing at the platform in front of the train with her cheek plastered to the window, but now she returned her gaze to the interior of the car. "She says she's sixteen," she whispered, scowling. "She's got some nerve. When did *that* happen?"

"I knew all about it. I couldn't say anything, though, because she didn't say anything herself."

"Oh, come on. It's just petty of you, acting like you're the only one who understands things. You're a *radio*." She glared at the machine by the window and pouted. They spoke in low tones, since most of the other passengers remained in their seats while they waited for the train to start up again.

"Actually, it might not sound like it, but I'm pretty grateful to you. You're doing lots of things to take real good care of Kieli."

"Stop that. Are you trying to annoy me? I just figured I could spend a few years with her to kill time, that's all."

"I'm saying even if a few years aren't much more than a 'killing time' type of thing for you or me or that idiot, *they're more than that to her. A year and a half is no small beans when it's only coming out of sixteen years total."*

"…I guess not. She was an ugly-faced brat up until just a while ago, and now suddenly she's sixteen? She's got some nerve." Repeating her earlier comment in a half-impressed, half-verbally-abusing sort of way, she let her gaze slide to the girl sitting on the platform, and thought, *No wonder she gets hit on sometimes,* again in a half-impressed, half-verbally-abusing sort of way.

Sixteen or not, she was still just a kid. But looking at her again with this new information, Beatrix did notice that her limbs had grown long and slender, and her childish look was fading away (though as to whether the girl had turned into a beauty, it was Beatrix's opinion that there was still nothing particularly special about her). It also rather seemed as though she'd been wearing a more mature, calmer expression lately—though perhaps "cold" was more accurate than "mature."

"Maybe I shouldn't have taken her away from South-hairo. She seemed about as cheerful as ever while we were there, but ever since we started traveling, she's been getting that look on her face more."

"Since we're traveling, she probably can't help remembering stuff. Especially on trains."

"…Well, you know," Beatrix sighed, propping her chin on

her arm in the windowsill so that her breath made the glass momentarily fog up, "even I didn't think that idiot would drop so completely out of contact for so long after he left her with me."

"He sent you word once."

"Only once."

"Even so, Kieli'd probably be relieved if you told her. Are you sure you shouldn't say anything?"

"It's not that I *won't* say anything; it's that I *can't* say anything!" she replied, wailing a little without meaning to. Her chin had jerked up from her hand as she spoke. She returned it and sighed again.

Beatrix hadn't told Kieli, but the truth was that the person who'd sent her the clue about Kieli's mother had been the very man for whom *that idiot* was steadily being established as a second name between herself and the radio. When they'd parted a year and a half ago, they'd set up a route of contact through the post office at East South-hairo Port. They'd never decided on a means of contacting each other before, but this time she could use the pretext that she was "looking after" Kieli, so she'd forced him to agree to the plan so that he wouldn't drop completely off the radar. There had been exactly one piece of mail from him via that route.

However, for a combination of unfortunate reasons, it was now difficult for her to honestly tell Kieli about it.

Reason 1: In the beginning she'd gone to check the post office about once a month, but there hadn't been any word from him at all, and eventually Beatrix herself had completely forgotten about it.

Reason 2: When she'd been near the port at the beginning of the summer to go shopping for summer clothes, she'd remembered and finally dropped by the post office again, and a single envelope had arrived for her. The date on its postmark was from the autumn half a year ago, and the place was the border of North-hairo parish. Even assuming it had taken a month or two to deliver because of problems in the postal system, that would still mean she'd left it lying there for several months, and it seemed as if that would make Kieli angry, so Beatrix hadn't been able to tell her.

Reason 3: She knew nothing of what had become of the sender after he'd mailed it. Given his personality, she could safely assume there was no chance he was still in the place he'd mailed it from, and it was also unlikely he'd left any clues about where he'd gone afterward. She thought it would depress Kieli even more to get her hopes up and then not be able to see him.

And Reason 4 was an even bigger problem...

The contents of the envelope in question were a memo with the scribbled phrase "Kieli's mother" and the address of the informant (though there were as many towns on this planet as stars in the sky, he had completely omitted *which* town the address was in and started right off with the street name; fortunately, she'd been able to deduce the town from the postmark, but the man's ability to communicate his intentions was hopelessly inadequate) and a single bill of a type of money that was no longer in use. Presumably this all meant that if Beatrix showed the informant the money as a sort of pass, she'd be able to get some kind of information about Kieli's mother — at least, that's the way Beatrix translated it. It was only just barely comprehensible to her and would have been unintelligible to anyone else.

That was all. He was the type of person who couldn't write a single considerate word explaining where he was and what he was up to, or asking whether Kieli was doing okay.

"...Do you really think anyone could be relieved after seeing something like that?"

"No. I guess it would just make her more dejected..."

"See?"

"That idiot," they cursed simultaneously, after which Beatrix glared at the radio with a look of heartfelt displeasure.

"And anyway, it pisses me off how we're weirdly compatible talking about him like this. You're just a *radio*."

"Well, excuse me. It pisses me off, too."

"This is partly your responsibility for not stopping him, you know!"

"How could I help it? A man has his own circumstances."

"You're not a man! You're a *radio*!" she cried, unintentionally loudly. The passengers in the next seats over darted suspicious sidelong glances at her, and she hastily pretended to be listening to the radio, averting her gaze out the window.

Watching the girl on the platform in the distance, she recalled that morning a year and a half ago.

"I thought she would cry..."

"That is just the kind of girl she is."

"There you go acting like you understand it all again," she began, voice starting to rise again before she forced it back into a soft grumble. "You're just a radio."

"You underestimate her about that stuff, but so does that idiot. She's not the type of girl who cries at times like those."

"Hmph." Beatrix moved her eyes from the platform to glare grumpily out at the wilderness filling the train window. It hardly changed even when the train was running, and now that they were just sitting still, it was boring enough to drive her crazy.

That morning she'd explained the situation to Kieli, whose face showed her worry at waking up in the bed of the three-wheeled truck to find the man who'd been there up until the previous night suddenly gone. Her "explanation" hadn't actually amounted to more than a rapid stream of words along the lines of *Ephraim went to the capital to look for word on Jude; you'd drag him down, so he left you here; I'm going to be taking care of you for a while since there's really no choice, okay?* Afterward she was inwardly anxious as she waited for the reply — Kieli had been listening with her mouth tightly drawn — but after she'd silently digested the situation, the girl merely asked if he would come back once he was finished.

Beatrix had answered, "Probably," with what even she recognized to be a pained expression, and a few moments later, Kieli appeared to accept it all surprisingly readily. "Okay. Then I'll stay with you, if it's not too much trouble." And after that, Kieli had never mentioned the topic again. She was so anticlimactically mature about it that Beatrix had let herself be reassured, figuring it must be okay, but...

Even so, she supposed it had been a year and a half. That man was just too...too...

Too stupid.

Her temples actually started to throb. She frowned and sighed for the umpteenth time.

If there's such a thing as a God on this planet, could He please do something about that idiot and the way his sensitivity is so radically lacking that somehow, even though he means no harm, he can walk out on a girl just turned fifteen and leave her hanging until she's past sixteen and a half?

Whoo-oo...

Hearing a faint whistle on the wind that whipped her hair, Kieli opened her eyes. When she squinted and peered through the sand-colored gas over the tracks, she saw another train pulling up behind their own stopped one.

"Oh, no!"

She was alarmed for a moment, but the workers clearing away the rubble in front of the train didn't seem to notice the new arrival at all, so before long she realized what was happening. The second train ultimately passed harmlessly through the first and slid up to the platform. With an almost unreal screech of friction, as if there were a thin film hanging between Kieli and the noise, the wheels slowly stopped turning, and the train came to a stop right in front of her.

Woof!

The dog beside her barked for the first time, standing up and beginning to wag its tail at the train. Passengers clattered down from the vestibules of each car and walked with slightly tired footsteps past Kieli as she crouched next to the ticket gate and looked up at them. As they cleared the gate, the old station manager saw them off individually with mild-voiced greetings. "Welcome back, good work this week. How's business in Westerbury? Have a good weekend."

After they passed through the gate and out of the train station's rectangular exit, one by one they disappeared from her sight as if melting into the milky-white light outside.

When at last a lone man in his overalls got off the train, the dog leapt up and bounded away from Kieli.

She automatically stood to watch it go, but it didn't cast a single backward glance her way. It danced around its master's legs, winding around them and then pulling away, and when its master bent down to scratch under its chin, it let its ears flop blissfully and stretched its neck as far as it could, trying to bring its nose to his face. When the man began walking, the dog started off with him, running in circles around him. And so the man and the dog filed through the gate and vanished outside the station like all the other passengers.

Fsssshhhhh…

Its passengers safely disembarked, the train slid away from the platform again in a hiss of steam.

All that remained were Kieli, the crumbling platform, the ticket gate, and the station manager in his dark green uniform. The sounds of the wilderness wind and the faint conversation of the workers returned to her ears. Still gazing at the station exit where the passengers and the red-haired dog had disappeared, Kieli stood unmoving by the gate for a while.

"They're lucky...," she whispered without conscious thought, and then averted her eyes and shoved her hands into her pockets, distracting herself. In place of the slight warmth she'd been feeling on one side, she felt the cold sting of the northern autumn wind cut through her coat.

"Are you waiting for someone, too?" The station manager prepared to close up the ticket gate as he asked, his day's work finished.

Kieli answered with a wry smile. Her feelings were complicated. "I guess so... But lately, I've started thinking maybe he won't come back."

"So you can just go see him, then."

"But I don't even know where he is."

"Then you can just go look for him."

He said this casually, as if it was obvious; gazing dazedly at his profile as he worked, she made a vague sort of "I guess so" reply and let her gaze escape to her feet.

She took a few steps backward and leaned her back against the concrete wall of the station.

She'd thought of searching for him so many times.

But then she'd thought that if he had left her behind because she'd drag him down, he might think of her as more of a burden if she found him. Also, if he really wasn't intending to ever come back, it would be scary to seek him out only to confirm that. And, more than anything else, she'd been angry with him this whole time for leaving without saying a single word to her. So if she went to look for him, wouldn't it be kind of like giving in and letting him win?

...And yet even as Kieli told herself this, she was heading toward the capital. *What am I doing?*

She was used to being patient and enduring. She'd done it since she was little. It shouldn't have been so hard for her to just wait until he got back...

Whoo!

This time, the sharp whistle that rang in her eardrums felt very real.

When she looked up, they had finished clearing the tracks without her noticing, and the train was slowly beginning to move. "Oh, no!"

"Kieli! What are you waiting for?!" Beatrix shouted, leaning out of the open window of their passenger car. She pointed to the end of the train and then immediately pulled her head back inside. The train gradually built up speed, pulling past the platform.

"Whoa, this is bad..."

As Kieli broke into a panicked run, the station manager's voice spoke up from behind her. "Miss — I'm glad I got to talk to you. Just eternally waiting all alone for the train like this is boring, you see."

"It was nothing," she said as she ran, only half-turning her head. "Good-bye. Take care." She thought maybe it was weird to say that, but she couldn't think of any other parting words.

"Good-bye. Have a nice trip." The station manager lifted the brim of his dark green cap to her in farewell, and continued with a smile, "I envy you for being able to go on a trip. You aren't like me or that dog; waiting here isn't the only thing you can do."

At those words, Kieli unthinkingly slowed to a stop after a running a few more steps with her head turned, and looked back into the face of the man seeing her off from the ticket gate.

"Kieli, are you planning to stay here?!" called Beatrix.

Startled, she faced front again and chased after the moving train. "Oh! I'm coming!" Beatrix, who had appeared at the rear vestibule, clung to the guardrail and screamed at her.

"If you want to live here forever, I'll gladly leave you behind! You'll have the run of all the empty houses!"

"I said I was coming!" Even as she scolded, Beatrix had reached out a hand, and now she hauled Kieli up as the girl leapt onto the train. When Kieli turned back to look over the guardrail, the train was picking up speed, and the cozy little ticket gate at the corner of the platform was left behind in no time.

Now she could see that the ticket gate had fallen into complete disrepair and was closed off by an iron railing. The faded dark green jacket and cap were merely hung on one wall as if long forgotten, and there was no sign of the station manager there.

I wonder how long he's been waiting there for the train that in the real world won't ever come back. I wonder how long he'll keep on waiting…

The urban district on the other side of the station filled the sky behind the train at first, then faded gradually from view. From a distance, the scattered rooftops of the ruined buildings looked like a thick cluster of gray tombstones.

An abandoned station, and an abandoned town where nobody lived anymore.

Kieli's eyes lit on two figures, one small and one large, standing a ways apart from the town. She gasped. Holding back the hair that flapped in the wind, she squinted at the disappearing townscape.

The larger figure was a man in overalls. The smaller one was the red-haired dog. It sat erect next to its master, seeing off the train by his side.

Kieli leaned over the railing and waved a little. *Bye-bye…*

Looking as aloof from the world as ever, the dog wagged its tail twice as if saying good-bye.

CHAPTER 3

A HARD GIRL WHO DOESN'T CRY

"...He died?"

Her voice as she whispered the words was more blank than anything else. She certainly wasn't upset by the news; she was taking it calmly, but, well, it was just that the idea hadn't occurred to her, so she couldn't quite think how to respond. Or something.

After a moment, she resumed: "Where did you get the info?"

"There's someone in Gate Town who was in contact with him. It was this past winter."

"And?"

"He was carted off by Church Soldiers."

"How do you know he's dead?"

"He was already dead at the time."

"I see," Beatrix responded neutrally, fiddling with the newly bought pack of cigarettes in her hand.

Night had fallen on the shopping district. She leaned against a streetlamp next to the small tobacco stand at the end of the street and absently let her eyes roam the stream of passersby. Travelers with large bags walked quickly by her, probably searching for a place to spend the night.

They were in a border town on the southwest end of North-hairo parish, on the line between it and Westerbury parish; it was also an inn town that housed pilgrims on their way to Gate Town, the literal gateway to the capital at the northern end of North-hairo. "If we go to Gate Town, can we meet with this person who was supposedly in contact with him?" she pursued. Her gaze was still on the road; to an outside observer it would seem as if she were talking to herself.

The man operating the tobacco stand responded in the same

manner, eyes resting on his newspaper with an expression of boredom. "If you want to meet with him, I can try getting in touch with someone who knows where he is...but everything from here on out is gonna cost a separate fee from what your friend paid me."

"...That's fine." Beatrix nodded, glaring at him out of the corner of her eye in silent irritation. The man could have just told her himself without bothering to bring another person into it, but the more well-developed an information peddler's network of allies, the more he tried to give you the runaround between them all and increase his profit margin as much as possible. These informants were shrewd operators.

"I appreciate your business. Okay, come back here in three days. You can pay me then — I'm treating you special 'cause you're such a beautiful lady."

"Thanks," Beatrix replied, wholly unmoved. She pushed up off of the lamppost and melted into the crowd without a backward glance at the tobacco vendor. Lighting a cigarette as she walked, she shoved the rest of the packet into the pocket of her trench coat, then turned up her collar to shut out the cold air of the deepening northern autumn.

North-hairo parish was the turf of the Church headquarters in the capital, and as soon as you entered it, the towns took on a somehow solemn atmosphere; even though Church doctrines didn't technically forbid smoking, there weren't many people here who brazenly walked around doing it on public streets. Some of the people walking by openly frowned at her, but she ignored them as she cut quickly through the crowd.

She eased off the smoking around Kieli, so she should at

least be able to do what she wanted when she was walking around alone. *I mean, I can't do it in front of her; we smoke the same brand. Damn it…*

It was true. She hadn't intentionally set out to match that idiot Ephraim, but she coincidentally happened to prefer the same brand of cigarettes he did. Over time, she'd stopped smoking much while Kieli was watching, not because she was being sensitive to the girl's feelings, but because she didn't want to be sensitive about something so stupid.

He… can't actually be dead, right…?

Putting her hands in her pockets, she idly looked through the trail of smoke at the nighttime cityscape and the backs of the people walking in front of her, turning over the information she'd just received in her mind. Apparently it had been last fall when Ephraim had gotten information on Kieli's mother in this town, left a memo with the informant, and sent that envelope to her in East South-hairo. That jibed with the date on the postmark. And according to the rumors, there had been a fuss that same winter about an intruder in a certain secret facility in the capital. Whatever it was, it had been serious enough to send a large number of security guards into action. Even the informant network didn't seem to have any details about the place other than that it had been constructed with Church funds on the site of an old power plant from the era of the high-level energy civilization and that they were doing something really big there. She assumed it must be the same facility she'd heard about from Ephraim (he hadn't wanted to tell her the details, so she'd forced them out of him), where the man from the ruined spaceship had worked.

From what Beatrix understood, for a while all the informant network could talk about was what the intruder might have found, and a lot of people had gone looking for him in order to buy the information. However, said intruder had dropped off the face of the planet that same day, and no one knew where he was. A while later word spread that a corpse thought to be his had been found in Gate Town bearing a horrible gunshot wound and had been carted off by Church Soldiers. The whole thing had left the information peddlers with the feeling they'd been given the slip, but talk of the whole thing had naturally died down over time.

He'd left this border town for the capital last fall, sneaked into some top-secret facility or whatever there that winter, and then been discovered as a corpse in the town that formed the gateway to the capital — there was no conflict between the course of action she could imagine Ephraim taking and the eyewitness accounts of this person who was supposedly him. It did seem highly probable that the information was trustworthy, but...

She heaved a smoky sigh.

Of course it had always been conceivable that someday one of them would be killed or captured before the other (in fact, it had been so conceivable she hadn't even bothered to specifically imagine it), and she'd never before supposed that she'd feel particularly strongly about his loss even if she did miss him a little, but circumstances were a little different now.

I swear, if you're really dead, I'm going to put a curse on you...

No way in hell did she want to be stuck taking care of Kieli for the rest of her life. The deal was that she'd do it for "a while," so he'd better get his ass back here to pick the girl up.

The information seemed trustworthy...and that was precisely why she wanted it to be wrong.

After looking up at the metal plate attached to the lamppost for a while, Kieli dropped her gaze to the old matches in her palm. She compared the lot number on the plate to the address on the matchbook. "Maybe it's behind here...?"

Right now she was at number 13, 4th Street. The address she was looking for was number 47, 4th Street. A little while ago she'd passed this place and gone all the way to the end of the road, but the building numbers facing this main street only went up to the thirties, and after number 31 they apparently doubled back onto a small backstreet on the other side of an alley before continuing.

The matchbook was a baffling little object. It looked as if it came from a bar or something of that sort, but the logo was scratched and it was hard to make out either the business name or the address—however, the address alone had been traced over by hand with a pen.

They'd pulled into the border station they were headed for before sunset, and Kieli had stuck close to Beatrix, who had grown quiet for some reason since their arrival, as they visited a tobacco stand on a street in the shopping district. It was a perfectly ordinary little stand, and the man running it was both unremarkable and unsociable. Beatrix had handed him an unusual piece of paper money, said a few words, and finally pointed to a particular brand of cigarettes from among the ones on display. The man had given her a pack of them along with an old matchbook that didn't look like something for sale there.

After a quick glance at the back of the matchbook, Beatrix had passed it to her and told her, "I have a little more business here, so you go on ahead to this address."

Kieli didn't get what was going on.

When she stepped into the alley next to number 31 4th Street there were no longer people around her, so she experimentally whispered to the radio. "It's pretty hard to tell what Beatrix is thinking, huh?" Beatrix was usually talkative to the point of being boring, but when it came to this trip she was strangely close-mouthed. Kieli could admit that she was probably a part of the problem for not pursuing the matter too deeply; thanks to a certain someone, she'd gotten used to people who hated explaining things.

"Well, I imagine she's got her reasons."

Kieli sulked a little. It wasn't precisely that she'd expected him to agree with her, but it was a shock to hear him take Beatrix's side like that. Walking with eyes fixed on the exit of the alley, she pouted. "You've been acting kind of weird, too, Corporal. Lately you come to her rescue all the time."

"What kind of immature thing is that to say?"

"That's not what I mean," she shot back angrily. Then she modulated her tone so that she *wouldn't* sound so immature, and continued, "Are you hiding something from me?"

"Wh-What would I be hiding from you?"

"Okay, then, so it's because Beatrix is pretty."

"Well, she is pretty, but…hey, wait a second!" Kieli didn't say anything, but the radio went right on, interrupting himself sharply in a flustered tone. *"That's not it! I was just voicing popular opinion, and it's got nothing to do with what I personally think!"*

She kind of wanted to ask what he *did* think, but she set that aside for now and glared at him with half-veiled eyes. "So are you hiding something from me, then?" she repeated. The speaker only leaked a queer, dry static, and no answer was immediately forthcoming.

"…Corporal, I'm not a kid anymore," she pressed impatiently. "If something's going on —" But then she came out of the alley into the backstreet, and a homeless man by the side of the road shot her a funny look, so she was forced to shut her mouth.

Business on the tobacco stand's street in front of the station had been as booming as you'd expect in an inn town. As she'd moved farther away from the train station, though, the crowd had thinned out so much that the bustle from before seemed like a dream; even the buildings lining the street became deserted-looking, and the distance between the streetlights grew larger and larger. This neighborhood was quite a ways from the station and bore no resemblance whatsoever to the image of an inn town bustling with pilgrims. In the corners of the dim patches of light created by the streetlamps stood piles of garbage, and she could see homeless people burrowed into them to protect themselves from the cold.

Kieli looked up at the address plates on the lampposts and found number 47. She transferred her gaze to the building there. The naked bulb hanging in front of it dully illuminated a small sign: LIVE MUSIC BAR — ADOLPH SAX.

"Live Music Bar…"

Kieli's eyes dropped to the matchbook in her hand. It was too scratched to read the name of the bar, but now that she'd encountered the phrase "live music bar," she could sort of almost make it out.

When she pushed open the heavy metal door, faint warmth, the smell of alcohol, and the strains of some sort of musical instrument leaked out from within. She wondered whether it was a wind instrument. Opening the door a little wider and peeking inside, she saw dim yellowish lights in a room on the other side of a dark, cramped entryway.

It wasn't a very big place. There were some tables set up in a dance-hall-style room with appropriately restrained lighting, but very few customers sat at those tables. Beyond their heads was a small stage that was lit somewhat more brightly than the rest of the room; a sturdy man stuffed into in a dark three-piece suit stood there playing a wind instrument, body hunched over. It was a strangely shaped instrument that she had never seen in her music class at the boarding school.

"Oh, ho, a sax, eh?" the radio whispered, impressed, and Kieli realized that was what it was called.

As she was craning her neck to look around, her eyes met those of a man polishing glasses at the counter on one side of the room. He was in the prime of life and wore a crisp shirt with a stand-up collar and a black vest — he was such a classic bartender that it was actually hard to find any distinguishing traits.

Kieli stiffened, but the bartender's face showed no change in expression; he merely said "Welcome" in a flat voice and looked back down, resuming his polishing of the glasses. The radio beneath her chin derided him for his unfriendliness.

The sax performance onstage went steadily on. Watching it out of the corner of her eye past the heads of the patrons at the tables, she advanced inside with somewhat fearful steps. When she finally stood at the bar, the bartender glanced at her and murmured, polite but distant, "Would you like some soda water or something?"

"Oh, no, it's about this." Kieli hastily drew her left fist out of her coat pocket and uncurled it on the counter. When she showed him the matchbook she'd been clutching, she thought she saw his narrow eyes widen just for an instant. "I was told to take this and come here…"

But the very next moment, he was flatly dismissing her. "That's not one of our matchbooks." Not expecting this sort of response, Kieli fell silent, perplexed. She'd only been instructed to come to this address; she had no idea what to do next.

When she looked down to the radio at her chest for help, a glass was placed on the counter in front of her. Inside the long, thin glass was an amber liquid. Kieli stared in surprise at the long series of tiny bubbles that rose up from the bottom to burst open at the surface of the drink.

"Go ahead," said the bartender's voice above her.

"Um, I don't drink alcohol…"

"It's ginger ale. Try it." As his words became friendlier, his voice seemed to soften as well. At his urging, Kieli sat down on the high bar stool and took the glass with its little rising bubbles in her hand. "Just wait there. It'll start before too long."

And without another word, he silently went back to his polishing.

It'll start? What is "it"? She cocked her head in confusion and looked down at the radio, but it merely released a questioning burst of static as if to express the same thought. Kieli rotated her bar stool forty-five degrees and cast a sidelong look at the room behind her.

A man and woman were chatting pleasantly at a table in the middle of the room, and a little distance away a single man was tilting his glass quietly to his lips; finally, when she turned her eyes to the corner of the hall, there was a lone customer slumped over his table asleep, surrounded by countless empty glasses. Even if she included herself, she could count the bar's patrons on one hand. And considering it was supposed to be a "live music bar," nobody seemed to be paying any particular attention to the performance onstage. The tone of the stooping musician's saxophone was lonely as it echoed through the hall.

It really ought to be more livelier, considering the time of day, but this place was so deserted it looked as though it might go out of business at any moment.

I wonder what Beatrix is doing... Unable to contain her discomfort, she shifted on her stool and faced back toward the counter. When she brought her glass lightly to her mouth, ice cubes clinked against her lips, and a complex taste, sweet and slightly bitter, spread across her tongue along with the faint tingling of the carbonation just beginning to flatten out.

Having nothing else to do, Kieli took her time savoring the glass of soda. Other than the lone instance he poured another round for the couple at the table, the bartender merely polished glasses without a word. The monotonous, medium-tempo sound of the saxophone droned on like a record stuck on repeat, bathing the bar in a languid atmosphere.

She realized something was strange after the couple paid their tab and opened the door to leave, when the man complained to his companion, "'Live music bar,' my butt! They never have a single performance here!"

It felt as if it was coming up on closing time, but Beatrix still hadn't shown up, and Kieli was finally well and truly bored. She was thinking about leaving herself when she heard the man's statement and whirled around in surprise.

The man who'd come alone had already left his money on the table and left, and the only other person in the now-even-darker bar was the drunk snoozing away in his corner. The sax player had vanished from the stage along with the ever-present sound of his instrument.

No, it wasn't that he'd vanished; he'd been invisible to the other customers to begin with.

"It's almost time," said the bartender from behind her. When she turned back to look at him, he was still polishing glasses, even though it looked to Kieli as if there were plenty of other things he could be cleaning up. She blinked and looked back at the rest of the room again.

"Huh...?"

The whole bar looked entirely different than it had just seconds ago, and Kieli doubted her own eyes.

There were suddenly so many people gathered there she could hardly believe it was the same place that had been so deserted before. They were all chatting happily, pleasantly tipsy, and watching the stage bathed in flickering spotlights. It was as if they were waiting for something to begin.

Who are these people...?

The whine of stringed instruments being tuned sounded through the hall, and as if on cue a hush fell over the crowd. Little by little, the stage was gradually illuminated by a blurry light. At first the sounds were nothing a person could call music — just each player in his own world tuning his own instrument. But eventually, even though they didn't seem to give each other any kind of particular signal, the sounds naturally blended together and a medium-tempo performance began.

Half-sitting on her bar stool, Kieli gaped in amazement at the stage over the heads of the enraptured listeners at the tables. There were four people in the band. It was a somewhat unusual combination: two stringed instruments, a drummer, and a saxophone, with one of the instrumentalists doing vocals. All of the musicians were men in their forties wearing dark suits, but they wore their clothes sloppily, their shirts and ties and suspenders slanting at rakish angles, and it looked sort of cool.

Applause rang out from the audience when their short introduction ended. Before that applause was over, they switched to a faster-paced, rollicking number, as if to say "Now the real thing starts." Kieli felt a sense of déjà vu, or more accurately déjà entendu: it was a melody she remembered — and a moment's thought told her exactly why.

"*Ah...*" breathed the radio around her neck in wonder. Yes; this was the radio's favorite music, and Kieli had heard it enough times to be able to hum some of the tunes herself. It was that genre called "rock," banned by the Church and played on unofficial guerrilla stations.

The Corporal's voice was overcome by emotion, and he whispered, enthralled: *"Hey, this is like a dream, being able to hear a live performance by a band like this…I'm so glad to be alive — no, I mean, so glad to be dead…"*

"You're so funny," Kieli giggled quietly. She softly closed her eyes and listened to instruments and the voice filling the hall.

The first song ended, and the listeners applauded again. As Kieli clapped with them hesitantly from the very back of the room (the Corporal only whispered *"Bravo,"* but she was sure he was clapping from within the radio, too), a voice called her by a completely unexpected name.

"Setsuri!"

She halted her hands in surprise and shifted her gaze from the stage across the room to the space in front of her. One of the customers sitting at the tables stood up so quickly he kicked his chair over, staring at her with wide eyes. The people around him turned around at the sound of his voice, too, and Kieli automatically straightened on her stool.

"Setsuri! So you're safe — thank goodness!"

"Where have you been?!"

Before she knew it, not only the man who'd first shouted, but also a whole crowd of people who appeared to be regulars had swarmed around the counter and were peppering her with questions and comments. Kieli shrank in on herself, hugging the radio to her chest, and looked up through her eyelashes at the faces of the people surrounding her.

She spoke up timidly. "Um, Setsuri was my mom…she's dead."

It was only after the words had escaped her mouth that she realized maybe she shouldn't have put it so bluntly. A chill immediately fell over the excited crowd of people. *Yeah, I guess that makes sense,* someone murmured in a horribly dejected voice.

After an interval in which Kieli tried to make herself as small as possible on the bar stool, feeling somehow responsible for the mood, she heard a calm male voice say from behind the crowd, "Hey, you guys, shut up and welcome her here. This is the girl Setsuri left behind." The bar's patrons parted a little to make space, and Kieli saw the man who'd just been playing the sax onstage. He looked somewhat older and more dignified than the other band members. She imagined he was their leader. "You're Kieli, right?"

"...Yes," she said with a nod, still shrinking back, and another round of cheers rose up from the crowd.

"Wait, Kieli, as in that little squirt? Seriously?"

"Whoa, you've sure grown! You look just like Setsuri! Do you remember me?"

"Hey, what about me?"

"Idiot, of course she doesn't remember you, she was too young. How old was she, again?"

A rapid-fire barrage of questions rained down on her, but Kieli could only open and close her mouth silently, unable to answer a single one. "U-Um..."

Behind the swarm of people seething with innocent excitement, the bandmaster quirked the corner of his mouth up in a smile. "Have a good time tonight. We'll make this a concert to remember." Then he went back to the stage, where the rest of the band was standing by for the next number.

The second song was a slower tempo, but it was a catchy, almost funny tune. As the performance began and the bar filled with lively sound again, Kieli succumbed to the fervent invitations of the people around her, and found herself led to a seat at a table in the middle of the front row next to the stage.

Frozen with discomfort at being the focus of discussion, she watched the crowd as its sounds of merriment shot back and forth over her head. People listening to the music and tapping their fingers or heels to the rhythm, people animatedly telling stories about old times with steins or glasses in one hand — when she realized that the words "Setsuri" and "Jude" were appearing frequently in their conversations, Kieli dropped her gaze and whispered "Corporal…"

But the radio appeared completely absorbed in the band's performance, and displayed no reaction whatsoever to the conversation. With a wry mental laugh that was half exasperation, she removed it from where it hung around her neck and placed it on the front edge of the table, so that it could be that much closer to the stage.

"Setsuri worked here for a while. She blew into town one day towing you along with her," said a friendly voice. She turned to look at the customer sitting next to her. It was the man who had first noticed Kieli and raised his voice to greet her. He was chubby and affable-looking. "You don't remember?"

She shook her head, and he nodded as if that was only to be expected. "I wonder how long ago that was? My sense of time has gotten pretty fuzzy… how old are you now?"

"Sixteen and a half."

"Oh, then I guess that was maybe fifteen years ago. Man, it's really been a long time."

The man, currently squinting his eyes as if to remember some long-distant past, was still young; he looked to be in his early twenties at most. He gave a little self-deprecating laugh. "I had a crush on Setsuri, actually. I mean, sure, she had a kid with her, but she was beautiful and she never put on airs, and all us regulars loved her. But then before we knew it, she up and got all friendly with Jude! I don't know what she saw in a straitlaced guy like that. I mean, he was a good guy, but I was much more—"

Somehow the conversation was turning more and more into the complaining of the brokenhearted, and Kieli, who'd been watching his profile as she listened, couldn't help laughing a little.

"I-I'm sorry."

"That's okay," Kieli giggled, then quickly stifled her laughter. But then the man let out an embarrassed chuckle of his own.

"Right, it doesn't matter about me. I'm glad I got to meet you. You really are the spitting image of Setsuri."

"Are we really that alike?" she asked, remembering the image of the mother she'd met on the Sand Ocean. Black hair and black eyes, with a face even Kieli thought was on the plain side. Their physical characteristics might have been similar, but she was pretty sure that she still bore no trace of her mother's most memorable feature: the sort of deep, calm aura she'd projected. What's more, Kieli doubted she'd *ever* have it.

"Yes, you're just like her." The man beside her grinned and then turned back toward the room, pointing at the counter where Kieli had been sitting not too long ago. "See?"

There was a woman at the bar.

She walked briskly around carrying drinks and food, exchanging friendly conversation with the regulars, sometimes pausing to catch her breath and bend an ear to the band's performance. Her long black hair hung behind her in a braid. Her white blouse and simple black apron suited her.

"Mom…"

Body twisted, Kieli half-rose from her chair and then froze in that position, staring at the scene playing out against a background of dimness and accompanied by faint noise.

Her apron-clad mother glanced to the end of the bar and smiled tenderly. Sitting there in the shadows of the already dark bar was a lone regular. His stubbly cheeks and large frame were straight out of her memories from the Sand Ocean. And there was one other person there — sitting quietly and stiffly between the large man's knees, looking bored, was a girl so very, very small and young she could hardly be self-aware yet. But when her mother came close, the girl lifted her face and offered a slightly shy smile.

That's me…

The scene of the happy-looking trio played in the corner of the hall like a faded, scratchy film. With a live band for background music —

"You really seemed like family." The man next to her was watching it, too, with his elbow propped on the backrest of his chair and his cheek in his hand. He gave a nostalgic smile and continued, "Jude was an unsociable guy, but you were real fond of him. Though you sure couldn't tell just from looking at the pair of you…but when me or one of the other guys would try to hold you, you would shake free like all the hounds of hell were after you and run away."

Kieli gave an embarrassed laugh. She could easily believe him. Forcing back the warmth welling up in her eyes, she bit her lip firmly and clenched her fists in the shadow of her coat.

She wouldn't cry yet.

She'd decided. Not yet.

The movielike image steadily faded under the weak lights of the bar, and scraps of the afterimage fizzled apart into particles of noise, eventually melting into the darkness.

Had those images been the memories of the people who once gathered here, memories now burned into the very air . . . ? There was no film playing in that corner of the bar now, but somehow Kieli still felt as if she might be able to see something there, and she stood stock-still beside the table for a while, unable to tear her eyes away.

Behind her, the band had switched to a slow ballad, a little dark but with a subtle warmth to it.

"How long were my mom and I here . . . ?" she asked the man beside her without moving her eyes, still somewhat dazed.

The response was hesitant and unhappy. "Ah, well, you weren't able to stay that long . . ."

Slowly she shifted her gaze, and swept her eyes over the hall with its crowd of excited concertgoers. There were the regulars happily drunk on music and alcohol. And the four members of the band, continuing to play proudly on that shabby stage under the lights.

What she saw was a lively and peaceful bar. But that stuffy atmosphere and smell unique to bars, the suffocating combi-

nation of alcohol stink and cigarette smoke and body heat, and the overflowing raw human energy — those things didn't exist here.

Kieli turned to the man at her side. "You and all these other people…" She hesitated a little, and then finished the question. "How did you die?"

About eighty years ago after the War, when the Church embarked on its campaign of "relief for our impoverished society" and took over the whole planet, acting like rulers as if it were only natural, several forms of music were banned. The variety called "rock," with its lyrics that were vulgar, violent, and impious by Church standards and its venal, noisy twang built around four- and six-stringed instruments and drums, was one of them.

From the Church's point of view, a live music bar where that barbaric music was openly performed was like a guerrilla radio station: a gathering place for heretics who might well plan acts of violence. So naturally as soon as such a place was discovered, Church Soldiers would rush there and thoroughly stamp it out.

It was fifteen years ago now that they had invaded this place.

"The raid was so merciless and thorough it was almost unbelievable. They must've made an example of us to the other bars. They didn't just arrest the employees and the band; they rounded up all of the regular customers, too, and anyone who resisted was killed on the spot."

It was late that night at the Adolph Sax, and the house lights had been turned off. Under the yellowish bar lights that just barely illuminated the counter area, the bartender in the black vest quietly told the story as he polished glasses.

Beatrix murmured a listless sound in response to this reminiscing, watching the thin trail of smoke from the end of her cigarette and leaning on the counter with her chin propped on one hand.

She'd arrived at the bar a bit before closing, but the secret late-night concert had started while she was still trying to think of what to say to Kieli, so she'd stayed leaning against the entranceway listening to the band. It wasn't a type of music she particularly liked, but it had a nostalgic air to it somehow.

By the time the concert had ended at well past midnight and the audience had vanished one by one, returning the place to the deserted quiet of reality, the only humans left in the bar were the bartender, one dead-drunk patron, and a girl sleeping in the corner.

"In the confusion of the raid, we pushed Setsuri and Kieli onto Jude and made him get them out of here. They were our first priority. Jude was hard to convince, but Kieli was so small; someone had to make sure she escaped safely, and besides, if he were arrested and they found out who he was, this would turn into more than just a raid on an illegal music house. We'd be charged with a serious crime, harboring an Undying, and everyone would get killed, even those who otherwise could've lived. The bartender convinced him—half threatened him, really—by telling him 'There are plenty of people here who have no idea about you. Do you want to get them mixed up in this, too?'"

Every so often in his story, the bartender used the word "bartender" referring to someone else. The bartender of this place at the time had been executed along with the bandleader and a few others as the principal offenders. This man running the place now had been one of the band members, and according to him, he'd been released a few years after the incident, come back to the then-deserted building, and quietly opened a new bar under a new name. "See, I was at the bottom of the food chain, just filling in for somebody," he explained self-deprecatingly, "so they didn't prosecute me as a principal offender." His wry smile was somehow wistful, as if he would rather have been executed along with them.

"A little while after I opened up shop, I started to sense people's presences here after closing time. It got livelier as the days went by, and eventually I started hearing familiar music, and I realized my friends had come back. Maybe this is why I survived. To create a place where my friends could live it up again."

"You've got some spiritual sensitivity, huh, Chief?"

The bartender nodded with lowered eyes. "Only a little, though."

Moving her cigarette up and down with her lips, Beatrix studied his face interestedly. It wasn't as if Kieli was the only person with strong spiritual sensitivity that she'd ever met, but it was certainly rare.

"From what I understand, Setsuri had some, too. It showed up even stronger in her daughter, and apparently that's why she took Kieli and left home. She didn't tell us who she was or where she was from, though, so I don't know the details."

"So we still don't know anything about the dad, huh…," Beatrix muttered to herself. She racked her brains trying to come up with an idea. A woman named Setsuri from God only knew where had rolled into this bar with a little kid in tow and started working here, had met a regular customer named Jude (whom the bartender said had also appeared out of nowhere, and was helping out the town's firefighters), had run away when the Church Soldiers raided the place, and had never been heard from again. Putting that together with what she'd heard from Ephraim about the events on the Sand Ocean, she imagined they'd probably failed in their attempt to escape directly to Westerbury, and were trying to sneak into that city by taking a detour and going from the far-east port through Easterbury.

At any rate, it was clear now that Jude wasn't Kieli's father. Beatrix and Ephraim had both figured he probably wasn't when they'd had their conversation about it. According to Ephraim, that one-hundred-percent ascetic, super-straitlaced man wasn't fool enough to forget the position he was in and irresponsibly father some child. (When she'd half-teasingly replied that *he* was a fool, so he might be capable of it, he'd regarded her with a meek look that might have been a joke or might have been serious. What a total idiot.)

So who the hell *was* Kieli's father?

At this point, a part of her felt as if that might not really matter anymore. The girl must have more important things to her right now than her origins or her past.

When she removed her chin from her hand and turned her head to survey the room, the blind stinking drunk patron was drooling all over his corner table in his sleep. Beatrix wondered how long he'd been there. Ignoring him, she shifted her gaze to the depths of the room.

A single light remained on in the darkness, illuminating the deserted stage and the profile of the girl breathing softly in her sleep in front of it, cheek pressed to the table. The stage was buried in dust and showed no sign of having been used in recent memory. There was also no trace of the applauding audience that had filled the room only a short time ago.

In place of the band's live music, the radio on the table enveloped the girl's immediate vicinity with the faint, staticky sounds of stringed instruments.

A sigh escaped Beatrix. *Sheesh, now what?*

She'd thought that if they came to this town, maybe they could get a line on Ephraim's whereabouts. Then she could show Kieli the memo, explain the circumstances, and make her decide on their next course of action. But now…

The only information she could claim to have found out was the worst possible kind: the news that he might be dead.

Beatrix was starting to get seriously pissed off, somehow. When you really thought about it, why should she have to strain her nerves so much over Kieli and that idiot? Whether he was alive or dead, it was a sure bet that it had never occurred to a single neuron in his tiny little brain how much *she* was fretting.

She turned back to the counter and abruptly said, "Give me a drink, Chief. Something really strong." The bartender, polishing his glasses as always, gave her an annoyed frown.

"We closed a long time ago."

"Come on, don't be such a square. Booze!" She screwed the butt of her cigarette into the ashtray, grumbling about her misfortunes. As soon as the glass of amber liquid was placed in front of her, she grabbed it and tossed it down straight.

"Hey, take the time to actually savor that stuff; it's expensive!" the bartender grumbled with a sigh, still holding the ice he'd had no time to put in her glass.

He showed his face to the guard outside the detention center and was waved through the gate. "Master Julius," said the warden of the solitary confinement unit, who had come to the entrance to greet him as he came inside.

He gave a brief grunt in reply and followed the warden down the hallway lined with iron-barred communal cells. Hearing the two sets of footsteps echoing eerily off the bleak concrete walls and ceiling, a few of the prisoners lying lifelessly in the corners of the cells turned annoyed stares at them, but before long they looked away as if it was all just too much work, and flipped over to face the walls.

Glancing out of the corner of his eye at their display of slovenliness — these prisoners almost seemed to suck the will to live out of him as well — Julius wrinkled his face at the smell of rust and filth permeating the building. No matter how many times he visited this place, he couldn't get used to the stench. Not that it mattered, since it certainly wasn't something he *wanted* to get used to.

"Still, you didn't have to take the trouble to come here all the way from the capital..."

"It's fine; school just let out for the post-finals vacation. You say he can talk now?"

"Yes, for what it's worth."

They left the communal cell area, passed through a bolted door with a grated window on the other side of the hallway, went down a steep, narrow staircase, and came out into the area where the solitary cells stood with their iron doors with the tiny barred windows. Because not as many of them were occupied, meaning fewer people, the stink of filth was less oppressive, and Julius breathed a sigh of relief. However, the smell of rust was horribly accentuated here. The cold damp that soaked through the walls and flooring clung to his skin, and he turned up the collar of the greatcoat he wore over his priest's clothing.

The warden stopped in front of one particular cell at the most remote end of the hallway, checking its interior through the little window before turning back to him. "He can speak, but I don't know if you'll be able to get an actual conversation out of him."

"That's fine. I'll try talking to him. Open up."

"But wouldn't that be dangerous?" the man asked timidly.

Julius frowned and turned to look at him. "Can he move that much already?"

"Well, no, I don't think he can move yet...," said the warden evasively, seemingly trying to judge Julius's mood before continuing. Then he stated the obvious. "But you know, he is an Undying."

"So?"

"You never know when he might go berserk and try to bite you."

Julius was silent. *Does he think Undyings are a kind of wild animal or something?*

Maybe the warden noticed his mounting irritation, because he began mumbling excuses under his breath and grabbed the bunch of keys hanging at his hip, applying them to each of the keyholes in turn. The door had been carefully supplied with a full four locks. Finally he removed the bar and pushed the door open with a rusty creak. Obviously getting cold feet, he only let it crack open just wide enough for a person to slip through. "Um, if something happens, I don't want to be held resp—"

"I know. I'll talk to him alone. Close the door once I'm inside."

"Right…" With this halfhearted answer, the warden stepped back a few paces and cleared his way to the door. The very instant Julius walked past him and set foot in the cell, he heard the door shut behind him with a heavy sound, and then heard the bar being pushed firmly in place. *You sure closed that faster than you opened it,* he thought contemptuously.

A single bare bulb hung from the low ceiling, illuminating the cell with a rusty glow. The room was small. You could walk across it with five steps. Since Julius had already walked one of those five, he was now less than three steps away from the form lying curled in a ball in one corner of the cell.

"Hey. You alive?" he asked, and then waited a bit. After a few seconds, the form twitched in response, lifting his cheek from the floor and looking up at Julius, but then his eye closed again as if uninterested.

Julius sighed and gave up on conversation for the time being. He observed the prisoner from his three-step distance.

Apparently the man had not yet recovered his energy, and he looked horribly weak. But other than the giant patch of gauze covering his right cheek and eye, his major external injuries had mostly disappeared; for lack of a better way of expressing it, he finally looked as though he wasn't *dead*.

When Julius had visited the previous month, the majority of his face was still unbearable to look at, covered with such gruesome wounds he looked as if he had been run over by a train. He hadn't even been able to move his mouth, though, since his throat had been crushed as well, Julius doubted he would've been able to speak anyway. Even so, the man seemed to be conscious and had glared at Julius sharply with his single copper-colored eye on each of his roughly monthly visits, so Julius was fairly certain his prisoner at least recognized him. Undying though he might be, apparently his prosthetic right arm wouldn't heal on its own — when you thought about it, it was only obvious — so a useless, tangled mass of warped metal frame and cables dangled lifelessly from his upper arm onto the floor.

Julius remembered when he'd first collected the man last winter. True, over a year had passed, but that day he'd been barely breathing, and now he'd healed this far without any treatment at all. Seeing the reality of an Undying before his very eyes like this, he felt a fresh sense of horror.

...But at the same time, he also thought it maybe made the

man more pitiful to watch than a normal human. A normal person would die from those wounds and that would be the end of it, but *he* was never carried off to his heavenly peace; his body knit itself back together little by little as he lay in utter, excruciating pain. That's what it looked like to Julius.

"...What do you...want...?"

Maybe the man sensed Julius staring down fixedly at him and grew uncomfortable; he actually spoke up with an annoyed frown. His voice was still horribly scratchy and his speech was garbled, but still, this was the first time Julius had heard him speak since finding him. "Why did you sneak into the capital?" Julius demanded.

The man completely ignored him. It had actually looked as if they'd successfully have a conversation, but now silence descended on the room again. Left with no choice, Julius softened his tone somewhat and switched his line of questioning to something more personal. And after all, this was what he'd most wanted to ask about anyway. "Did you come to the capital alone? Where's Kieli?"

After another period of blankness that was less as though Harvey was ignoring him and more as though he'd frozen up, the moody, grouchy answer came. "...I don't need to tell you."

"Hey." Julius sighed briefly. "I saved your life, you know. If it hadn't been for me, you'd definitely be dead right now."

"You should've butted out. Damn brat."

"I'm not a brat anymore."

"Brat," repeated Harvey with a cluck of his tongue, and Julius fell silent with a feeling of half exasperation and half discontent. *Your attitude is way brattier than mine.*

It had been almost two years now since the winter he'd met the two of them on the Sand Ocean ship. He'd looked much younger than his age at the time, and in truth he might've been a little immature, but he'd learned a lot since then, and gotten taller, too. Lately he'd even started martial arts training out of personal interest in addition to his studies at seminary and his job.

Julius remembered having to crane his neck quite a bit to look up at this man, but now he was the one looking down at Harvey. Sure, it was because the man was lying on the floor, and it seemed as if there was still a decent difference in their heights, but in a few years his height and age would catch up for real. Kieli wouldn't treat him like a child anymore, either.

"What's Kieli up to? Is she doing okay? She doesn't know you're here, right?"

"... Shut up. Why should you care?"

Managing to control his irritation at this characteristically harsh response, Julius doggedly countered, "No, I mean, isn't she worried about you?" He didn't know how this guy had wound up coming to the capital alone, or where Kieli was and what she was doing, but at the very least, Harvey wouldn't have been able to contact her for the more than six months since Julius had picked him up. "Don't you want to see her, too? If you know where she is, I can contact her —"

"I said shut up."

When Julius clammed up after his attempt to pursue his questioning was thus completely shut down, the other man's cheek remained slightly raised from the floor, and his left eye cracked open. The copper orb, whose color in a way reminded him of rusty-red blood, glared sharply up at him. "Just try saying another word about her. I'll kill you."

Harvey's voice was lowered in tone, and Julius actually heard a threatening growl behind it. He reflexively gulped in surprise. *You never know when he might try to bite you.* The warden's words, which he'd swept aside minutes ago, abruptly sprang up in his mind with a new immediacy; he had the illusion that the three-step distance had suddenly shrunk until they were nose to nose.

But the murderous rage that had swelled up from Harvey in that moment was quickly swept away by a lazy weariness, and he spat in his usual tones, "Go home. I'm tired." Then he laid his cheek back down on the floor and closed his eye again. It looked as if speech was using up the last reserves of his strength.

Surreptitiously letting out the breath he didn't realize he'd been holding, Julius answered with forced calm, "Okay. I'm in town all this week, so I'll come again." Then he turned on his heel. When he signaled through the tiny window, the warden released the bar and opened the door.

"Are you all right?" whispered the warden in his ear.

"Why shouldn't I be?" he bit back crossly. It wasn't until after the words left his mouth that he realized his expression had frozen in place.

When he moved to step through the door, feeling bitterly frustrated somehow, a voice called out behind him. "Julius." He turned, internally somewhat afraid. The owner of the voice was still lying in the corner of the dim cell like a rag doll; he parted his thin lips a fraction and started to say something, but in the end all that came out was, "Never mind. I'm tired. Next time." Then he broke off and lay still as a corpse.

Next time. Maybe Harvey wasn't particularly rejecting the idea that he'd come again? Bewildered, he nodded with a short "Sure" and left the cell.

Come to think of it, he had a feeling that might have been the first time the man had actually called him by his name.

She found a mop and bucket in the locker in the corner of the room. She put all the chairs in the bar up on the tables and mopped every centimeter of the floor. Then she took the chairs back down, thoroughly polishing each one as she went. Next, she tidied up as much as seemed appropriate all the parts of the counter and kitchen she figured it was okay for her to touch, and polished the sink. She'd been at this since first thing in the morning, so even with all of that work, when she was finished there was still a fair amount of time before the bar opened for business in the evening.

"You're going overboard," said the radio in exasperation from its place at the end of the counter.

"But I'm bored." Her eyes roamed the bar, and settled on the stage; she began to clean it. It wasn't that she particularly liked cleaning, but once she got started she was always compelled to do a thorough job of it.

The stage looked as if it hadn't been used in years. Both the floor and the sound equipment were covered with dust, and it was pretty satisfying to clean them off. As she wrung out a washcloth over the bucket, sweating even though it was deep into autumn now, she felt someone's presence behind her.

She turned around, crouched over the bucket, and saw the black-vested bartender standing at the bottom of the stairs to the second floor and gaping at her.

Kieli shot to her feet with a gasp, unthinkingly shifting the washcloth behind her back. "I'm sorry for doing this without asking. I mean, I owe you so much…"

"No, no, that's not it," said the bartender quickly. He seemed just as flustered as she was. Passing his eyes over the bar that was now sparkling clean (if she did say so herself), he walked up to her. "You didn't have to do this. Thanks."

"It's no problem. I worked in a place like this once, and so I guess I just got fired up."

As she'd cleaned, she'd been thinking back with fondness to the month she'd worked at Buzz & Suzie's Café in West South-hairo. And even while she and Beatrix had been drifting around East South-hairo, Beatrix had always pulled her "capricious woman" act, coming and going with no warning, telling her to earn her own keep; it made paying rent on an apartment seem like a waste, so for a period of time Kieli had worked in a restaurant that gave her room and board.

It was the third day since she'd first visited this live music bar on the parish border. She hadn't had the time for a proper talk with Beatrix, who kept wandering out into the city, and she didn't know what they were doing next, so without really planning it Kieli had ended up sleeping in a bedroom on the second floor above the shop. She'd wanted to help out with the bar in return for the free room, but frankly it was practically out of business, and with so few customers there wasn't much she *could* help with during open hours. So today she'd decided to use the time before opening to clean the place up.

"I'm almost done," she said. As she picked up the bucket, thinking she'd change the water before continuing, a single drop of water splashed down in front of the bartender's shoe. She looked down in surprise at the tiny stain on the floor, and then lifted her head.

"It's nothing," he said, covering his surprised face with one hand and wiping away the tear track there with his palm. "It just felt like Setsuri had come back. Lots of times she'd be cleaning like that when I came here early for practice...I'm sorry, I'm being childish."

"No, I don't think you're childish at all..." Kieli couldn't think of anything else to say; she ducked her head down, bucket still hanging from both hands. An uncomfortable silence fell on the desolate bar as the two of them stood there all alone.

The bartender coughed as if to cover up the awkwardness, and opened his mouth again. "If you want to, you can stay here forever."

"Um..." Kieli was silent a few more moments, searching for the right way to answer. "...I'm sorry." She bowed, bucket bobbing with her. "I can't stay forever. I'm thinking of going to look for someone."

"Oh, right, the redhead —" The bartender broke off his automatic answer at almost the same moment as Kieli's head jerked up to stare at him. Water splashed out of the bucket and soaked her feet.

"Redhead...? Wait, do you know Harvey?!" The sound of

her voice shaping that name was horribly rare and strange to her own ears somehow, and it felt unnatural on her lips. It was a name she'd automatically avoided saying or even thinking about up until now.

Swallowing once, in a dry voice she said it again. "Did Harvey come here?"

"Well, I didn't catch his name. And I promised not to say anything..." The bartender mumbled this last sentence with a stricken look on his face.

Nobody told me anything about this! Kieli thought, gazing at him flabbergasted. "*Who* did you promise not to say anything?!"

On top of the counter, the radio let out a strangled groan whose meaning she couldn't decipher.

Beatrix visited the tobacco stand three days later as promised and received the name and address of the cleaner who was supposed to have seen Ephraim in Gate Town, but as she pushed open the door of the Adolph Sax, she still couldn't decide what to do next.

She thought it was about time for the sun to set and business to start up, but of course this bar didn't have the kind of praiseworthy regular customers that showed up right away at opening time. When she walked unceremoniously into the hall, the black-haired girl at the counter turned to look at her.

"Welcome back, Beatrix."

"Uh, right..." Much as she hated to admit it, her answer was exactly the kind of unsatisfactory one Ephraim might give. Behind the counter the bartender's face twitched oddly, and the radio spewed a burst of obnoxious static in her direction for some reason. Kieli turned around her entire bar stool in order to face Beatrix.

"Did you find out anything about where Harvey went?"

She said it in such an ordinary voice that Beatrix responded without thinking. "Well, I do have a sort of clue, for what it's worth…" she answered, making a face and playing with her hair. Then her heart did a somersault in her chest. She immediately tried to talk her way out of it, but she completely failed, and wound up incoherent. "I mean — wait — wh-wh-what do you mean?"

Kieli looked calmly up at her through her eyelashes. When Beatrix cast her eyes around the room for help, the bartender behind the counter twitched his face apologetically at her, and the radio spouted static that seemed to say *Crap, that's done it.* She squeaked, opening and closing her mouth silently a few times before releasing a long, groaning sigh and hanging her head in defeat.

"What's this all about? Were you in contact with Harvey without telling me?" Kieli's quiet but relentless voice hit the top of her bowed head like an arrow. Beatrix shot a glance up and saw the girl sitting straight up on her barstool, hands on her knees, eyes glued straight on Beatrix's face.

It felt as if the girl had gotten the drop on her, and she lost the energy to bull her way through it. Letting her shoulders drop, she answered.

"It wasn't what you'd call 'being in contact'…"

"Is it true you got a letter?"

Beatrix glared at the radio out of the corner of her eye. *You told her that, too, you old fool?!* But at Kieli's urgent "Beatrix," she snapped her eyes back to the girl, sighed in defeat, and reached a hand into the inner pocket of her trench coat.

She practically shoved the beat-up envelope at Kieli. Kieli stood up from her stool to take it, and after flipping it over to examine both sides, she opened it and drew out that memo that might as well have been the dictionary definition of "curt."

"Er, so you see, when I said I had an informant who'd dug up a lead on your mother, that informant was Ephraim. But he dropped off the face of the planet after that, and I don't even know whether he's alive or dead, and that letter is just awful, you know? So I couldn't tell you. So in other words, it's all his fault. Right. Yes…" The memo was short enough to read in less than a second, but Kieli was just staring at it unmoving, so Beatrix began nervously rattling off excuses. However, doing that didn't help her nervousness in the slightest, so in the end she tapered off awkwardly.

Still staring at the letter in her hand, Kieli quietly opened her mouth. "You knew too, didn't you, Corporal? You teamed up to keep it from me."

"Uh, um, it wasn't that we were KEEPING it from you," acknowledged her accomplice feebly.

Kieli merely said "Hmm," and raised her gaze to Beatrix again. "And? Where is Harvey now?"

"That's what I'm telling you: I don't know…"

"You just said you found a clue."

She gulped and slid her gaze to the radio, but no help seemed forthcoming from that quarter.

"Beatrix," Kieli prompted again.

"…Oh, for goodness' sake." Evading the issue was becoming

a pain anyway. Beatrix decided on total surrender. "Okay, fine. I'll tell you. That's what you want, right?" But as soon as she'd made this decision, she suddenly started to feel defiant; when she considered that the whole reason she'd never said anything before was out of consideration for this troublesome girl and that insensitive man, it seemed unfair that she should be criticized. Illogically angry, she puffed out her chest and put her hands on her hips as she said, "*You're* the one who wanted to know, so don't blame me. Listen up, then: the 'clue' is that he might be dead."

Kieli listened without a single change of expression, eyes angled downward, as she went on to report everything she'd learned from the information peddler at the tobacco stand: about the supposed disturbance at the secret facility at the capital, the cleaner who'd witnessed him in Gate Town, everything.

Beatrix concluded by explaining that the information might be false, of course, but if he really had been taken away by Church Soldiers, there wasn't much chance he was still alive, twisting her lips in a frown and thinking for no reason she could clearly explain, *There, did that teach you a lesson?*

There was a silent pause. She was inwardly anxious as she waited for the girl's response.

When it eventually came, it wasn't tears or anger; Kieli merely murmured in a flat voice so expressionless it was actively scary, "I see. So I'm the only one who didn't know those important things all this time." Then a customer saved the day, choosing that moment to come into the normally deserted bar, and so the conversation was set aside unfinished, abandoned until the following morning.

The issue was nowhere close to being resolved, but Beatrix

was relieved they'd been able to let the matter drop for the moment…

"She got us," Beatrix muttered blankly.

It was the next morning. She was standing in the doorway of Kieli's now-empty room.

This bedroom in a corner of the bar's second floor had apparently once belonged to Setsuri and her little daughter, and that grown-up daughter had been sleeping here up until last night, but now there was no sign of her. Her luggage had all been cleaned away as well, and her bag and coat were gone. The only thing left was the battered little radio sitting on the bed made neatly as if in thanks for the hospitality.

When she ran up to the bed and seized the radio, Beatrix found its power off. She violently switched it on. "Hey!"

"*Hey, Kieli, wait!*"

"She's long gone!"

"*What?!*"

They simultaneously let out little squawks, wordlessly traded glares for a while, then calmed down somewhat and resumed the conversation.

"What's going on? When did she leave?"

"*She was sleeping like normal. Just like normal! Then all of a sudden she shot out of bed real early in the morning and started packing her bags, so I tried to stop her, and then just like that she turned me off!*"

"Damn it, she looked like she'd sort of accepted it, but that was just a feint?! How dare she —"

When she grabbed the radio's cord and dived out into the

hallway, the bartender was just coming out the door kitty-corner to Kieli's room, still in his nightclothes. His job must have turned him nocturnal; he stared at them with sleep-hazed eyes and muttered something like *What the hell is this racket so early in the morning*, and half-filled with misplaced rage, Beatrix grabbed him by the collar and yanked him to her.

"What time is the train to Gate Town?! Can we still make it?!"

Whoo! Whoo-oo-oo — The whistle of the train about to depart had been sounding for some time, but now it cut off with a halfhearted echo, and the bustle of the passengers became oddly tentative, too, for some reason. A strange quiet briefly enveloped the platform.

"Wait! I'm getting on!" Kieli dashed up the step into the vestibule just as the railroad employee who'd been looking up and down the train to make sure everything was in order was about to give the sign that they were clear for departure. She dived into the passenger car through the connecting door.

The passengers in their seats all looked at her oddly as she leaned on the door panting for air, so she quickly found an empty seat and slid into it. When she'd seated herself and placed her sports bag next to her, there was a clattering vibration as if the train had caught on something, and the scenery out the window began to slide slowly by. While she took soft, deep breaths and tried to catch her breath, she watched the platform disappearing from view.

Unbidden, words sprang into her head. *I'm sorry, Mom...*

This was the town she'd lived in as a very small child with her mom. She was sure it was filled with memories of the two of them together — Setsuri and Jude, the man she had wanted to protect even if it meant making enemies of the whole rest of the world. The bartender had been kind enough to tell Kieli he wanted her to stay forever, but right now there was something else she absolutely had to do.

She had been hesitating, but the words of that station manager she'd met in the ruined station had given her the push she needed. *Then you can just go look for him. Waiting here isn't the only thing you can do.*

What had she been waiting for all this time? She should have gone looking for him right away, and not decided to wait. No matter what, she would find him, and meet him, and see his face —

— And tell him off.

Kieli took her right hand out of her pocket together with the objects it clutched, opening her fist. A cheap lighter and a crumpled envelope. She gripped the lighter and took a memo, also crumpled, out of the envelope.

The prose was dry as dust, and the handwriting was crude in a way that went beyond the simple issue of skill or lack thereof; she imagined this message that so failed to meet even the most minimal requirements of real communication had been jotted quickly with his left hand. She couldn't recall ever seeing him writing anything except for signing his name at the various inns they'd stayed at, plus the time Kieli had written the introduction to her Church history report on a momentary whim and he'd made unsolicited spelling corrections (and yet, she would like to point out, he'd completely forgotten how to write several easy words). Still, the handwriting of this letter definitely matched the handwriting in her memory.

As she gazed at it, anger welled up from deep inside her.

What the heck did he mean by just scribbling down his *business* and nothing else? He could've at least added one more sentence. One more sentence about anything.

He'd left without saying a thing, and sent her no word for a year and a half, and what had he been doing while *she'd* been wondering whether he meant to stay away forever? Investigating her mother! How could he be considerate enough to do a thing like that without her even asking, and yet not give a single thought to how she must feel waiting for him? On some fundamental level, the man was a born airhead. *I swear, I'm going to tell him off so bad…*

You'd better say your prayers, she vowed silently, and clenched the lighter and memo in both hands. Closing her eyes, she pressed her forehead firmly to her clasped hands as if in prayer. *I'm going to tell you off. I'm going to tell you off, so…*

"You have to be alive…"

There was nobody there to respond to her whisper. She'd left the radio that had been her constant and unfailing companion on her travels back at the bar. The rhythmic vibrations coming from below her seat and the subdued conversations of the other passengers shrouded the four-person box where she sat alone in a sort of only-faintly-real static cloud.

I've never traveled alone before…

Carrying solitude and unease and restlessness and a faint, precarious hope, the train sped due north to Gate Town, the gateway to the capital.

CHAPTER 4

LONG NIGHT BESIDE A DEEP POOL

She didn't know who the hell had first confidently suggested that the world was round, but it was definitely a lie.

No matter how far you went there was nothing but relentlessly flat, rocky wilderness, and she didn't see a scrap of sensory proof that they were inhabiting a spherical planet. The distant, low-lying bluish shadows of the northern mountain range actually looked as though they were getting farther and farther away the more she walked, and she couldn't imagine she was drawing any closer to them.

Surely this land was on a sort of conveyor belt that looped backward beneath her the exact same distance that she walked forward, and those snide mountains sprawled majestically at the end of the world, someplace that she could never, ever reach, where they lived in comfort and laughed mockingly at all travelers. Damn it.

"Now that I think about it, I should've just waited until tomorrow morning and gotten on the next train. Why am I following her on foot?! It's getting my clothes dirty, and damaging my hair, and chapping my throat, and who's going to take responsibility if my soft, maidenly skin gets burned by UV rays and I get a rash?"

"Are you really an Undying? Quit bitching like such a sissy."

"That is total discrimination. A problematic statement. Look, it's not wartime right now, you know. It's an era of peace. What's wrong with having requirements appropriate to the times?"

"Okay, okay, just stop swinging me around!"

It had been half a day since she'd started walking along the railroad tracks, dragging with one hand the clattering cart to which she'd affixed her trunk, and now with the other hand swinging the radio vigorously by its string. Naturally she hadn't seen any trains pass, but the fact was she hadn't even seen a single truck driving along the rutted road that ran next to the tracks. The sand-colored sun peeking through the dust storms had long since passed its peak in the sky and started to travel west.

She should've turned around the moment she realized that the most effective way to overtake Kieli was certainly not to go to Gate Town on foot, but rather to wait for the next morning's train; however, by that time she'd already walked far enough that the thought of turning back pissed her off, so she was stubbornly pressing on.

"This is all your fault to begin with. If you call yourself her guardian, at least trouble yourself to predict what she's going to do!"

"Don't ask for the impossible! Even I never thought she'd just run off on her own! And anyway, when you get right down to it, this is YOUR fault for not showing that letter to her when you got it; the secrets just piled up after that, and that's how things ended up this way."

"Well, you knew about it and you never said anything, either, so you're just as guilty! Besides, the reason I couldn't show it to her was because what he wrote was just so insensitive, so, yeah, the whole mess is because *he's* stupid and thoughtless. Why should I be —" Suddenly she realized something and broke off talking, stilling her steps at the same time.

The sounds of her own incessant chattering and of the trunk dragging along the ground temporarily stopped, and the lonely wilderness silence that blanketed her surroundings made her feel oddly hollow. The dust clouds dancing over the tracks flapped at the hem of her trench coat as if to tease her.

"*What is it?*"

"We're turning back."

When she pivoted on her heel and began returning the way she'd come, dragging the trunk behind her, the radio spoke up in a panic: "*Hey, wait a second, are you serious? When we've come this far already? At this point it's going to be hard work going back, too. I'm telling you, it'd be better to keep going and hope for a car to come by.*"

"She's the one who left all on her own. Why should I have to go out of my way to chase after a troublesome girl like that? She can just do whatever she wants. Die in a ditch somewhere, wander into a bad neighborhood and get captured and forced into prostitution, whatever."

"*Idiot, that's not funny!*"

"Why should I care? I've babysat her more than enough to fulfill my promise to Ephraim. Any more than this wouldn't be worth it even if I made him be my errand boy for life to pay me back. That's *if* he's even alive."

Beatrix had been briskly walking as she delivered this fast-tongued assertion, but after about twenty steps she stopped again.

"*Sheesh, what now?*"

After silently glaring at the ground for a while with a sour face, she turned around 180 degrees again and began quickly picking her way back north.

"*. . . Beatrix.*"

"What?!"

"You've got an unprofitable personality, huh?"

"Shut up or I'll leave you here."

Beatrix considered doing exactly that, but walking and shouting all by herself in the middle of the wilderness would feel more empty than anything else, so in her heart she firmly resolved to sell him off as soon as she got to town. Just then, a faint new sound caught in her ears, which had become accustomed to nothing but the sounds of her own voice and the radio's, the clattering trunk, and the ambient noise filling the wilderness.

She stopped and looked back over her shoulder. Dust clouds were rising up over the rutted road that ran parallel to the tracks a short distance away. As she stood there squinting, the faint sound of a fossil fuel engine drew steadily closer, and a three-wheeled truck with its canopy up came into view.

"I'm in luck!" she murmured excitedly. She shifted her grip on the trunk and ran from the railroad tracks over toward it. As she did so the truck did its own part to close the distance between them, and when she got to the side of the road, cart rattling wildly, it was just pulling to a stop before her.

"Thank goodness! I was really in a bind. Would you mind giving me a lift to Gate Town?"

"Oh, now you play the nice girl."

Swinging the radio's string behind her back and letting the machine slam into the corner of the truck, she flashed her full-wattage professional smile and looked up at the driver's seat. The truck driver stuck his head out the sand-grimy window. He gave her face a quick, appraising look with his elbow propped on the windowsill, and immediately grinned. "Wow,

I'm pretty lucky today, picking up such a fine-looking lady in a place like this."

Huh? Beatrix frowned, feeling as if she'd heard that lightly flirtatious voice somewhere before. At that moment, the driver's eyes fell on her trunk and his mouth made a little "o" of surprise that sparked her memory.

It was the young man who'd been trying to pick up Kieli in Toulouse. He hadn't looked as if he was on a pilgrimage, so she had taken him for an ordinary tourist, but judging from the sight of him driving the truck, he must be a merchant. "Wow, what a coincidence," he said. "Isn't that other girl with you?"

"Never mind, I don't need a ride," she answered. She turned ninety degrees to the left and set off walking again.

"Hey!" a flustered voice called after her. "What the heck? Come on, get in. You want to go to Gate Town, right? Even by car it's still more than a day away, you know. There's no way a woman could walk that far."

"Mind your own business." She half-turned, thoughts rather contradicting the antidiscrimination rant she'd delivered to the radio earlier. *Don't make me out to be the same as all those normal women!* That was when she first noticed the driver had companions in the passenger seat.

Two small heads were peeping out at her interestedly from over the driver's shoulder. There was a girl who seemed a few years younger than Kieli and was what she might politely call "unassuming" (or, to put it another way, she was plain and screamed "country girl"); with her was a boy about another four or five years younger.

The boy's face immediately brightened, and he let out a cry. "Hey! It's that lady who was with the witch!"

"Il! You're being rude!" The girl blushed and forcibly ducked his head back down. Beatrix was impressed that he'd recognized her; she'd been in her disguise at the time, after all. Anyway, it was one thing for the guy to go after sixteen-year-old Kieli—now he was trying something with kids of *this* tender age?

"You're seriously misunderstanding this, aren't you? It's not like that at all. I just let them ride with me out of the kindness of my heart."

"I wonder." She shot a hooded glare at the driver.

He raised both hands in front of him and waved them in a pacifying gesture. "Okay, then, if you get in, too, it'll prove that I've got no ulterior motives. Sound good?" He smacked a fist into his palm as if he'd just come up with a brilliant idea, beaming at her with a face that betrayed ulterior motives all too clearly.

The far-northern mountain range beyond the fortress walls was still a long way off, blurred with sand-colored gas that made it seem like a mirage. But from here, if she squinted she could start to make out a dark gray city lying solemn yet strangely eerie in the heart of it. It was a skyscraper city with tens, or maybe hundreds, of towers jutting up toward the heavens, each looking different from all the others—if you looked at it a certain way, it seemed like a collection of gravestones twisting and writhing in pain, all twining around each other looking for help.

So that's the capital, the mechanical city…

Kieli stood still for a while, gazing at the shadow of the distant city.

The pictures on the walls of the boarding school had fired her imagination with the idea that it must be a glorious view, but seeing it with her own eyes now, it didn't inspire any particularly deep emotion. A feeling like awe bubbled up in her for just an instant and then vanished, and that was all.

When she shifted her gaze from that distant scenery a little closer, the milky-white fortress wall ringing in the northern part of the city loomed over the roofs of the houses uptown. The corresponding wall to the south had crumbled during the War, and to this day had never been rebuilt; the downtown area had expanded in slow stages and was now a sprawling slum.

This city might be the "gateway to the capital," but beyond the gate in the northern wall there was still a wearyingly long road and a steep climb waiting before you got to the center of the mountain range. Apparently lots of the pilgrims from all over the planet who stopped here on their way to the capital ran out of steam and ended up just settling down here.

Uptown, with its houses of the historied high-born who had received the favor of the capital, and downtown, where the lower class and the pilgrim settlers lived — Gate Town had a unique structure: it was divided into two radically different neighborhoods by its midtown, where the station and the church were. Its other defining characteristic was its vast network of underground waterways, which Kieli understood had been built drawing on the groundwater from the capital's mountain range. It was a relic of the prewar era, but it had hardly changed since then. It spread below the entire town.

She'd spent about a day and a half vibrating along with the train, and had arrived here from the parish border town the afternoon after she'd boarded. She'd gotten a grip on the basic layout of the city at the station and set out for the downtown area to the south. From downtown to the higher ground of uptown ran layer after layer of staircase-like inner walls, probably also left over from the War; maybe they'd protected the city from invasion back then, but now they just divided the various city neighborhoods and made traffic difficult. Kieli had been told that the "underground waterways" were not always underground downtown, since the neighborhood was already at such a low elevation, and that sometimes they actually passed through those inner walls towering above her.

As she walked down the paved, zigzagging stairs along one such wall toward the slums of downtown, the dry air of the city got gradually moister. The sun was still relatively high in the sky, but already an exhausted fatigue was settling about her shins. The walls and ground gave off a smell like soaking-wet laundry that refused to completely dry, and it stuck in her nose.

When she reached the bottom of the stairs she saw a line of arched openings like windows at the base of the inner wall. From them, dreary tunnels stretched on into the wall. Apparently this area had once functioned as a part of the waterways, too, but now the waters had receded, and the trails they left behind had become perfect refuges for pilgrims and vagabonds.

The fading sunlight of afternoon hit the tunnels at an acute angle, providing just enough light to dimly illuminate them. Kieli stepped inside one of them and made her way toward its depths, flinching a little at the unfriendly stares from the people lying scattered around on both sides of the tunnel.

As she was debating with herself over whether to ask anybody for help, she noticed a table set up deep within the tunnel, with a crowd of people around it enjoying a card game. Though it was still the middle of the afternoon they already reeked of alcohol, and most had a beer in one hand; still, they seemed far easier to strike up a conversation with than those people who were just lying there in the shadows and glaring at her like she was a nuisance. *Those* people seemed half-dead.

"Excuse me…," Kieli ventured, standing behind the ring of players. However, they appeared to have gotten to the most important stage of the betting, and they were all so caught up in the game that no one responded. Just as she started to get worried, her eyes met those of someone leaning one hip lightly on the end of the table and surveying the game.

It was a woman, wearing disheveled makeup and clothes open wide at the breast. She craned her neck over the heads of her companions and spoke to Kieli. "Hi. What's up?"

At first Kieli was relieved that someone was giving her a friendly response, but she quickly felt something was off. She hesitated a little, but in the end there didn't seem to be anyone else she could ask, so she walked over to the woman.

Just at that point the game ended, and under cover of the

noise of the players all crowing about who'd won and lost, Kieli asked her question. "Um, is there anybody around here named Hans?"

"Hmm, there are all kinds of people named Hans in this world."

"I heard he was a cleaner who worked around the wall."

"Oh, him." The woman sounded as though she knew whom Kieli meant, and Kieli's breast filled with hope. But then she added, "I hear he's dead."

And those brief words were all she said.

"Dead...?" Kieli echoed dumbly.

"Yeah, so I hear," the woman repeated. She thrust a hand into the hair piled up on top of her head and mussed it, continuing, "I forget how long ago it was, but he went to work one day and never came back. Everyone's saying he must've fallen into the waterways. Even if he's lucky enough to get found, he'll probably be a swollen-up floater by then. It's not too unusual for someone to go missing in the waterways."

The woman's interest returned to the next game, which had just started, and she left it at that.

For a while Kieli just stood stock-still behind her, utterly lost. She'd thought that if she could meet up with this person who was supposed to have seen Harvey, then even if she couldn't figure out exactly where Harvey was, she'd at least get a little bit of a clue about what she should do next. But now suddenly she had nothing to go by.

"Come to think of it," said the woman, as if she'd just remembered something. Kieli raised her eyes to look, and saw that the woman had craned her neck around to face her again.

"About Hans — people say he was going on about some pretty weird stuff before he went missing. Something like, 'If I die, I want you guys to know that it's because I saw the procession of the dead, so they came for me.' But you know, he was living just like normal even after he started saying that. When people die, it's sudden and it's over before you know it, huh?"

"The procession of the dead?" Kieli had never even heard of it. Or seen it, of course.

"You go on now. This is no place for a girl like you," the woman said coldly, and then turned around again. Kieli gave up on finding anything in this place, thanked the woman softly, and turned her back on the circle of people living it up over their card games.

What do I do now?

Should she just head straight for the capital? But if she went there, she really had no idea what her next move should be. Naturally she didn't know anyone there, plus now that she thought about it, she didn't have much money left.

Wait... someone I know at the capital...

Just as she was on the edge of remembering something, suddenly a ruckus broke out at the waterway exit in front of her. Amidst the confusion she could hear the clanging of something metal, and against the sand-colored sunlight coming in through the archway appeared one huge black shape after another.

At the same time another commotion rose up behind her. When she turned around, the people who had been enjoying their betting were hastily gathering up the cards and cleaning off the table.

"I told you, hurry up and get going." The woman from before jerked her chin toward the exit. She was the only one composed in the midst of this storm of activity, still leaning on the edge of the tilted table. When Kieli only stood there stunned, her voice grew impatient. "It's illegal to gamble here. If you don't want to get thrown into the slammer with the rest of us, you'd better run away quick."

The dozen or so people who'd been participating in the card game feverishly tried to carry off the table, but by that time the group gathered at the exit had entered the tunnel, and they began to seize the screaming crowd one after the other by the scruffs of their necks.

White clerical robes were fortified with white armored plating over every vital point, and all of them carried nightsticks — these were the Church Soldiers charged with maintaining order in Gate Town, mainly by keeping the pilgrims who passed through the gate under surveillance.

The other residents who had just been lying around got caught up in the heat of the moment and started running away, too, and in the blink of an eye the tunnel had descended into chaos, with criminals and bystanders all running amok together. The Church Soldiers, for their part, seemed to more or less be hauling in anybody who crossed their paths without worrying too much about who it was. Before she knew it, a hand clad in rough gloves had grabbed her by her neck.

"Let me go!" Kieli struggled and wheeled her fists around, trying to get away. Then there was a crack on the back of her head and a brilliant flash that filled her entire field of vision, and she collapsed into the crowd.

For some odd reason something the woman had said to her before still rang in her ears, repeating itself over and over in her mind. *When people die, it's sudden and it's over before you know it, huh?* When Kieli had first heard it she'd just let it wash over her without thinking anything in particular about it, yet now…

He's not dead…

She'd almost begun to believe it in spite of herself, but now she stubbornly denied it. He wasn't dead. He wasn't like normal people; there was no way he'd die easily.

Her rear end was cold where it pressed against the ground, so she shifted slightly. As she did, she took the opportunity to lift her face slightly from where it had been buried between her hugged knees and take stock of the area. Into this damp space penned in by gray walls about twenty people had been crammed; they squatted on the ground like refugees. Among the crowd she could see the faces from around the card table, but surely half of these people had just happened to be in the tunnel at the time, and gotten caught up in things and dragged here with the gamblers.

"Yo. Your head okay?" said a voice next to her. She turned to look. The woman she'd spoken to in the tunnel was sitting beside her in the line of people next to the wall.

Kieli put a hand to the back of her head, and whispered half-jokingly, "I'm fine. I've got a hard head." In part she was trying to cheer herself up. It didn't work very well.

She hugged her knees again and propped her chin on them,

gazing with downcast eyes at the tips of her own boots. This was the first time in her life she'd ever been in lockup. Even though she hadn't done anything to be arrested for (in this case, at least), despair crept into her heart, whispering that maybe they'd keep her here and never let her go. This uniquely closed-off space where the damp and stink settled heavily along the ground might be pretty effective at making a person lose her energy.

"Well, you don't have to worry. They don't really intend to do anything to us, so they'll let us out soon enough. After all, if all they do is lock up a bunch of poor people and feed them for free, it might as well be volunteer work. We're actually grateful for it, and nobody ever learns anything from it, so all of us just repeat the same thing over and over again. This is basically a regular event."

The woman said this with a light laugh, and Kieli smiled back, cheered a little. She'd vaguely imagined that the people living in North-hairo parish, which was strongly influenced by the capital, would be even more devout than those in East-erbury, but it looked as if not everybody living in the slums was a pious believer.

"What did you want with Hans? It doesn't sound like you know him. From the look of you, you're not a pilgrim either. Did you come all the way here just to see Hans?"

"No…" Probably nothing more than idle interest had motivated the woman's question, but Kieli was at a loss for an answer. "I'm looking for someone Hans might have seen, so I wanted ask him about it."

"Huh. So, your boyfriend, then."

"Eh?!" she squeaked in surprise without thinking. It echoed unexpectedly loudly against the bare concrete walls, and everyone else in the cell looked at her funny. She stammered her denial in a flustered whisper. "N-No, it's not like that!"

"Sure, sure," agreed the woman in a teasing voice that didn't really convince Kieli that she believed her. "Well, I don't know what's going on, but I hope you find him." A tired but pretty smile appeared on her thin, makeup-streaked face.

"Thanks...," Kieli answered, looking down in embarrassment. Still hugging her knees, she leaned her back against the wall. Staring at the tips of her boots, she murmured softly, "But he might not be alive anymore..." As soon as she heard herself say it, she was disappointed by her own weakness. She'd denied it so vehemently just a few minutes ago, and now unease was already reasserting itself.

"You don't know he's dead yet, right? Why not search for him?"

Maybe it was nothing more than false comfort, but it had the same sort of scent about it somehow as what the station manager had said to her on the abandoned train platform. After a pause, Kieli gave a small smile. "You're right. Thanks." She'd just begun to search, after all. She had no intention of giving up yet.

Metallic footsteps approached. When she looked up, one of the Church Soldiers guarding them was standing on the other side of the barred door. Kieli stiffened in surprise, but her fellow prisoners merely turned sluggishly toward him; after he'd glanced contemptuously over the lifeless people in the cell, the guard began to noisily unlock the door. "We're finished with you. Scram."

Someone gave a low whistle. The woman next to her whispered, "You're a lucky girl. He's letting us out early today. Usually they leave us to stew here at least overnight." Kieli heard other voices nearby lament that it wouldn't have hurt to let them go *after* dinner.

The barred door was wrenched open, and the people confined inside heaved themselves up and started heading for the exit.

At the woman's voice urging "Go on, go," Kieli got in the back of the line and passed through the door as well. When she got into the hallway and turned back to look into the cell, everyone was out and it was empty.

The woman was nowhere to be seen.

"What's the matter with you? Get a move on," snapped the guard. She resumed her place at the rear of the line and started walking again, silently giving thanks. The woman must have realized that Kieli didn't know anyone else in the cell, and talked to her so that she wouldn't feel lonely and discouraged. *I wonder how she died…it must have been sudden and over before you knew it, just like she said.* Kieli even thought that kind of death would have suited her.

They came through the hallway lined with communal cells and climbed the stairs to the ground floor. There was an observation room right before the exit to the prison. Before it two Church Soldiers stood guard with identical expressions of practiced, robotic blankness, watching the prisoners leave.

Diagonally behind them, Kieli glimpsed another person standing there primly, seeming small compared to the well-built soldiers.

In contrast to the white clerical robes of the soldiers, he wore a long, jet-black robe with a high collar — priest's clothes, though somewhat plainer than those worn by the full-fledged priests. They looked like the uniforms of the seminary students who had come to visit the Easterbury boarding school to do their in-service training, but the boy wearing them seemed young for a seminarian, young enough to still be called "boy." It was odd how the brawny soldiers held their expressions rigid and stood motionless, as if unnerved by the boy behind them.

She watched him casually out of the corner of her eye as she passed, and their eyes happened to meet.

She held his gaze as she walked a few steps past him, until her neck couldn't turn any further, and then she stopped. Her neck still twisted, they gazed at each other across air that had grown tense for some reason.

The boy's mouth opened first. "... Kieli?"

Kieli whirled around, her whole body twitching, and gaped up at him in speechless silence.

... Gaped *up* at him?

It was true: the boy wasn't actually "tall," but he had a fair number of centimeters on Kieli. The eyes looking down on her from above were dark green. There too were the soft, light brown hair and the refined features.

"Juli...?"

At her dazed murmur, the boy's face lit up. His expression instantly became more childish, and he looked a full two or three years younger in one stroke. "Kieli, it *is* you!"

He came toward her with arms spread wide in greeting and a smile on his face, and seemed about to hug her around the shoulders before his hands froze as if he'd suddenly remembered himself. He recovered his attitude before the suspiciously frowning soldiers at his back, and spoke again in a restrained whisper. "Wow, Kieli, it's really you, isn't it?"

Kieli stared up at him in disbelief. "Juli, is that really you? But I don't remember you being so..." She compared this boy to the one in her memory of almost two years ago. *I don't remember you being so tall!* Kieli remembered actually being a little taller than he was. His voice was lower now than before, too, and it was kind of strange. But his way of talking and his expression did belong to the mischievous Julius she knew.

"You've changed, too, Kieli," said Julius, looking a little shy. He darted his eyes around them and schooled his expression again (which made him look old enough for a seminarian's uniform to suit him). "Well, never mind. Let's have a nice, long talk later." He bent down a little and brought his face to her ear, lowering his voice even more. "How did you know?"

"Huh?" Kieli said, bewildered.

Julius blinked his dark green eyes, still quite close to her. "Huh? Didn't you come because you knew? I thought I'd worried for nothing."

"Knew what?"

"Well, you know... that he's here."

"... Who?" she asked, and then abruptly realized who it must be. But even after she figured this out, she couldn't think for the life of her how to react. She stared fixedly up at Julius, frozen.

"He still looks pretty bad. Are you sure you want to see him? You'll be okay?"

"I'll be fine. Let me see him." Her expression was still frozen, but she nodded firmly. Julius signaled the guard of the solitary confinement cells with his eyes. The guard withdrew a jangling bunch of long keys and began unlocking the door.

Once they'd descended the steep stairs down from the communal cell block even deeper into the building, Kieli had been led to a hallway of long, narrow doors with tiny barred windows in them. Perhaps the underground waterways were directly underfoot now; it was chilly, but she felt a layer of moisture settling on her skin, and the sound of her footsteps here was subtly different than it had been on the floor above. The echoes bounced off the walls slightly diffused, as if she were ringing bells in a cave.

In a corner of the hallway were a steel desk and chair; on top of the desk were a logbook, a rusty kettle, and a camp stove. On the wall beside it was a coat hook with a dark gray coat on it. That must be where the guard stayed when he wasn't on his rounds. Working in an environment like this, just keeping watch all alone all day long, must be enough to drive you crazy.

The guard released the bar and peeked through the small window before slowly pushing the door open, creating a gap just wide enough to admit one person. Then he whispered something to Julius, who replied with a brief "I see" before turning to face Kieli.

"Perfect timing. It sounds like he might look a little better now. Wait here just a little longer," he said. Kieli had no idea what he was talking about, but she nodded, and then Julius slipped through the opening and disappeared into the cell by himself. She could hear the low rumble of voices through the door.

Kieli unconsciously fumbled one hand into her coat pocket and gripped the thing her fingers found there.

Her pulse sped up. The thumping of her heart threatened to rise into her throat, and she swallowed thickly against it.

"Kieli."

It felt as though she'd waited a long time, but really it had probably been less than ten seconds. Julius was craning his head around the door frame. He gestured with his eyes for her to come inside.

She walked somewhat stiffly to the door, hands still stuck in her pockets. On the threshold she stopped and looked slowly and nervously around the cell. It was a tiny, damp room hazily lit by a dim bulb hanging from the ceiling. The first thing her eyes fell on was a middle-aged woman wearing classic black clothes. She nodded a brief greeting at Kieli with a smile on her plump-cheeked face, as she bustled about the room tidying up the debris of dirty clothes, bandages, and washbasins lying scattered around it.

The frozen tension in the air was finally broken by the sight of this unexpected figure; then the woman withdrew to the side as if to make room, and past her Kieli could see someone else.

Sitting with his back against the undressed concrete wall that looked as if it couldn't possibly be comfortable was a tall, lean young man. Despite the fact that three other people were crammed into the tiny space with him, he displayed no interest in his surroundings, merely staring down with lowered eyes at a random spot on the floor.

It seemed he'd just had his clothes changed, and now he was comparatively neatly dressed, but she could see festering wounds all over the skin peeking out at the throat and cuffs of the shirt he wasn't able to wear quite properly. He looked even more emaciated than he had before; his collarbone and the bones of his hands jutted out sharply.

"Hey," Julius said in an exasperated voice, and at last the man irritably lifted his head of washed-out, damp copper hair.

The moment she saw his face, Kieli's heart gave a great lurch in her chest.

Half his face was covered by huge patches of gauze plastered over his right cheek and eye and held in place with tape. In the glow of the bare dull-yellow lightbulb, the snow-white gauze looked awfully, spitefully clean, harshly emphasizing the painful scar on the man's face and the bleakness of the room.

She unthinkingly started to look away before she caught herself and tightened her fists fiercely in her pockets against the impulse. "Har...vey...?" she murmured in a trembling voice. He was right there in front of her eyes for the first time

in so very, very long, and yet her lips and tongue fumbled the name.

At the sound of her voice, the man sluggishly turned his face toward her. He squinted his one remaining copper-colored eye slightly, as if straining to see her (maybe his eyesight was bad?); after a beat, he frowned in undisguised suspicion. "...Who are you?"

Those were the first words she heard out of his mouth.

Her vision was abruptly shrouded in a white cloud. She froze. "...It's Kieli, obviously," Julius ground out next to her, sighing.

"Ki..." the man mumbled brokenly at Julius. Then he turned back to look at her face, checking. It still took several more seconds before he looked as though he finally understood.

"What the hell are you doing he—"

But before he could finish the sentence, Kieli drew her right fist from her pocket and threw the object she'd been holding in his face. A lighter wrapped up in crumpled paper hit the gauze over his right eye. In that instant she regretted it a little—but only a little.

"What do you mean, what am I doing here?! D-Do you have any idea how much I..." *Oh, no, I'm going to cry!*

The moment she thought it, she spun 180 degrees and flew out of the cell.

"Wai—"

The voice behind her ordering her to stop was cut off, and then she simultaneously heard the clatter of the washbasin or something similar being knocked over, something collapsing onto the floor, and someone saying "Ow!" She ignored all of it.

The guard standing at attention outside looked at her in surprise, but she ignored that, too, slipping past him and running out of the hallway and up the stairs at full speed.

He immediately tried to follow her, but when he got to his feet he tottered unsteadily and tripped over the washbasin, and then somehow it didn't even occur to him to get up. He turned his attention to the feel of the damp concrete against the cheek now planted against the ground and the faint sounds of moving water.

The wet cold slowly but surely oozed up through the gauze over his face and began eating at his wound like a swarm of microbes. With the remaining half of his vision, he hazily glimpsed the same sickeningly familiar walls and ceiling of undressed concrete that he'd seen day in and day out for so long — to the extent he thought he could probably close his eye and reproduce the sight down to the details of the water stains.

He heard a rusty scraping sound and flicked his gaze upward a fraction. Out of the bare thirty-centimeter gap between the open door and its frame (the guard here was always terrified, and never opened the door wider than this, so that if something should happen he could close it instantly, abandoning the visitor inside if necessary) appeared a boy in priest's clothes.

The other two people in his cell had left to chase after the girl who'd gone running out, but apparently the boy had now come back alone.

From his position on the floor, Harvey glowered at him and asked in a low tone, "Where's Kieli?"

"I'm taking her home with me for today."

"Let me see her again."

"Not today. Even someone in my position will get questioned if I let visitors come in and out of here too frequently."

"I don't give a shit about your position," he spat, but even to his own ears it just sounded like venting, so he clicked his tongue in annoyance and fell silent. Julius sighed and leaned against the door behind him. They regarded each other in silence for a while. The quiet didn't become unbearable to Harvey or anything, but eventually he spoke up anyway, figuring he'd rather hurry up and ask what he wanted to know and then put a stop to this unpleasant atmosphere. "Did you call her here?"

"How could I? You refused to tell me where she was, remember? She came all the way here looking for *you*. She had a terrible experience, getting mixed up in their sweep of the slums and tossed in jail, and then when she finally got to see you, you responded like *that*?! Do you remember what you just said to her?"

Harvey was silent. The boy's lecture made him incredibly pissed off, all the more so for the fact that he couldn't actually refute any of it. Why should he have to be scolded by a little brat like this?

"Cool your head a little, will you?"

"Shut up. It *is* cool," Harvey shot back, mouth twisting. He turned his head away, pressing his forehead to the cold ground while he was at it.

Whatever the boy might say, *she'd* been the one at fault here. Just showing up out of the blue, and suddenly looking kind of different and more grown-up...as if anyone would be able to recognize her like that!

He glared up at Julius's figure in the door frame out of the corner of his eye and internally chided himself. *Look how big that little snot-nosed brat has gotten! He's even giving you lectures like some big shot now. If you'd actually thought about it for a second you'd have had to realize that Kieli must've grown up a little, too. You just never actually expended the effort to think about it.*

"All right, I'm leaving, too," Julius said, straightening. He peered through the window and signaled the guard, but then turned back around as if he'd just thought of something. "Maybe I'll invite Kieli to go out sightseeing tomorrow. Just the two of us, to celebrate finally getting to see each other again. You can get a good view of the town from the corridors at the top of the walls. It's beautiful at night."

The boy was blatantly rubbing it in his face, and Harvey felt pretty seriously murderous. He let it show in his attitude as he kept glaring; Julius seemed to shrink back a little, but nevertheless flashed him a triumphant smirk.

...He's still just a brat after all. Harvey looked away, feeling ridiculous, and spat, "Do whatever you want."

"I'm really going to invite her, then. Don't you regret those words."

"I won't." Maybe the disinterested response took the wind out of his sails; he just let out an annoyed breath and turned to go. The guard outside removed the bar and, as always, pushed the door open just wide enough to let someone slip through.

Harvey thought of something, and called out to the boy's retreating back. "Julius."

The boy paused on the threshold and turned back to look at him one more time. "What?"

"... Why did you save me?"

It was the question he'd almost asked before, then put off with a "next time." It had been lying unspoken and unanswered ever since.

Julius paused as if in thought, and then answered him seriously. "I wanted to try talking with an Undying."

"Liar." *What, that's all?*

"It's not a lie," he said flatly, and then lowered his voice, maybe out of concern about the guard outside. "The Church teaches us that Undyings are barbaric monsters, repugnant beings who go against God's order. But you look just like a normal human being. And you can speak and understand just like anyone else — not that you seem to want to speak with *me*. I don't know if Undyings really have to be captured and put down the minute you find them, like rabid dogs. I don't really understand why we have to go that far."

"Heh, you're a heretic? Your parents would cry if they heard you."

"I'm sure my father would understand if I spoke seriously with him about it."

"You're dreaming," Harvey snorted derisively, figuring he'd

get a little of his own back for Julius's victory before. "If the Church would change its tune based on one thing a little kid said, the world would be a real happy place." Julius fell silent with a glum look on his face.

After a while, Julius changed the subject with an abrupt arrogance. "I'll tell you one thing: don't assume I'll just unconditionally release you when you're healed. You're my prisoner. Your life is more or less in my hands, you know." And with a final "I'll be back," he left the cell for good this time.

The door was closed with the same rusty creak it had opened with, the bar was shoved back into place, and the four locks were turned one by one. Harvey felt they were being unnecessarily careful with him. He didn't warrant *that* much security. He'd become too used to the sounds, though—lately he'd started to think that maybe his apartment in South-hairo had had four locks, too.

Two sets of footsteps echoed against the walls of the corridor, getting farther away. The guard must have gone with the boy to see him off. All at once, as soon as the signs of their presence disappeared, an exhaustion so great he hardly felt like breathing descended on him. Harvey let out a strangled breath and planted his cheek back on the floor. After that, he didn't move a muscle for a long time. He concentrated on the flow of blood in his body, experimentally tracing the path it took outward from his core. He'd learned this clever feat only a few months ago, lying in this cell with too much time on his hands, conscious but unable to move.

When he lay still, he almost felt as if he could actually hear the blood moving slowly through him, carrying little regenerative particles along with it, and he began to feel somewhat more at ease.

It seemed almost the entire capacity of his core was used up trying to regenerate the damaged parts of him, and there wasn't enough leftover energy to maintain his regular biological activity or his bodily functions — at least, this was how he'd vaguely grasped his situation while, again, lying in the cell. That must be just how much the functions of his core had been impaired. Before the Incident, he was pretty sure injuries like this had always been healed by this time.

Apparently this was the result of the crack to his core back on that spaceship in South-hairo.

At the very far reaches of his dim field of vision, he could see his own arms lying flung out on the floor. He'd wrecked his prosthetic right arm escaping from the capital, and now he couldn't move it at all...or maybe it wasn't quite accurate to say *he couldn't* move it. After it had begun to tear off during that incident in South-hairo, though the external wounds had healed and it had been connected again on the surface, it had never again fused with his nerves like before, and since then he'd never been able to move it of his own will.

However, it had moved independently on his behalf, almost perfectly intuiting his will, so he hadn't suffered any handicap. In fact, it had been more dexterous than his original arm. After he'd left South-hairo and set out for the capital, it had always aided him as his lone personal (mechanical?) travel companion.

But now he couldn't feel a trace of the soul he was sure the arm had housed.

"Hey," he tried calling out to it, but as expected there was no response from the cruelly warped metal, only the faint sound of its motor running. It was as if it had never been anything but an ordinary prosthetic arm. As if it had never once moved by itself. Though when he thought about it, he supposed that was only normal.

Where do you get off just up and breaking down, you idiot? he inwardly complained, unreasonably. He sighed silently. Then he tamped down on his feelings and transferred his attention to his flesh-and-blood left arm.

He directed his energy into it. After a brief time lag the message reached his fingers, and he balled them awkwardly into a fist, but there was almost no strength in his grip. Or rather, he couldn't really remember how to *use* his strength.

It took a certain amount of effort just to grasp the lighter in front of him, with its scrap of paper that looked like trash, and bring them toward him.

Huh, I think this is mine..., he thought, gazing at the lighter. But it was the kind of mass-produced one you could get anywhere, so there was no way to conclusively determine whether it was his. He couldn't really say. It wasn't worth enough to insist on his ownership rights either way.

However, when he unfolded the scrap of paper he'd thought was garbage, he did recognize it: it was in his own handwriting. But it was just a memo he'd jotted down in two seconds and handed to the information peddler. He only remembered what he'd written after rereading it.

...I asked her what the hell she was doing here. Recalling the stupid thing he'd said to Kieli just a little while ago, he was

thoroughly disgusted with himself. Obviously she'd used the memo to trace him here. His mind had short-circuited, and his mouth had basically been running on nervous reflex.

"She's the one who should be asking me that…" Of the two of them, he was less sure what the hell *he* was doing.

He opened and closed his left fist a few times. He hadn't really moved his body in a while, and now it was out of shape; it felt alien, hardly like his own body at all. But before long he started steadily getting sensation back, and remembering how to use his strength. His body had maintained a low temperature, but now he could feel it beginning to rise, as if he were switching to active mode.

He felt a presence on the other side of the closed door. Apparently the guard had come back. From just the sense of presence and the sounds, Harvey could clearly picture his every movement as he sat down in the folding chair at the desk, making it squeak.

Still prone, he stared at the door. This time he clenched his fist tight.

I guess this would be the perfect warm-up…

"Here."

A delicate teacup was placed with a light tapping sound on the subdued tablecloth at the dining table. Kieli sat primly on her chair and looked down at it. A dark-brown liquid filled the cup to a refined three-quarters, sending up a trail of steam and a sweet aroma.

"This will warm you up. Or are you too old now for hot chocolate?"

"Oh, no, I like it. Thank you," she said, wrapping her hands around the cup. She felt pressured; it was a beautiful cup, and it would be terrible if she dropped it and broke it. "I'm sorry for troubling you. I'll leave tomorrow."

"Please don't worry about it. We don't mind having you here at all. You *are* a dear friend of the young master's."

Kieli hadn't noticed it at first, but she recognized this gentle-voiced woman. She was the lady in the maid's uniform who'd been there the first time she'd ever seen Julius as their sand ship was leaving to cross the Sand Ocean, standing at the pier waving good-bye with her handkerchief. She'd been Julius's nursemaid, and now that her duties in that area were finished, she'd come back to the family home in Gate Town's uptown district. Kieli was informed that Julius usually stayed in this house when he visited Gate Town; now he had arranged for her to spend the night here.

"I owe Juli... I mean Julius... *Master* Julius so much for all his, um, assistance... and I've got to... I mean, I *must* thank you both for what you've done for Harvey, too..." She tripped awkwardly over the unfamiliar polite language. As she stared down at the cup in her hands as if searching for help — though of course it wasn't as if there were a guidebook written there — the lady laughed softly.

"It's perfectly all right for you to speak as you normally would." On the whole, that did seem like a safer idea.

Putting the rim of the cup to her mouth, Kieli looked up

through her eyelashes at the face of the woman sitting kitty-corner from her, who had begun peeling a piece of fruit.

According to her, she'd been visiting the prison once a week on Julius's orders to take care of Harvey. Although he was an Undying who wouldn't die even if left alone to rot, he still had certain minimally necessary bodily functions that had been working during his recovery. However, he'd been more or less a vegetable up until recently, and hadn't been able to do anything for himself.

"Um, you have close ties to the Church, don't you...?"

Kieli couldn't bring herself to say *If you're so religious, why did you help one of the "infernal Undyings"?* so it came out as a very roundabout question. The lady seemed to understand what she meant, though, and began talking with a smile, staring down at the hand holding her paring knife. "I merely do what the young master wishes. I don't ask unnecessary questions, and I don't tell a soul. After all, I imagine he has his reasons. Though it's true he was once an impish little boy, and I used to scold him for it," she added, her smile a little wry. Then her expression softened again into the mild smile with its restrained pride. "He suddenly started studying quite a lot after he returned from his trip alone to South-hairo last winter, and he's been at the top of his class ever since he advanced to the high school division of the seminary."

"Yes, Jul—*Master* Julius has turned out really...er, *quite* wonderfully," she said, still a little stiffly, and remembered afresh her reunion with Julius that evening at the prison. All traces of his mother's ghost, which had followed him everywhere when they'd first met on the ship, had vanished. She must have realized to her relief that he'd be okay by himself now...

"He has turned out wonderfully, but he doesn't seem to have any friends of his own age, and I've been worried. I feel much better now that I know he has a charming friend like you."

"Er, right..." Kieli's eyes darted around the room. She wasn't quite sure how to respond to that. She was embarrassed, and more than that she was guilty. It had been almost two years since she'd practically run away from Julius at the South-hairo port, and she'd barely thought of him since, yet Julius still thought of her as a friend, and had harbored Harvey even though he knew he might face terrible punishment if he were found out.

He'd done so much for her; she could never be grateful enough.

She took a sip of her hot chocolate. The sweet taste she hadn't experienced in so long was delicious, and somehow comforting. But at the same time, she also felt it bring home to her that when all was said and done, she was still a little kid that sweet hot chocolate suited.

She'd always had someone protecting her. When her mother had been alive, and when she'd been staying with her grandmother, and when she'd been at boarding school, and when she'd traveled with Harvey, and this past year and a half when she'd been with Beatrix and the radio, too. The Corporal was a given, of course, but even Beatrix had always stuck with her, for all her complaining.

If Kieli had thought about it at all she must have known that they were considering her feelings, trying to keep her from being hurt, and yet in a moment of distrust, she'd thrown a childish temper tantrum and left them behind.

I wonder if they're worried about me. Forget that; they must be angry.

And Harvey must be angry, too, huh?

It must have hurt. His face looked so awful... The image of the painfully white gauze on his face and the wound she could see beneath it were still burned into her brain. He'd been so injured, and she'd thrown the lighter right at his wound with all she had. And now that she thought about it, that might have been the first time she'd ever actually *thrown* something at Harvey. When she'd last looked at him, he'd been staring at her with frozen-faced shock.

But this is Harvey's fault, too, she murmured in her heart. It half-sounded like an excuse. After all, that reaction had just been too cruel when they'd just been reunited after so long. How much did he think she'd worried, hearing that he might be dead?

...But when they'd just been reunited after so long, she'd cut off their conversation almost before they'd said anything, and run away.

What the heck did I come here for, anyway? I left everyone behind, and then I fought with Harvey, too.

It was as if she'd suddenly been cut off from everything she'd been connected to before, and left all alone. And she'd brought it all on herself, too.

Seeing Kieli staring silently down at nothing, the lady stopped peeling fruit and gently said, "You must be tired. You should take a bath and go to bed early. Let's go visit him again tomorrow."

"But…" She closed her mouth, eyes still on her hot chocolate. Today, tomorrow, it was all the same; she still didn't know how she could face him. She wasn't confident she'd be able to speak calmly to him next time either, and he might be angry, too.

"I thought he was more frightening at first," the lady said in tranquil, clear tones.

Kieli looked up at her face, astonished. "You mean Harvey?"

The lady nodded and continued, furrowing her brow as if a little troubled. "Naturally I thought Undying were fearsome things, and he was so horribly injured, with one eye gone; in the beginning that was frightening enough that I couldn't look at him… And above all else, his good eye was always glaring at something. He had such a harsh expression on his face…"

To Kieli this speech felt somewhat unexpected. She didn't have many memories of Harvey seeming scary. If she had to pick a most-common Harvey expression, it would be the one in which he looked as if he wasn't thinking about anything at all.

"Last week, though, he finally started speaking to me a bit. That day I'd dressed his wounds and helped him change his clothes as usual, and as I was about to leave, he said, 'Thank you for your help.' It was almost a whisper, but he said it." And with that, the lady smiled and brought the tale to a close.

Kieli gazed speechlessly at her for several seconds, then dropped her head to her chest and answered with what few words she could manage before the tears came. "Yes…that's the kind of person he is…"

Boom!

A huge noise suddenly rang out from the other side of the isolation cell door, and the guard sitting in the chair outside felt both his heart and his rear end leap a full five centimeters into the air.

He'd seen off Master Julius and returned to his post. There was still a little time before someone from the night shift came to relieve him, but nothing in particular for him to do, so he was sitting at the desk writing in the logbook.

The log itself was purely a formality; they only wrote in it the kinds of harmless things that could be reported to their superiors. Only a very small number of people knew the truth about who exactly was imprisoned in this solitary cell: Master Julius, the prisoner's guarantor; Julius's hired woman; the tiny band of soldiers under Julius's command whom he'd had bring the prisoner here; and the guard whose salary the young master's pocket money was supplementing in exchange for staying silent and keeping watch over this place — in other words, himself.

Rather than keeping watch to prevent the prisoner from escaping, his main job was in fact to vigilantly guard against anyone else *seeing* the prisoner.

What was that noise? Putting down his pen, he stiffly craned his neck around to look at the door. But there was only silence in the wake of the original crash; now the cell was so devoid of sounds or any signs of living presence that it sent a chill up his spine. He started to get up, intending to check on the prisoner; but while he was still only half-standing, he hesitated.

When the prisoner had first been brought here, he was such a tattered half-corpse that the guard had almost expected to smell the stench of rot. But not only had the prisoner not died, he'd gradually recovered to the point where the guard felt he was capable of going berserk any second. The man wasn't human.

Still, Master Julius trusted him to guard this prisoner. He'd never be able to face the young man again if something should happen to his charge...

There were some who didn't think well of Master Julius, saying he had only gotten his position through the influence of his family, but the guard and most of his colleagues felt the boy wasn't so bad. True, he came from one of the super-privileged families of the capital, and he made full use of that authority doing things like keeping a mysterious prisoner here, but it wasn't as if that had unduly messed up their work or anything. There were probably plenty of kids from powerful families who had the potential to become uncontrollable tyrants, but that boy was (though he knew this was a strange way to put it) a tyrant with a true conscience.

Aw, damn it. Okay, I have to do this for Master Julius...

Resignedly he prepared himself, praying all the while that nothing would happen.

He kept his eyes fixed on the door as he felt about with one hand for the nightstick at his waist and withdrew it. Then he fearfully approached the cell in a timid crouch, walking noiselessly. Brandishing his nightstick in his right hand, he brought his face to the bars at the window and darted a look inside —

Whoosh!

That instant, a hand suddenly shot out from between the bars and grabbed his wrist. He shrieked. Then he tried to turn around and run, but the prisoner's arm immediately slid up to his neck and dragged him back, and his own captured arm ended up bizarrely crossed with the prisoner's in a choke hold at his throat.

"L-Let me—"

"Don't speak," whispered a low voice behind his head as it was pressed up against the window. He gurgled in answer. Even if he'd wanted to speak, the other man's arm was biting into his neck, and he could manage only sporadic snatches of breath.

"Unlock the door."

The voice was blunt and commanding. The breathing at his ear sounded like a low, canine growl. Inwardly trembling with terror that the fiend might latch its teeth onto him at any moment, the guard nevertheless screwed up what little courage he had and managed to shake his head a fraction in refusal. The hand holding the nightstick was captured, but the other one remained free. By contrast, the prisoner had only one arm.

He tried prying off the enemy's grip with his free hand, but to his surprise, it didn't even budge.

Of the two, he was clearly in better shape. The prisoner's arm was so emaciated that it had fit through the barred window; the bones and veins stood out starkly. There was no way that arm could possibly be stronger than his. And yet, no matter how hard he yanked, the prisoner didn't move.

The guard whimpered.

"Unlock it. I could kill you easily." The arm at his throat

tightened as he repeated his order. The guard thought he heard a strange snapping sound coming from that arm, but he was so out of his mind with fear that he couldn't think anymore; he fumbled at his waist for the keys and began unbolting the door behind him.

He had to do it by feel, and on top of that his hands were shaking and unsteady. He couldn't quite get the keys to go into the locks. As the time passed the prisoner's arm bit more fiercely into his neck, and he had trouble breathing. A sense of heavy, sharp malice like a mad dog stifling its growls pressured him from behind.

He's going to rip me apart...!

The guard continued to work feverishly, praying for divine protection, and somehow managed to undo all four locks before his neck was broken or his breathing cut off. (Why were there *four* of them?! The inconvenience was unforgivable.) He drew the bar out and dropped it on the floor.

The arm around his neck momentarily relaxed, and he had just enough time to be fervently relieved before it tightened again and slammed his head hard against the window's bars.

While he was lost in a fit of dizziness, he found himself dragged into the open cell and thrown into one corner, the prisoner passing him in the doorway as he slid out. Then he heard the bar slide into place outside.

"Oh, hell..." Shaking his throbbing head, he hastily stood up, pressing his face to the window and peering through the bars. "Huh?" He hadn't heard any retreating footsteps, but somehow the prisoner had already vanished from the hallway.

The guard was utterly bewildered for a moment, but when

he looked down he realized that the Undying had simply collapsed right at the bottom of the door; however, in no time he stood up again and ran with a somewhat unsteady gait to the stairway. He grabbed the guard's coat from the wall on his way out.

"W-Wait!" All the blood drained from his face at once. "Hey! Somebody come here! Hey!" He grabbed the bars with both hands and rattled the door on its hinges, screaming for help, but of course there was no one else within earshot. That was exactly why Master Julius had decided this would be the safest place to hide the prisoner.

Wh-Wh-What should I do? Forget about taking a pay cut; if I'm unlucky I could be fired for this, or maybe even driven out of the Church. "Somebody, please...!"

For lack of any better idea, he rattled the door madly. He felt hopeless. After a while, though, he noticed the crossbar starting to come loose. Maybe the prisoner had been in a hurry; apparently he'd mounted it carelessly and it wasn't firmly secured in place.

Taken aback, he shook the door even more violently. The crossbar slid a few centimeters at a time from its perch across the metal fittings on either side, eventually coming loose on one end and sliding to the floor with a clatter.

There was no time to stop to breathe. The guard flung open the door and bolted down the hallway. Before he could give it much thought, he flew to the alarm on the wall and sounded it. With its furious wail as background music, he seized the phone.

The tinny voice of his coworker in the guardroom above greeted him. "Man, what's up? I'm eating right now and —"

"This is no time to sit around eating! We've got a prison break on our hands, do you hear me?! And I've told you a million times: bring me some food before you dig in!" he bellowed back in irritation, and then threw the mouthpiece at the wall before grabbing a flashlight and running off in the direction the prisoner had escaped.

The hallway spat him out at the foot of the stairs leading up to the communal cells. He stopped there for a moment and looked up into the darkness above. There were windows high up on the wall of the landing to let in light; perfect square slices of the blue-gray night sky stood out against the gloom. Someone built like the prisoner might be able to squeeze through them, but realistically speaking, it would be impossible for him to climb up to them.

He dropped his gaze to his feet. In the muted light of the bare bulb overhead, his shadow lay pale and blurred on the floor. Letting his eyes travel across the floor, he saw a forty- or fifty-centimeter water drain in front of the steps. Its grated metal cover wasn't sitting quite right.

He was regretting that he hadn't waited for his colleague to join him before coming down here, but it was too late. Fearfully casting the round beam of his flashlight before him, he squelched along the pitch-dark underground waterway. With each step came the sensation of the soles of his shoes being sucked down into the moist ground, the feeling of damp cold, and the sound of slow-moving water. It all combined to form an air of perfect eeriness.

On top of that, there was no telling when that wild dog of a prisoner would leap from the darkness and tear out his throat.

He lamented the bad luck that had landed him in this horrible situation. *Oh, why does this have to happen to me? God, did I do something to wrong you?*

Letting the prisoner escape had been a mistake, of course, but so had ringing the alarm on the spur of the moment like that. If the situation got out of hand and others found out that the prisoner was an Undying, even Master Julius would be in a very awkward position, and his own head could roll. Possibly literally. *Oh, I should never have let the special bonus lure me into taking this side job! It's just like they say: humans should humbly live with faith as their only joy. Yeah.*

He felt water lap at the tip of his shoe. When he trained his flashlight on the ground, he saw a rippling pool of black liquid right in front of where he had put his foot.

The hallway that formed the riverbanks broke off suddenly into a sharp vertical drop.

"Whoa, that was close...!" He drew his foot back with a shiver and wiped the cold sweat from his face.

Then he heard a low growl behind him, like something clearing its throat —

The instant he whirled around, the tall shadow suddenly standing there behind him shot out a long arm. Before he even had the chance to scream, five bony fingers clutched his throat, and he had the rare experience, both his first and his last, of hearing his own neck breaking.

❧

"Temple flush! How d'ya like *that*, eh?"

"Full house, cruisers and swords."

Julius flung his cards to the table with a cry of dismay, leaning far back on the couch and tipping his head up as if in appeal to the heavens. "I lost again! I never expected you to be such an expert at cards, Kieli."

Gathering up the cards from her seat on the sofa facing his, Kieli gave a pained smile of embarrassment. "I'm not good enough to be called an expert."

She'd taken advantage of the lady's kind offer and had a bath. As her body warmed up she'd become pleasantly sleepy, but just as she was thinking of going to bed, Julius had come home. So now they were playing cards and living it up reminiscing about the past.

The subject of what they'd done after parting at the South-hairo Port came up, and she told him a safely edited version of her job at Buzz & Suzie's Café in the mining town and about her life in eastern South-hairo. Of course there were some parts she couldn't go into detail about, like the Corporal, who was a radio, or Beatrix, the other Undying besides Harvey.

Julius had stayed in South-hairo for a while and then gone back to the capital. He had now advanced to the high school division of the seminary. Two things surprised Kieli about his story: first, although she'd thought she was at least two or three years older than Julius, she now discovered they were only one school year apart. Second, Julius's family was even more wealthy and famous than she'd ever imagined.

Julius's grandfather was a prominent member of the Church's highest body, the Council of Elders. Likewise, his father was second-in-command of the Church's Security Forces — in other words, he was Number Two in the organization that united all of the local outposts of Church Soldiers across the entire planet. To put it in extreme terms, thanks to his father's influence Julius could come and go freely from any of those outposts and do whatever he wanted.

The Council of Elders was made up of eleven high-level clergymen who were said to descend from the Saints, and below them fell all the individual organizations, like the Security Forces responsible for the Church Soldiers and the Preaching Department responsible for all the priests. Kieli personally doubted that the "Eleven Saints" had ever really existed, but at any rate Julius's family was one of the planet's eleven greatest houses, and Julius himself might become one of the Elders someday.

When she heard this, Kieli found herself staring at Julius as if he were literally from another world. She said, "Juli, you're like the prince of some noble family" (and there had never been any nobility on this planet, so the old tales of nobility must have come from the mother planet), and he smiled broadly at her and told her, "And the girl who marries me can be a princess."

"I just know she'll be lovely, too."

"No, that's not what I meant…" At Kieli's blank stare, his smile slipped slightly for some reason. "Well, whatever," he sighed.

Julius kept insisting on another round, so even though Kieli was starting to get seriously sleepy, she'd gathered the cards and begun cutting them again when the lady appeared in the living room doorway.

"My, you seem to be having fun," she said, taking in the sight of them. Then she gestured to Julius with a look. "I'm sorry to interrupt you, young master, but you have a call from the guardhouse."

"At this hour?" Julius frowned slightly and stood up from the couch. He left the living room with a promise that he'd be right back. The lady disappeared with him, and Kieli was left alone; with nothing better to do, she let her eyes wander around the room as she continued to meaninglessly cut the cards.

Sofas, curtains, low tables, cabinets: all its furnishings were elegant without being showy. It probably didn't hold a candle to Julius's family home, but this house was surely upperclass in its own way. She'd heard that Gate Town's uptown was filled with the estates of the capital families' cousins, as well as of the families who had served the capital for generations. It probably wasn't even worth bringing up, but she couldn't help wondering why there was such a gap between their lifestyle and that of the failed pilgrims who lived in the abandoned waterways of downtown, when they were all members of the same faith.

She drew her legs up onto the sofa and hugged her knees. *What should I do tomorrow...?*

"Kieli!"

Julius's sudden return caught her by surprise. She lowered her legs from the sofa in a panic and straightened her spine a little to sit formally as she turned to look at him. He was standing in the doorway, all the color drained from his face.

"Is something wrong?"

"They say he ran away!"

"Huh?" She blinked, gazing back at him. Julius wasn't doing much better than she was. He was standing still as stone and looked half-dazed. "...Huh?" she whispered again, and then after a beat she shot up from the sofa. "What do you mean?! Where did he go?!"

"I don't know! It looks like he escaped into the underground waterways, but...Anyway, I'm going over to the prison right now."

"I'm coming, too!" Kieli cried eagerly, but he refused her with unexpected sharpness.

"No."

Somewhat surprised, she swallowed the rest of her words. Still, she gazed into Julius's dark-green eyes in earnest appeal.

After a while, he sighed in defeat. "Fine. Go get your coat. It's cold outside."

Kieli nodded. "Okay, I'll be right back!" She flew out of the living room and headed for the guest room on the second floor, where the lady had put her for the night. *What does he mean, "ran away"? Harvey, why would you do that when you're so beat-up?!* Her heart began to pound, and not just because she'd sprinted up the stairs.

Now she bitterly regretted the short temper that had sent her running out of the prison so fast earlier that day. She hadn't gotten to do more than see his face for a few moments. She hadn't said anything to him yet. Somewhere inside, she'd assumed that she could just make up with him the next time she saw him, and she'd let herself relax. But too late she realized there had been no guarantee she'd get a "next time."

When she dived into the bedroom, she couldn't bear taking the time even to turn on the light. She found her coat by the faint glow of the streetlamps through the window and grabbed it. She was already turning to leave the room, shoving her arms through the sleeves, when the door slammed shut with a bang.

She heard a key turning in the lock.

"What...?"

Unable to grasp the situation, she simply gaped at the closed door in shock. Then with a start she seized the doorknob. It just clicked back and forth as she turned it; the door didn't budge.

"I'm sorry, Kieli," said Julius's voice from the other side. The doorknob passively continued to bar her way. It had a picture of a sheep etched into it. She let go of it and plastered herself against the door, pounding with both fists.

"Juli?! What is this? Open up!"

"I'm sorry, but you need to stay here until I get back."

"No! Take me with you! Why are you doing this?!"

"It's kind of a bad situation. Depending on how things go, even I might not be able to protect him any longer. But no matter what, I'll guarantee your safety, I promise. So just stay here."

"I don't understand what you're saying! What is this? Did something happen to Harvey?!" she demanded, pressing her face to the door.

The answer came in a cold, clipped voice that was horribly unlike Julius. "It's the other way around." He sounded annoyed, or disappointed.

"Juli…?"

"They found the body of the guard who went after him in the underground waterway. He was murdered. His neck was broken."

"Mur—"

"There's a search force in the waterways now. They've got permission to shoot him on sight if he puts up any resistance. If they do that, it's only a matter of time before they find out he's an Undying." This speech came out in a voice deliberately stripped of feeling, and then Julius fell silent, as if declaring the explanation over. While Kieli stood there thunderstruck, she heard him start to walk away, leaving a few words of instruction to the lady.

"Wait…wait! It's not true! Harvey didn't do it!" she cried hurriedly through the door, but his footsteps continued down the hallway without pausing.

"Juli, wait! Please, let *me* go! I'll find him and ask him what happened. I know this is some mistake! Please, take me with you!"

She kept pounding the door with her fists, but the footsteps didn't turn around. The lady's thin, rather trembling voice told her, "I'm very sorry. I'll come back later." Then her footsteps disappeared down the hallway, too.

"Wait…"

Kieli stayed glued to the door even after all signs of human presence disappeared from the hallway, but after a little while she heard mumbling voices behind her, and she spun around like lightning and ran to the window on the opposite wall.

As she looked out through the glass, a black truck that

blended into the nighttime darkness was just pulling away down the road in front of the mansion. It was a Church Soldiers' truck. It must've come to pick up Julius.

She tore her eyes from the window and looked around the room, but there weren't any exits other than the locked door. Turning back to the window, she pressed against the glass and ran her eyes over the surrounding walls outside. Below her she could see light spilling from a window on the first floor. It was some distance down, but if she hung off the window ledge she should be able to manage a jump.

When she unlocked the window and opened it, the nighttime autumn winds of North-hairo stirred her hair. Feeling genuinely sorry for the trouble she was causing Julius, she climbed out onto the ledge.

Unfortunately I wasn't raised well, so nobody ever taught me to always enter and exit a room through the door.

Since Harvey's right arm wouldn't move, he opened the pack of cigarettes he'd just bought with his teeth and pulled one out with his lips. With his left hand he returned the pack to his pocket and grabbed the lighter instead, halting his steps just long enough to light up.

As he brought the flame to the tip of his cigarette, he stared at the lighter and silently racked his brains. *I just don't get it...* It was the lighter Kieli had thrown at him, but looking at it again now, he still didn't have any memory of owning it.

His attention was on the lighter, so he sucked in the smoke

out of habit without thinking too much. His lungs immediately seized up and he fell into a violent fit of coughing.

While he was underground, he'd been the extremely ungrateful victim of a strict no-smoking policy; now that he thought about it, it had been a pretty long time since he'd last inhaled smoke. Maybe he was now oxygen-deprived, because the world swam before his eye and he stumbled slightly. *Crap.* Now all the pedestrians around him were giving him dubious looks. He pulled his hood farther down across his face and sped away from them.

Grabbing that coat he'd spotted hanging on the wall had been a good call, if he did say so himself. There had been a little cash in the pocket, which he'd gladly taken to buy some smokes before melting into the crowds and welcome darkness of the city night. Now he was walking toward uptown. No pursuers seemed to be following him through the city streets yet. To be honest, he hadn't expected the guards to fall for such a simple ploy, but luckily they seemed to think he'd headed into the waterways, just as he'd hoped they would.

Now that he was forcing his body to move, his core seemed to have transferred its energies from healing his wounds to more everyday activities; even though he'd been so weak at first that he'd immediately collapsed after escaping his cell, his awkwardness had steadily faded and now he was starting to be able to move normally.

His right eye and cheek had begun to throb painfully, though. He hid that conspicuous gauze under the hood of the coat and rushed along the edges of the city, puffing on his cigarette with odd stubbornness even though it didn't taste that good, and periodically coughing.

Incidentally, he'd also injured a muscle in his left arm using that absurd strength earlier.

They'd been treated as the strongest of soldiers in the War because they'd been able to ignore their physical limitations and go wild, since no matter how much damage they did it would heal right away anyway. They didn't actually have inhuman strength or anything. He'd heard rumors that when they were manufactured, the scientists had chosen the corpses with the best parts to use on them, which frankly seemed likely — but even if that were true, it still meant their superiority or inferiority was measured on the same scale as a normal person's.

Shit, this is taking forever...

Pain still shot from his elbow to his shoulder when he flexed his arm. He realized once again that if he unthinkingly went too far, his regenerative powers probably wouldn't be able to keep up with him. Looking back on it now, he thought his decision to rip out the remains of his own crushed eyeball because the odd loose feeling of it had annoyed him might have been too hasty. At this rate, it was going to take a fair amount of time for the eye to fully regenerate. He couldn't get a handle on his depth perception, and he'd come close to knocking over several passersby before he'd gotten used to walking around with only half his vision.

The woman had given him an overall explanation of the city's layout before, so he found the house he was looking for comparatively easily. It was in a corner of a quiet uptown residential district. In this neighborhood the mansion could be rated "cozy"; there was an agreeable refinement to the white walls that jutted up into the blue-gray night sky.

He felt somewhat relieved to see that it was more or less as he'd pictured it. Then, in an act that sharply contradicted this peaceful feeling, he darted his eye in either direction to confirm that the coast was clear and began climbing the gate. From the top he dropped down soundlessly to land in the estate's front garden.

"Now then…" So far he'd acted without hesitation, but now that he was actually standing at the front door, he came to a halt. He hadn't given any concrete thought to what would happen next.

If anyone was here besides Julius or that woman who'd been his nursemaid or whatever, he couldn't very well just waltz right in, but on the other hand, even if he sneaked in somehow, he sure as hell didn't know the layout *inside* the house. And even if he got past those hurdles and managed to meet up with Kieli…

What do I even intend to say?

He considered this for a few seconds, then mentally shrugged and decided it would work itself out somehow. He was casting around for a good point of entry when the front door suddenly opened.

The rectangular patch of light from inside illuminated the garden. He made as if to hide, but then the female-shaped shadow who'd flown out the door tripped on the step and started to fall. Without thinking, he reached out to support her.

With a cry of surprise, the woman in his arms lifted her face. When she recognized him, her mouth opened in the shape of a scream, so he hastily covered it with his left hand. He bent his mouth to her ear and said in a fast whisper, "I'm not going to do anything to you. I heard that Kieli — I mean, the girl who came to see me this evening — was here."

No sooner did the woman give a tiny nod than she began shaking her head wildly, eyes wide. He realized something was wrong and removed his hand. She immediately grabbed his arm with an awful expression on her face. "I'm so sorry! She's gone from her room and —"

"Gone?"

"I'm sure she went to the underground waterways to look for you. This is all because I took my eyes off her for a minute... Oh, how will I apologize to Master Julius? No, that's not important; what if something happens to our guest?! Quick — we must go look for her —"

"Hey! Okay, I get you. Calm down." Faced with this woman wailing at him as tears and makeup ran down her face in streaks, he was a little at a loss. He pulled away. "How long ago was it? Do you know which way she went?"

"It can't have been long... I'm so sorry, I don't know which direction she left in. This is all because I took my eyes off her for a minute! However can I apologize to Master Julius?!"

"Okay, okay, I get it." *You said that before.* "Look, go back inside. It's okay. I'll go look for her," he said as sincerely as he could, holding on to the woman's shoulders. As he spoke, half of his mind was focused on bringing up a mental map of the city and orienting himself to where the possible entrances to the sewers were. If not too much time had passed, he should be able to catch up.

The woman wiped her tears with the handkerchief clutched in her hands and lowered her eyes in embarrassment. Apparently she was feeling a little calmer.

"I'm sorry for getting so upset...."

"It's fine." He let go of her shoulders and bowed his head lightly. "I should apologize to you for all the trouble."

With that he turned on his heel and started to leave, but feeling eyes on him, he looked back again to find the woman still at the front door, staring stupidly at him, her face streaked with tears. When their eyes met she dropped her gaze hastily. "No, I'm sorry, it's just...you sounded like such a normal person, and I wasn't expecting...oh!" Harvey had no idea what that "oh" was supposed to mean, but the woman shrank back and fell silent without continuing the thought.

Well, excuse me for being so unexpectedly normal.

Unsure how to respond, he eventually turned around and left without any expression registering on his face.

"Il, it's late. Go to sleep."

A boy's voice cheerily answered the girl's. "I'm not sleepy yet!"

Beatrix peeked at the bed of the truck through the small window in the back of the cab and stifled a sigh. The girl had made a little bed out of blankets in the space between pieces of cargo in the back, and now the boy was rolling around on it with cries of delight.

What a peaceful scene.

"So like I said, when that innocent little brother and sister told me they were going to their relatives' place in North-hairo all by themselves, I took them aboard out of the pure kindness of my heart. A man wouldn't be able to sleep at night thinking of some bad guy catching them, taking all their money, and selling them into slavery, right?"

"Yeah, yeah, quit going on about that," she answered carelessly, sliding her gaze to the man in the driver's seat, who was chattering fluently as he gripped the steering wheel. Well, she guessed he was probably telling the truth. He might have an ulterior motive — perhaps he guessed that these relatives were a rich family with ties to the Church and hoped to force their gratitude and get some reward money, and with luck, some business connections — but she was under no particular obligation to worry about that.

According to what he'd said, he was a merchant who traveled between Westerbury and North-hairo, mainly dealing in rarities and collectors' items for fanatics. It was true that there was a comparatively large number of rich people in those places who could afford to pour money into such interests. Of course, it was still just a handful of the elite.

He'd been making a pit stop in Toulouse when a black-haired girl with a cool expression and some real talent who'd happened to be at his table in the gambling parlor had caught his eye, and so he'd gone after her to try to pick her up. And the rest was history.

"But man, talk about a surprise. You were wearing such a weird, no, I mean *eccentric* getup and covering your face, so I thought you must be a real ugly woman. But you're a total babe! I should've asked *you* out that day."

"If you had, I would've done more than hit you with a trunk. And there were extenuating circumstances that day." *"Eccentric" isn't any better than "weird"! I know you mean the same thing by it!*

"What circumstances?"

Beatrix turned away irritably. "None of your business."

"Lady, why did the witch girl leave you behind?" broke in a guileless voice from behind her. When she turned around, the young boy was sticking his head through the window with a grin on his face. She didn't really like or dislike children, but if nothing else she was bad at talking to them. While she hemmed and hawed, grimacing, the boy's older sister grabbed him and yanked him away from the window. "Il! I told you not to bring that up anymore!"

"She's right, Il," nodded the merchant, assuming a brotherly expression for no reason Beatrix could see. Addressing his audience in the rearview mirror, he launched into a specious lecture. "The story that the Witch of Toulouse was a black-haired woman in black clothes is pure fiction. The souvenir sellers who've set up around the bell tower invented it based on eyewitness accounts from people who said they saw a ghost there or whatever. What the reliable sources say is that the witch was a beautiful woman with blond hair and blue eyes."

As he spoke, he darted a look at Beatrix out of the corner of his eyes. Unable to judge how much he meant by it, she confined herself to glaring expressionlessly back at him. Could he be gauging her reaction? Maybe she was overthinking things, but…

"Anyway, the witch's ghost couldn't exist in the first place. Everybody calls her a witch all the time because that's easy to understand, but the actual Witch of Toulouse was —"

"No!" the girl cut in suddenly, halting the merchant midsentence. The loud cry echoed in the back of Beatrix's skull, and she instinctively leaned away a little. She turned, wondering if it was really something to shriek about like that, only to see the girl crouching in the truck bed with her arms protectively around her brother. He squirmed to get away, whining "What was that for, Monica?!", but she kept her hands clapped firmly over his ears.

"That's a dirty word that you mustn't ever say! It's even worse than 'witch.' Our parents *and* the Church priests were v-very strict about it…!" In her passion, the girl was actually convulsing. Both flabbergasted, Beatrix and the driver exchanged blank looks.

"Wow, now I really feel like I'm in North-hairo," joked the merchant with a grin.

"…Yes," Beatrix agreed shortly. Then she turned away and looked out the windshield at the scenery. There was nothing much to be seen there, however: just the headlights cutting white circles into the heavy blue-gray of the nighttime world, casting shadows on the rutted path through the wilderness.

That kind of thing wasn't limited to North-hairo, the lap of the capital. To the totally average devout family, it was totally average for Undyings, and the word "Undying," to be thought of like that.

Boom!

An explosive sound like something pounding against an invisible wall suddenly reverberated through the back of the truck, jerking her thoughts back to her surroundings. Then music began to play at high volume.

"Wh-What the hell is that?!" the merchant cried in surprise. Equally shocked, Beatrix covered her ears and turned to look into the bed, and almost jumped out of her seat. The little boy sat frozen on the blanket, stunned. In his arms was a small radio. She'd tossed it back there with her trunk; the boy must've picked it up and fiddled with the controls.

"Give me that, you idiot!" Leaning her upper body out the window, she snatched it out of his hands. She immediately turned the sound down with a sigh of relief, but the girl, who had also sunk to the floor of the truck in a daze, frowned at her.

"What was that? Savage music like that is banned, you know!"

"Well, excuse me for being say —" the radio began, protesting. To shut it up, Beatrix tossed it onto the floor of the front seat without looking.

"Um, you see, this isn't mine. I'm just holding on to it. If it were up to me, I'd throw it away right now, but it isn't."

Things were starting to get kind of troublesome. She was fed up with it all, but she bluffed it out for the moment and glanced at the driver to check his reaction. He kept on driving casually with his elbow on the wheel. "Eh, loosen up. It's not like anybody's going to take you to task for it out here in the middle of the wilderness. Go ahead and let it play; I don't care. Like they

say, good company on the road makes the shortest journey."
He beamed, winking at her.

This guy is a little too understanding. "…Thanks," Beatrix
said grudgingly, and decided not to let her guard down
around him.

She sensed something lurking beyond the darkness in front
of her.

She tried beaming the flashlight hanging from her neck at
it, but the light was swallowed up right away by the darkness
of the tunnel, and she could see only a little way ahead. Underground, darkness must be higher on the totem pole than
light.

"Harvey…?"

No voice answered her weak call. The echoes of her own
voice just bounced eerily back to her off of the walls of damp
and dark that enveloped her. For lack of a better idea, Kieli
trained her light on the pathway along the water and went in
that direction. It'd be trouble if she ran into the Church Soldiers' search team, so she couldn't very well wander around
shouting for him.

She'd found the flashlight sitting in front of Julius's nursemaid's house and grabbed it, silently apologizing for her terrible upbringing. She thought it had been a little less than an
hour since she'd climbed down into the underground waterways from a drain in the uptown residential district and
started walking along the water. A moist cold seeped through

her coat, chilling her to the bone; it was completely different than the dry, biting winter wind that blew across the plains. The wet sound of her feet striking the dank concrete floor echoed weirdly off walls slimy with muck and moss. She was already nervous, and the sour smell and the claustrophobic feeling of the underground tunnel only made her feel smaller.

She hadn't *thought* she was walking aimlessly, but now she was gradually losing confidence. It made sense that to get from uptown to midtown, where the prison was, she should follow the water downstream. But in this part of the tunnel the current slowed down, and it was hard to tell which way was downstream. When she cast her light on the surface, viscous black water like used oil undulated with the deliberation of a lazy animal.

The underground waterway network was built by the advanced pre-War civilization, and boasted a grand scale that was probably impossible with today's technology. People said it spread out underneath all of Gate Town, crisscrossing itself like a labyrinth. Walking down the concrete path that had been built along the water, Kieli sometimes saw gaping arched caverns along the wall beside her. Water flowed into these thin sidestreams and out of sight.

The passage she was walking along now followed a fairly large stream; the puny glow of her flashlight didn't reach the other side. However, considering how wide the tunnel was, it wasn't very tall. The uneven ceiling coated with muck that hung low over her head deepened her feeling of claustrophobia.

After she'd gone down the tunnel awhile, she started to hear the sound of rushing water coming from the darkness ahead. She walked a little farther, shining her light around her, and came out into a slightly wider space where two streams met. At the point where the two currents ran into each other and grew stagnant, she could see a sort of black embankment stretching across.

It looked like all the debris that the water carried with it, large and small, had accumulated in the center of the stagnation, combining with the muck and lumping into a small dike. The dammed-up water flowed out through cracks in the dike, past which it broke out of its stillness and coursed in a fast current downstream.

Kieli could understand now what had been blocking up the flow of the river behind her. As she squinted at the dike, the toe of her boot slipped into the water with a splash, and she hurriedly drew it back out. Maybe the pathway she'd come down was starting to crumble beneath the surface; the concrete slanted down into the water before her and the hallway was cut off.

I'm at a dead end…

If the presence she'd felt earlier hadn't been a figment of her imagination, then there must still be a path forward somewhere (as long as that person hadn't dived into the water, and that was why she hadn't seen him…). She let her light play over the water slowly so that she wouldn't miss the smallest clue.

Various bits of flotsam were stuck right in front of the dike and were bobbing slightly up and down on the black surface of the water.

Among them was what looked like the back and head of a person floating facedown.

With a cry, Kieli realized she'd stepped farther down the path and into the stream without really thinking about it. Luckily, there wasn't a sudden drop-off or anything, and the water only came up to about the tops of her boots. She sloshed along, sending up splashes of the cloudy water churning around her legs.

She managed to scramble up onto the dike where a part of it had rotted and crumbled, and walked along to the floating body. Hesitantly, she shined her light on it to see if it was still alive.

Oh!

In hindsight, of course she hadn't been sure it was Harvey; she'd just seen a person floating and so she'd come closer to investigate, that was all. And the thing that had looked like a person was just a big piece of trash tangled up in a tattered, waterlogged blanket.

She was relieved, but at the same time a little deflated. Maybe she'd leapt to the wrong conclusion because she'd heard that it wasn't unusual for people to go missing in the waterways.

It looks like I can keep going from the other side . . .

When Kieli let her light shine on the other bank from her perch on the dike, it looked as though the path hadn't crumbled into the water on that side. If she crossed over, she could probably keep going downstream.

She started walking down the dike to the opposite bank. Muddy gunk coated the trash it was formed out of, and it was easy to slip. She moved cautiously forward one step at a time, paying attention to the surface under her feet.

She thought she'd been careful enough. But she'd been so focused on where she stepped that she was taken by surprise when her foot slipped inside her water-filled boot.

"Wah!"

She lost her balance and slipped down the other side of the dike, splashing into the water backside-first. "Oh…uh-oh!" The water on the other side of the dam was moving faster than she'd thought. She was almost swept away before she knew it, but at the last second, she grabbed the dike with both hands.

She'd just barely managed to hold her ground, but now she couldn't move. She was sure the slightest motion would throw off her balance and she'd be swallowed up by the current.

It hadn't bothered her when she'd first stepped into the water, but now the wet hem of her coat was unexpectedly heavy, twining around her legs and threatening to drag her into the current. As she somehow resisted, clinging to the dike, painfully cold water was seeping through her clothes, soaking her to the core. She started feeling pins and needles in her hands.

Even as she panicked, she still couldn't quite grasp the situation. The flowing sands of the Sand Ocean had been smoother, and had never clung to her like this. And far from being this cold, the sand had actually had a slight warmth to it.

What should I do? I'm in trouble…

She'd never known water was so heavy and cold.

"I'm so stupid…," she mumbled to herself.

"Yeah," a completely unexpected voice agreed.

Kieli looked up from her humiliating pose sitting butt-first in the water and clinging to the dike with both hands. The flashlight around her neck was submerged, too, but luckily it didn't seem to be broken; enough wavery light broke through the water's surface to win her a small field of vision.

On top of the dike in front of her, she saw the hem of a dark-gray coat and a pair of long legs. Sliding her gaze up a little further, she made out the shape of a man standing with both hands shoved into the pockets of the coat.

She lifted her chin a little farther still and looked up at his face. He was a young man of about twenty, with white patches of gauze covering his right eye and cheek.

She breathed a little noise of relief and started to smile, but —

"What's wrong with you? That foolhardy personality hasn't improved at all. A normal person would at least think about the fact that if she got in the water unprepared she might get swept away."

— The very next moment she was mercilessly cut down, and her thawing feelings froze over again at once. She couldn't see him clearly in the dimness, but all the same the look of exasperation in his copper-colored left eye was plain as day.

"...Well," mumbled Kieli. Embarrassed and offended, she looked down, sulking. *Well, there were no waterways in Easterbury or South-hairo, and it's easy for him to say a normal person would have thought of it, but I never have. It's Harvey who knows too much about this stuff... especially considering he doesn't even know where chickpeas come from.*

After she'd stared at the dike in miffed, stony silence for a while, she heard a sigh and saw a hand thrust down toward her. She looked up to see Harvey crouching there, his right hand still in his pocket, his left hand reaching out to her.

"Here. Hurry up and give me your hand."

"..."

She gazed at the hand in front of her for a few seconds. Various different emotions flashed through her mind. Long fingers and a big palm — they were slender and bony, but she could still see the rough muscles there. It was no different from the hand etched into her memory.

For a moment, she thought of grabbing it.

But in the end, she turned her eyes angrily away. "No thanks. I don't need your help. I look after myself."

"Obviously you *can't,* or you wouldn't be in this situation! What's with the weird stubbornness?"

"Excuse me?!" Kieli looked right back up again. She felt as though she'd just been letting him insult her for this whole conversation, and she didn't like it. "This is all your fault in the first place for running away! And Juli took good care of you, too, and then you caused him trouble! I'll have you know he was angry about it!" she shot back in a wild voice.

Now Harvey was the one who looked miffed. "Look, you! I only did that because *you* stormed off without listening to me."

"Well, *that* was because *you* —" she started to argue, and then her hand slipped from the dike.

Two panicked voices cried out in chorus. She immediately dug her fingers into the slimy sludge of the trash heap and got her grip back. When she lifted her bloodless face to look at Harvey, his own face was equally ashen; he stood there paralyzed with his hand still stretched toward her. For several seconds they gazed at each other, speechless.

Eventually Harvey appeared to give in. "Okay, fine," he said with a grimace and a sigh. "We can call it all my fault. I'll listen to you complain all you want later, so for right now just give me your hand. You're giving me a heart attack."

This made Kieli even madder, since he sounded as if he was only letting her win out of necessity. *He says I haven't improved, but his habit of just agreeing with people because arguing is too much trouble hasn't improved at all either!*

"Kieli, come on, grab it. Please."

"No. Leave me alone." She started scooting herself sideways along the dike to get away from that outstretched hand. She could probably climb up on her own if she could get to a place where the current was weaker. After all, she'd gotten along without stupid Harvey this long.

"Hey, watch out —"

She felt the place she'd grabbed for a handhold squish and sink underneath her fingers.

She was suddenly holding on to nothing but handfuls of half-rotten garbage plucked from the dike, and in no time she was propelled away by the black, rushing water, and then she didn't know what was happening anymore.

"You little id —" Harvey managed to bite out before other concerns became more pressing. He'd managed to grab Kieli's wrist at the last moment, but when he instinctively tried to reach out for purchase with his right hand, naturally it didn't respond. Unable to keep his balance, he ended up getting dragged into the water with her instead.

Kieli seemed to be unconscious. He drew her to him by the

hand and held on to her body with his left arm. Since that left him no way to resist the suddenly faster torrent, he let it knock them about, sending them slipping through the dark tunnel. The roar of crashing water bounced off the walls and ceiling and assaulted his eardrums from all directions.

If it had been completely dark, he would've lost his sense of direction in no time, but the flashlight around Kieli's neck managed to cast a dim, blinking light as it bounced off the surface, sunk, and reemerged again.

Damn it, how far does this thing go...?

He strained his eye, following the light downstream, but the arched tunnel just stretched on and on into the blackness in a slightly weaving line. He couldn't even guess how far they might be carried. With a silent growl of irritation, he tightened his one-armed grip on the limp girl clutched to his chest so that she wouldn't get wrenched away. He just hoped she hadn't breathed in too much water...

When he returned his attention to the tunnel in front of them, he let out an involuntary groan. The end of the road had abruptly come into view. Maybe "end of the road" wasn't quite the right term. At any rate, the black torrent broke off suddenly, leaving only a horizon line, beyond which there was nothing but darkness.

He realized the danger, but there wasn't anything he could do about it; by that time the brink was already right in front of him. He slid cleanly off it and launched into the dark.

At the horizon line, the water cascaded straight down. Buffeted by the churning current, Harvey fell with it and was smacked into the surface of the stream at the bottom several seconds later. For a moment his awareness dimmed. Then he realized with a start that he'd almost let go of Kieli as they sank underwater, so he reasserted his grip on her, kicking up to the surface.

"Kieli!" The roar of the falls was so loud he couldn't even hear his own voice. He propped her head on his shoulder and briefly checked the color of her face before surveying their surroundings.

They were in an almost circular open space, like an underground lake or something. The ceiling was high. When he let his eye travel up the vertical waterfall, it was swallowed up midway by darkness, and he couldn't tell how far they'd fallen. He guessed it was about a dozen meters, or maybe a little more, but it didn't really matter, since he couldn't see any way of getting back up.

Directly below the falls, where the loudest of the roaring was coming from, the water sprayed up violently and churned in muddy whirlpools, but otherwise the water here was comparatively calm. Gentle black waves reflected the light. Judging from the fact that the water level seemed to be constant, there might be a drain somewhere on the floor underneath them, but the water was pretty deep, so that didn't really matter, either.

He saw a bank along the far wall that looked low enough for him to crawl up it.

Hmm, that's a little far away...

Given that he could only use one arm *and* he was holding onto Kieli, it would be tough to swim that far. Irritated at his own body, he bit the girl's neck in his teeth so that her head wouldn't slip beneath the surface; and he began to swim, pushing at the water with his now-free left hand.

The waves were gentle, but their wet clothes made their weight feel many times heavier, and the sluggish black water clung to his limbs with what seemed like deliberate malice. With enormous effort, he closed in on the bank. Just when it was almost within reach, he heard the girl's groans amid the rush of water filling his ears. "Ugh…nnn…"

It sounded as if she had come to.

Harvey suddenly had a bad feeling about this. It was painfully obvious that she couldn't swim. She probably had never experienced being in water so deep she couldn't touch the bottom…

After a few seconds, enough time for her to take in the situation, his fears were confirmed.

Kieli suddenly gave a shrill scream, eyes rolling sluggishly around the room, and she clutched his head as if trying to use it to crawl up out of the water. "Stop that, you moron!" With her pushing his head down, his face started to sink below the water, and of course Kieli started to sink with him, which only terrified her and made her clutch more desperately at him.

They came close to drowning together, but Harvey somehow reached the bank before his breath ran out, and he seized one of Kieli's flailing hands and forced it to grab the side.

"Climb up!" he spat in annoyance, pushing her from behind. Kieli clung frantically to the bank, hauled herself up, stumbled a little farther on as if to put whatever distance she could between herself and the edge, and then dropped down on all fours and began to cough.

"Sheesh..." Immense exhaustion poured over him, and for a while he just leaned his upper body against the wet concrete, panting. After he caught his breath, he finally pulled himself up one-handed onto the bank. "You really had me panicked there. Were you trying to kill me?"

"But—"

Harvey cut off whatever excuse she was going to make and bellowed, "'But,' my ass! You have no clue how dangerous the water is!"

Kieli shrank back at his shout, but she was apparently still upset with him over something, because she turned away with a sullen look on her face.

"...Whatever. Do what you want; I don't care." He couldn't deal with her anymore. Sending off splashes of water every time his feet hit the ground, he walked a little ways away and sat down.

He couldn't see the whole room from where they were, but it seemed to be a pretty big circular space. Along the gentle arc of the wall, a sort of lakeshore stretched out to their right and left. In one direction the path had crumbled a little ways ahead and sunken into a pile of flotsam and jetsam by the edge, but in the other direction it kept going on into the darkness; they might be able to get somewhere by following it.

For right now, Harvey didn't feel like doing anything.

The path was less than a meter wide. If he stretched out his legs, his heel could touch the brim. He bent his legs a little and sat there, leaning his back against the wall. Every centimeter of his body was soaked through, but he couldn't work up the energy to dry himself past swinging his head a little to shake

the droplets out of his hair. His heavy, freezing clothes stuck to his skin in a thoroughly unpleasant way.

The noise of the falls crashing in the distance faded into a nice static here, easing the silent atmosphere. Letting the sounds of the water flow over him, he stole a sidelong glance at the girl sitting next to him. Like Harvey, she was sitting with knees folded and streaming water like a drowned rat. Her face was bluish white, and her lips trembled a little; she pressed them into a thin line and wrung out the hem of her coat with the same violence someone might use to throttle their parents' killer.

"You're cold, right?"

"No."

"Liar."

"Leave me alone."

"...I see. Fine, I won't say anything anymore."

Conversation over.

He had no idea how they'd gotten on such bad terms. He couldn't remember anymore what the direct cause had been. While he was avoiding her gaze, he turned his face up to the blackness above them and sighed. He thought quite sincerely that if there were someone looking down on them from the sky, he wished they'd tell him what had happened — but then again, even if there *was* someone there, it was hard to believe they could see all the way down underground to where he and Kieli were anyway.

Her clothes were soaked right through to her underwear, and every time she moved even slightly, they squelched. It felt gross.

Even though her hands were so numb she could hardly feel them, she forced them to squeeze out the hem of her coat as she stole glances at Harvey's profile. He was sitting against the wall, long legs folded, staring at a random spot on the shadowy surface of the water with a faint scowl of annoyance on his face. As she watched, he irritably tore off the tape that had half peeled free from his cheek. Underneath the gauze a nasty wound was still festering horribly. The tape over his right eye was wet and peeling too, but maybe he didn't want to take that gauze off. Instead, he pressed his palm to his face and forced the tape back down.

When he'd held out his hand to her earlier, she hadn't really noticed anything, but now she realized that his *right* hand had been stuck in his pocket this whole time. She wondered whether that meant he couldn't move it anymore. Come to think of it, she had the feeling he hadn't used his right arm while he was dragging her here through the water, either.

Why was this man always so tattered every time she saw him?

It's not fair, she thought. When she saw him like this, she started to feel as though *she* was the one in the wrong. Now it seemed as though her stubbornness was just causing problems for an injured man.

...Before, we could have made up and been friends again so easily.

The year-and-a-half void hit her in an unexpected way. How *had* she talked to him before? Was she cheerful and honest? Or had she been more reserved? If nothing else, she knew she hadn't been this pigheaded and contrary.

Harvey was probably the same as he'd always been. She must be the one who had changed. He was right there within her reach, so close, yet the deep rift that year and a half had made seemed to yawn open between them.

Kieli shifted to sit with her hands around her knees, and gazed into the wide, dim space in front of her. With nowhere to go, the murky water that was neither clean nor clear grew stagnant, its ripples sluggish. Soon it started to look like a mass of tentacles waiting to drag any prey that got near the edge down into the black depths, but when she drew her feet away a little in fear, the surface was tranquil again, and it began to seem like nothing more than gentle, dark waves.

Maybe the water here was a mirror that reflected a person's state of mind.

If I can manage to talk with Harvey like I used to, will this foul water seem clear? She tried to imagine a beautiful, clear lake, but she couldn't really picture it. She hugged her knees and shrank inside the coat that was now just heavy and cold.

CHAPTER 5

LET'S GO HOME SPLASHING THROUGH THE PUDDLES ON THE DRIZZLY ROAD

Kieli remembered reading in a book once about how somewhere in this universe had been a blue planet where there was lots of water on the surface, not just underground. The resources of that planet had long ago been devoured, and it had become a dry sphere of nothing but wilderness and desert just like this one. So even if mankind regained the technology to fly into space someday, she figured they probably couldn't find it again.

While she was thinking about this, hearing but not really listening to the distant crash of falling water, the cold woke her up.

Her body had gone stiff as a board. When she awkwardly sat up, the coat she'd been using for a blanket slipped off her shoulders.

Within the bonfire that had died down to black cinders, the last of the flames sizzled and smoldered. Judging from the fact that almost all its heat was gone, she guessed she must have fallen asleep for several hours.

They'd dragged all the scraps of wood that seemed burnable from the debris that had washed up onshore. The lighter had been wet, too, but after a few tries it had worked; so they'd started the pile burning and then poured all the lighter fluid on top of it, too, eventually managing to build enough of a bonfire to give them some heat. If they hadn't done that, maybe by now she'd have frozen to death in her waterlogged clothes.

Looking down at the man's coat that lay on top of her own duffle coat, Kieli thought for a moment, then looked anxiously around her. The flashlight she'd set on the ground created a fuzzy patch of light, but its glow was slowly yet steadily getting weaker.

All she could see within the small circle of light was a gray wall slimy with dampness and moss, the rim of a great lake, and jet-black water so deep she couldn't make out the bottom. Unease instantly started eating at her.

Where did he go…?

She realized that amid the far-off sounds of the waterfall and the nearer sounds of slow water, she could hear a faint clattering ahead of her in the darkness. Her eyes fixed in the direction of the noise, she pulled on the boots she'd left drying upside down by the fire. They were still cold and clammy, but most of the water that had invaded them had drained out again, and her feet wouldn't slip around inside them.

Kieli picked up the light and began walking along the wall with the coats under her arm. The weight and unpleasantness of her still-damp clothes wore her down, and it took more energy than she expected just to walk. When she lifted an arm, heavy as lead, to hold up the light, she saw the back and copper-colored head of a man crouching by the wall.

Relieved, she opened her mouth to call his name, but he noticed her and turned around before she made a sound. The light seemed too bright for him, or perhaps he just couldn't see very well with one eye; his squinting stare cut right though her. She unthinkingly swallowed what she'd been about to say and pressed her lips together, which ended up making her look angry. Maybe that upset him. He silently looked away and went back to what he'd been working on.

Everything was still strange between them somehow.

Kieli shyly directed her beam of light over his shoulder to see what he was doing. There was an arched tunnel in the wall that poured water into the lake. It looked as if Harvey had found a tributary like the one they'd been swept down — but luckily not so high up.

If they followed the tunnel upstream they could probably get out of the depths of the waterways where they were trapped now. The problem was that it was blocked off with iron bars just like the ones from the communal jail cell.

Harvey was crouched at the bottom of the entrance, scraping away at the groove where the iron bars met the ground with what looked like a rusty pocketknife. She guessed that he'd found it in the pile of garbage. If he could get one or two bars loose, they'd probably be able to squeeze through.

After a while she thrust the light at him and asked gruffly, "Isn't it too dark? You might as well use this."

"It's fine. I'm used to it," came the equally gruff response.

After opening and closing her mouth a few times searching for something to say, Kieli eventually left his coat and the flashlight kitty-corner behind him and retreated a little ways off to sit hugging her knees.

Looking around, she saw that some of the moss on the wall was giving off a very faint natural gleam, just enough to ease the inky blackness a little. Harvey was right: even without the flashlight, it wasn't a perfect darkness. When she lifted her chin to look up, the belt of hazy light stretched all the way to the ceiling far above them.

She returned her eyes to Harvey and his work. He really was only using his left hand. It looked very inconvenient, but she knew at times like these he could do finicky work with unexpected perseverance, without a single complaint.

After hesitating for several seconds, she asked, "What happened to your right arm?"

"It broke," he replied shortly, without turning around. But when she thought about it, that was more or less his normal way of talking.

Now that she'd asked one question and gotten an answer, other words came, even if she had to whisper them while staring down at her boots. "Thank you for finding out about my mom...I guess."

"Sure."

"Did you go to the capital?"

"Yeah."

"Did you find out anything about...Jude, or anything?"

"...Yeah."

"Is he alive? I'd like to meet him someti —"

"No. He's dead."

He said it matter-of-factly but so quickly that he cut her off, and Kieli's mouth clicked shut. When she lifted her head, he was just working steadily, with no change of expression. She gazed at his profile for a little while, and then looked down again. "Oh...I see."

"Yeah."

Silence fell.

Kieli pictured the stubbly sand-colored beard of the large man who'd set her tiny self on his knee at the live music bar. She didn't really know whether she was sad or not. But at the same time, she did feel a certain emptiness in her heart.

A while after that, Harvey clenched his fist and gave one of the bars a sharp blow with his wrist. It pulled free from the groove with a loud clang and splashed into the water on the other side. After several seconds of studying it with a thoughtful expression, he turned to her. "You can get through there."

"No," she answered immediately. Harvey seemed to have more or less expected this. He showed no particular reaction before turning back and starting on another bar.

"Wait there, then."

And so Kieli had to wait even longer. She couldn't think of anything to talk about at the moment, so she sat there with her arms wrapped around her knees, feeling uncomfortable.

When she wasn't doing anything, she couldn't think about anything but the cold seeping into her body. She dug her jaw into the collar of her coat, but it still trembled, and her teeth chattered softly together.

"Wear that," Harvey said abruptly. When Kieli looked up at him through her lashes, he spared a moment from his work to kick his coat toward her.

She shook her head, stiff-faced. "I don't need it. You wear it." Then Harvey huffed a little in displeasure, and she wished she'd just borrowed it graciously.

After some time had passed, the second bar slipped free like the first, and it splashed down on the other side the same way when Harvey hit it with the base of his palm. The space still wasn't wide enough to give him any leeway, but tall as he was, he was definitely on the bony side, so they should both be able to get through.

"Time to go," Harvey said.

He picked up the light and the coat and stood, so Kieli got a grip on herself and dragged her heavy body up to a standing position, too. "I wonder what time it is?"

"Dunno. Maybe it's morning already." He gave her the flashlight and told her to hold on to it. She accepted with a nod. She slid the strap over her neck with a practiced hand, if she did say so herself, but Harvey's movements were clumsy as he pushed his left arm through the sleeve of the coat and drew it up with his teeth. Halfway through the process, he seemed to notice for the first time that something was missing. He blinked at her with his good eye. "Where's the Corporal?"

Kieli squeaked, remembering.

"And Bea. Aren't they with you?"

"They were, but…" Hesitating, she avoided his eye. "It's kind of a long story."

Harvey frowned suspiciously, but then quickly seemed to lose interest. He faced forward again and slipped through the opening in the bars. Kieli hurried after him, afraid he'd leave her behind.

When she slid through the entrance and stepped into the passageway, water splashed at her feet. The river had risen to encroach on the corridor beside it, and a shallow film of water covered the floor, lapping at her boots.

She looked up at the back of the man in front of her. Harvey had come to a halt just beyond the entrance and appeared to be squinting into the dimness upstream, illuminated only by the faint glow of the moss on the walls. However, as she stood behind him to wait, he glanced at her over his shoulder and said, "Well?"

"Huh?"

"The story."

Huh? So I should have kept talking? She gaped at him, then realized he'd already faced forward again and resumed walking.

"You said it was a long one, right? We have a long way to go before we get to the exit."

"Oh. Right." Kieli jogged after him, splashing water behind her. To anyone listening it would have sounded like such a faltering conversation, but it felt oddly comfortable. Maybe it wasn't that they'd forgotten how to talk; maybe it had always been like this.

The sky was starting to brighten.

Shielding her eyes with one hand and squinting into the distance past the wilderness that spread out before her, she could just make out milk-white city walls standing against the sky with its light-sand-colored morning sun.

When she'd been making her way on foot, she had been sure she would never reach Gate Town. Having a vehicle was a magnificent thing. She could see why people said that out of all human inventions, evolving means of transportation had the greatest power to transform eras.

As long as the engine didn't stall.

She looked behind her. Standing there was a hooded three-wheeled truck broken down in the center of the rutted path. As if it had lost its temper after being worked hard for over twenty-four hours, the truck had overheated just as their destination was getting close. Right now they were all taking a break and giving the engine a chance to cool off.

"I think it's not too far to walk now," said the radio hanging from its strap in one hand.

Beatrix nodded grudgingly. "True. Even if I don't want to." For one thing, she still didn't trust that merchant, even if she didn't have any proof against him. It would probably be best to cut off contact before they got into town.

"Kieli got into town a long time ago. I just hope she hasn't gotten mixed up in something dangerous."

"Now you're just being overprotective. She's not a little kid anymore. I hate you old men; you're such worriers."

"And you Undyings never mature enough inside for people whose lives are so long."

"Shut up," she spat back, lips twisting. The cover over the truck bed lifted a crack, and a plain girl came out, stifling a small yawn. Shrugging her shoulders slightly against the cool air of morning, she noticed Beatrix and walked toward her. "So the truck isn't fixed yet."

"Where's your brother?"

"He's sleeping. He wore himself out playing all evening," she answered, glancing toward the truck bed with a wry smile. Beatrix inwardly grieved that this girl was overprotective even though she *wasn't* old yet.

The girl stood next to her and squinted quietly for a while at the distant walled city. There wasn't anything going on, and yet oddly it wasn't a perfect silence. The wind whipped at their hair with its constant, faint white noise.

"Are your relatives rich?"

"That's what they told me. But my family was normal. My parents died last month, so that's why they're taking us in."

"Huh," Beatrix answered listlessly. The answer wasn't unexpected. She couldn't imagine a young boy and girl from such a common family (well, that had been her prejudiced guess, but apparently it was right) would travel alone for no reason, so she'd more or less assumed that was the case. "He doesn't know they're dead, does he?"

That had been a hunch, too, but it looked as if she'd been right again. The girl nodded, face clouded. "I don't know what to tell him…"

"They went to be with God, right? There's nothing to be sad about, really. They got what they wanted." She'd started out wanting to mess with the girl a little, but it felt so childish that she stopped before long. She had no desire to get into a fruitless argument with a true believer about views on life and death. Instead, with a little disclaimer of "Well, this is just a little piece of advice, but," she switched gears. "Once you hide it from him, it'll never be the right time to say it. If you hold back, thinking he's a child, that just basically means you don't trust him."

"…All right." The girl nodded up at Beatrix, bewildered. Just then, a babyish voice called out "Monica!" from behind them. She turned to see a young boy rubbing his eyes and near-falling out of the truck.

"I gotta pee."

The girl hurriedly ran up to him, taking him by the hand and leading him behind the truck. "Hold it in for a minute; you can't do it there."

As Beatrix watched, sighing, the smug-faced — well, smug-voiced — radio piped up, *Speaking from experience there?* She swung it viciously around by the strap and started back toward the truck, when a figure in the driver's seat caught her eye. She could have sworn that just a moment ago he'd been lying down on the front seat taking a nap, but somehow he was awake and fiddling with what looked like a small communications device.

Communications —

Before she realized it, her body had slipped into motion. She reached for the driver's-side door and yanked it open. The merchant jumped in his seat, hands still on the communicator. "What are you doing?" she demanded.

"U-Uh, nothing?"

Beatrix lifted her eyebrows at this obviously flustered response, then reached out and snatched the communicator. The merchant yelped and pulled his hand back. She shot a glare at him before looking down at it. It was a fairly high-tech video communicator, even for a city with display screens. "Who were you call —" she began, when light suddenly glinted off something in the hand he'd hidden behind his back. Sheer knee-jerk reflex sent her leaping aside. At the same moment, she heard that familiar thick sound like a ball of compressed air being suddenly released. It had been a long time since she'd heard it, but she sure hadn't missed it.

It was so unexpected for a civilian to have that kind of gun that her response was a split second too slow. A fragment of the bullet that had exploded at the edge of her field of vision flew at her and cut her face. Covering the wound with one arm, Beatrix skittered backward to put some distance between herself and the merchant in the driver's seat, eyes glued on him and the object he held. A hefty big-bore gun wielded in both hands with back braced — the carbonization gun carried by Undying Hunters.

"... That's a dangerous toy for a novice."

"Now, I can't have you treating it like a toy. It's a knockoff made in Westerbury, but it's just as effective as the real thing. It's one of the things I sell. See, these are all the rage among the North-hairo rich lately. They buy 'em for self-protection."

"Uh-huh. Self-protection." *And what exactly are they trying to protect themselves from? If they thought a bunch of Undyings were going to come attack the citizens en masse, that would be one thing, but…*

"Hello there and nice to meet you, Witch of Toulouse," the merchant said mockingly, holding her off with the gun. "I got a photo from my contact in Westerbury on a hunch, and boy, was I right!" He climbed down out of the truck.

Beatrix felt no particular urge to play dumb. She dropped the arm from her face. She'd avoided a direct hit from the bullet, but a thin piece of shrapnel had pierced her temple, and the blood dripping down her face obscured half her vision. She started to get really pissed off. Not because of the abrupt change in the man's attitude — she didn't really care about that, since he'd smelled fishy to her from the beginning. No, more importantly, he'd hurt her *face*.

"Beatrix," the radio whispered urgently. She nodded slowly, eyes never leaving the enemy.

"You fell apart in the endgame."

"What?" The merchant's eyes widened.

"Too bad. I have a projectile weapon, too." Air swelled up around the radio, and the shock wave flew —

— Or it would have an instant later, if she hadn't wound up and pitched it at the merchant.

It was a pretty good sidearm, if she said so herself.

The radio spun at him like a fastball to dead center, and a corner of it hit him square in the face. He started backward with a hoarse cry.

Beatrix had seized the opening to run right up to him. She braked hard with one foot, at the same time using it as a pivot to spin a half-turn and deliver a sharp reverse roundhouse kick at the man while he was still moaning and clutching at his face. The back of her knee connected beautifully with the back of his neck, and he flew several meters through the air, sending up a cloud of dust.

You're still wide open! Without missing a beat, she followed and kicked the gun out of his hand. She had just whirled around to face him again when he cried out in a shrill voice, still flipped over on his back, "W-Wait! It was a joke! Just a joke! Come on, don't take that seriously!"

Does he really think it isn't too late to worm his way out of this? Beatrix ignored him. She began to drive her leg down. "P-Please spare me! Don't kill me!" he begged. The expression on his face was so pathetic that she lost her motivation.

As soon as she quit moving, the merchant looked as if he thought he was safe. So on reflection, she canceled her decision to cancel, and kneed him in the solar plexus.

He passed out with a strangled grunt, foaming at the mouth. Beatrix looked down at him with a "hmph." He'd probably broken a rib or two, but that was getting off lightly. "I'll let you off the hook with that," she said. It would be a waste of energy to kill him.

"Beatrix! Why, you —" The radio let loose a stream of invectives from where it lay abandoned on the ground. *"Don't throw me around, you stupid bitch!"*

"Excuse me, *who* are you calling a stupid bitch?!" She picked it up and brought it to eye level. "Good job; you were very useful as a projectile," she said calmly.

The radio growled even more angrily. *"That's NOT what 'projectile weapon' means! And I've built up frustration, too, you know! Let me do some fighting!"*

So that was his problem? The radio continued to gripe. Letting its voice pass in one ear and out the other, Beatrix moved on. She looked around her. The merchant might have already reported her to the Church Soldiers' station in Gate Town. *Maybe I'll take the truck and run.*

"Hey, what was that?!" cried an excited voice behind her. She turned around to see the little boy running out of the shadow of the truck. He darted up to stand beside her, eyes shining. "Wow! You're really tough, huh? You're so cool!"

Beatrix was sure he hadn't really taken in the situation, but he was totally worked up. At a loss for how to respond, she pulled away. *That's right; I forgot about these two,* she thought, inwardly irritated. *I can't just run off with the truck and leave them out here.*

His sister was there, too, behind him — and when she saw the girl, Beatrix froze.

She was carrying the carbonization gun Beatrix had kicked out of the merchant's hand. She clearly wasn't used to holding one, and both hands and both knees were shaking wildly, but her finger was firmly on the trigger with the mouth of the gun pointed at Beatrix.

"Come here, Il," the girl ordered the stunned boy in a firm voice. "You need to get away from that woman." When Beatrix put a hand on his shoulder, her face went utterly rigid. "Please don't touch my brother!"

"…Well, that's certainly not a nice thing to say. What do you intend to do with that, exactly?"

"Was what he said true? Are you really an Un…Un…" She broke off on the crucial word, as if it were too unspeakably disgusting. Beatrix gave a jaded sigh. She couldn't work up any anger about it.

"You go," she told the boy, nudging him toward his sister. "You're in my way." He kept looking back at her uncertainly as he walked. When she saw him get halfway there, she fixed her gaze on the girl. She mopped at the blood on her face with her sleeve.

She'd bled heavily, but the wound wasn't deep. Her tissue had already started to regenerate, and the laceration was closing up.

The girl's eyes were wide with shock and fear.

"Well? What do you want to do about me?"

"I'm going to call the Church Soldiers here. P-Please turn yourself in quietly."

"And if I say no?"

"If you try to resist, I'll shoot," the girl threatened in a low voice. Most likely the only thing the kid would accomplish by firing that thing would be knocking herself over with the recoil, but at any rate, Beatrix believed she meant what she said. Her eyes looked glazed. "You go against God's natural law. You shouldn't exist. But if you give yourself up, God in His mercy will forgive you. I know the Church will deal with you in good faith, too. So please, just surrender."

"…What are you, stupid?" Beatrix found herself sighing a

second time. "Do I need someone's permission to be here? I'm not looking for anyone to forgive me, and I don't think I'm some creature who shouldn't be allowed to live without someone's forgiveness, either." ... *Well, maybe I do want to apologize to Kieli just a little. But that's all.*

She closed her eyes for a moment. She wasn't upset with the girl. If anything, she was fed up with herself. She'd been playing Ms. Softhearted, a role that wasn't even in character for her, and look where it had gotten her. She should never have let herself get emotionally involved with any damn humans in the first place.

She drew in a breath and opened her eyes.

In front of her was the familiar sight of the vast wilderness. And in the center of it, a human standing and pointing a gun at her. Therefore the human registered as an enemy. Obviously.

"...Since you're pointing a gun at me, I assume you're prepared for the consequences."

"Beatrix, don't do it. She's a kid," the radio whispered in a hushed voice. *"Hey, wait—"*

Without answering, Beatrix let the arm holding the radio dangle and let go of the strap. She heard it strike the ground at her feet.

It all happened in almost the same moment: Beatrix taking a step forward, the frightened girl pulling the trigger out of what was probably pure reflex — and the boy suddenly leaping forward and yelling "Monica, stop!"

Beatrix wanted to curse at herself. *Why did my body move like that?*

The instant she'd judged that the boy had leapt directly into

the line of fire, she'd snatched him into her arms and twisted
their bodies around.

She took the hit to the shoulder. Immediately and clearly,
she felt that unpleasant sensation of rending flesh and vapor-
izing blood that was unique to the carbonization gun. Monica's scream rang out and was swallowed up by the peaceful
sand-colored sky of the wilderness.

"You're such a kid..."

At this exasperated remark, Kieli pursed her lips in displeasure. "I know," she grumbled at the back of the tall man walking in front of her.

Along the way, she'd stumblingly explained how she'd left
Beatrix and the radio behind at the live music bar on the parish border. At the time, she'd run away out of mistrust of the
two of them, but when you got right down to it, Harvey's
thoughtless letter had at least partially caused the whole thing.
He had no right to make one-sided, exasperated comments
about her immaturity.

She was glaring huffily at his back when he casually muttered, without turning around, "Well, I caused Bea trouble,
too. Want to apologize to her together?"

Kieli blinked and momentarily stopped walking. "...Yeah,"
she replied, nodding. Then she hurried to catch up to him.

The sounds of rushing water and two pairs of feet splashing
through the puddles echoed in the gloom of the tunnel. By
now the light around Kieli's neck was only bleeding a weak

yellow glow, but the luminous moss crawling along the walls and ceiling lit their path with dull bands of light.

She closed the distance between them until she was just behind Harvey and to the side, and stole a glance up at his profile over his shoulder. She felt as though the angle she saw it from had changed, even if only just a little; it must be that she had gotten taller. Gauze still covered his right eye. The right sleeve of his coat was empty, the cuff stuck into the pocket. His right hand was inside the pocket of his work pants underneath the coat.

She still hadn't heard anything about what had happened in the capital.

According to Beatrix, he had sneaked into a secret Church facility or something, but what could he have done there to get such horrible injuries? Kieli figured it must be an important facility since the information peddler said he wanted the inside scoop about it. Was there something about that place above and beyond Harvey's goal of looking for Jude…? If it was something to do with the Undyings, then of course it would have been dangerous for him to go there. So the fact that he'd gone anyway must mean that Jude was there…but he'd said Jude was dead.

Now that she thought about it, what were the circumstances of this "he's dead," anyway? Had Harvey found his body? Or had they been able to meet first? If so, had he died after that?

The more she thought, the more her disorderly imagination ran away with her. She could probably just ask Harvey himself, but she was strangely certain that he'd give her some vague, evasive answer. And she didn't really feel as though she could bring it up now anyway. He was talking to her just like always — in fact, a little more gently than usual — but all the same, he had an air of inapproachability that probably wasn't just Kieli's imagination.

Right now she could almost understand why Julius's nurse-maid had thought Harvey was frightening.

Abruptly she heard Julius's voice in her head saying, *They found the body of the guard who'd gone after him in the underground waterway. He was murdered. His neck was broken.*

No, of course it couldn't be Harvey. There was no way. But if Harvey hadn't done it, who *had*?

Kieli shook off the thought that had momentarily blossomed in her mind. She was horrified. Not at the idea, but at herself for letting that doubt enter her, even for an instant.

Harvey turned back toward her from his position a little ways ahead, and she realized that she'd unconsciously stopped moving. She rushed to catch up. Without any particular change of expression, he glanced at her with his left eye, which had somehow taken on the color of dried blood in the semi-darkness, and quickly faced forward again.

"Um, hey...," she ventured timidly from behind the shoulder of his dark gray coat. She hadn't been aware of it before, but looking closely now she saw that there was a small pin at the collar of his hood—a gun and a sword symbolically crossed. The emblem of the Church Security Forces. "Is that coat from one of the prison—"

Before she could finish the question, out of nowhere Harvey's hand shot toward her and clapped over her mouth. She gurgled. "Shut up," he whispered sharply. He wrapped her up in his arm, hand still over her mouth, and plastered them both against the wall so that her cheek pressed up to the stone.

Unsure what was happening, she grew scared and felt confusion starting to sweep over her before her ears picked up a faint sound that was new and different.

There was someone upstream from them. "Kill the light," Harvey hissed into her ear. She turned it off without looking at it.

The moist sliminess of the cold wall made it stick to her cheek. At her back was the warmth of Harvey's body and his breath. In contrast to her own pulse, which was racing with anxiety, the heartbeat she could feel behind her seemed to switch to war-ready mode; all signs of living presence vanished, and hearing him breathe.

It's Church Soldiers. She could tell from the metallic scraping noise of their plate armor and the unique tone of their conversation. Flashlight beams flickered up ahead.

"Kieli." The soft whisper was pitched so that only she could hear it. "We'll see how things play out. If worse comes to worst, I'll hand you over to them. I'm sure Julius will take you under his wing right away, so —"

She tried to make an angry sound of protest. The hand over her mouth clamped down tighter, as if Harvey had expected this response, so instead she shook her head as hard as she could trapped between him and the wall.

They both raised their voices without thinking. "Calm down, idiot. I said we'd see. If it looks like we can get out of this, I won't —" "Nngh!" Then they heard a loud hail coming from upstream, and both froze stock-still.

Holding her breath, Kieli peered in the direction of the voice. It seemed they hadn't been found after all. Another soldier had come to deliver a message to his comrades. She could hear several voices talking at once. Eventually their sloshing footsteps and the beams of their flashlights disappeared back into the darkness upstream.

"Why did they turn back?" muttered Harvey, glaring doubtfully after them. His hand still covered Kieli's mouth. His long fingers dug into her cheek with biting force. When she protested with a pained groan, he finally relaxed them as if he'd just now noticed what he was doing.

She reflexively jumped a half step away from him and put a hand up to her aching cheek.

"Sorry. I panicked."

"Harvey, was it you who killed the prison guard...?"

It chilled her to hear the mistrust in her own voice. The moment the words were out of her mouth, her heart stung with regret. She'd never spoken to Harvey in a tone like this before. It was just that for a second, she'd been frightened...

In the shadowy glow of the moss, she could see his face go blank and expressionless. After a pause, he said, "What are you talking about?"

"Juli said someone found the guard who went after you... and he'd been murdered. And they have permission to shoot you on sight because of it..."

"Don't know anything about it," Harvey answered promptly. He sounded as if it were news to him, and Kieli felt a little relieved.

"Then I was right; it was some kind of misunderstanding," she began somewhat excitedly, when Harvey's voice interrupted her in the same awful tone she'd used on him earlier.

"Did you believe them?"

The words lanced at her heart a hundred times more heavily and sharply than when she'd said it herself. For a moment she couldn't breathe. "N-No, that's not what I…" She started trying to explain it away, but then she remembered how she'd started to let that tiny bit of doubt invade her, and she hesitated. "I'm sure if you explain it to Juli, he'll understand right away. It'll be all—"

"No," interrupted Harvey, cutting off the reassurance she'd unthinkingly twisted around. He looked somehow dazed, or maybe even really dismayed. "More like, if *you* don't trust me, who would?"

It felt like a terribly dry wind had blown through the damp underground tunnel.

Kieli stood paralyzed, unable to come up with anything to say to that. After a short silence, Harvey gave a little sigh and looked away. "Whatever. One false charge doesn't really matter at this point."

"Harvey…"

"First things first. I guess we'd better get out of here." And with that, he put an end to the conversation, turning on his heel and walking rapidly down the path again.

So in the end, Kieli hadn't been able to say anything for herself. She hurried after him.

A while past the place where they'd seen the Church Soldiers' lights, the stream they'd been following ended, and there was a meter-high wall in front of them. Harvey issued the one-word command "Light"; she thought for a second and then trained her flashlight on it from behind him. At the top of the wall was a path along another branch of tunnel that intersected with this one. It must be the main river. The low, violent sound of a large current reverberated off the walls and ceiling.

Harvey put his left hand lightly on the ledge and jumped up ahead of her, then turned and squatted down to offer her a hand. He didn't say "Grab on." He didn't say anything else, either. Kieli looked up at his face and found him silent and expressionless, just waiting. This time, after only a split second of hesitation, she meekly gave him her hand and let him pull her up.

She was just getting one knee on the ledge when suddenly a shadow fell overhead.

Huh?

By the time she lifted her head to see what it was, Harvey was already looking over his shoulder at the tunnel behind him. Straight afterward, what looked like a long arm reached out and grabbed him by the throat, dragging him into the waterway before either of them had a chance to speak.

Her hand abruptly wrenched out of Harvey's, Kieli lost her balance and tumbled down with a shriek, landing backside-first in the hallway she'd just climbed out of and sending up a shower of water in all directions. At the same time, she heard another, more dramatic splash on the level above her.

She immediately jumped to her feet and clung to the ledge, shining her flashlight around the river. She let its beam play along the surface and found Harvey's head bobbing above the current. But he seemed to be grappling with something underwater that clutched at his legs and tried to drag him down.

That something broke the black surface of the foamy, turbulent water just long enough for her to catch a glimpse of it. It was a giant human shape, grossly bloated as if it were filled to the bursting point with water — in fact, she wasn't sure she could call it "human" at all. It definitely had the rough shape of a human, but its skin was greenish with rot. That skin couldn't possibly belong to a living person.

…What is that thing…?

Harvey was being swept downstream as he fought with it, so she scrambled up the wall on her own power and began to run along the bank. "Harvey!"

By then he'd managed to shake off his attacker, but he seemed to have lost all sense of direction. His head peeked out above the surface, and he was looking around wildly. Kieli had to shout at the top of her voice to be heard above the roar of water that filled the tunnel. "Harvey, this way!" He appeared to notice her, and started paddling one-handed toward her side of the river.

She ran a little farther until she came up beside him, and then got down on her knees and leaned forward to yank at the shoulders of his coat and help him crawl up onto the pathway. He promptly doubled over and began coughing.

Kieli rubbed his spasming back. "Are you okay?"

A great crash of water sounded nearby. When she looked toward it, the humanoid shape that had gone after Harvey was hauling itself up onto the bank a little way downstream.

There was a wet squelch. Sloshing a liquid that was far thicker than the muddy river water onto the concrete floor of the passageway, the *thing* drew itself up to its full height.

It was way too eerie to call "human." But if she were forced to assign it some kind of human condition, maybe the rotting corpse of a drowned man would be the closest. Its green-tinged skin swelled up in patches as if it was covered with hundreds of blisters, and through their translucent membranes, she could see the blood vessels beneath pulsing unsteadily. Various blisters had burst and were oozing that viscous liquid. As for its face, both skin and flesh had half rotted off, and it retained no trace of its original shape. Maybe it had once had hair, but if so that had all fallen out, too. Its lidless eyes bulged grotesquely out of their sockets.

From the way it stood, back rounded and arms dangling in an animal stance, and the way it sluggishly let its eyes rove around the passage, it didn't seem capable of much thought. But what Kieli couldn't come to grips with was that it was precariously wrapped in what looked like scraps of cloth. Maybe it had worn clothes once. So did that mean it really was human after all ...?

Kieli just watched the strange creature for several seconds, petrified. Then her instincts kicked in and snapped her back into reality. *We have to get away.*

"Harvey, hurry!" she said, standing up and turning to look behind her. But Harvey was still collapsed on all fours, staring frozen at *it* with a face even paler than Kieli's.

"What's wrong? ... Harvey? Harvey?!" she called again. She seized him by the collar and pulled. His shoulders twitched once, and he swiveled his eye toward her, looking startled. Then he let out a cryptic little "Ah" sound, and with no warning he grabbed her wrist, sprang hastily to his feet, and began bolting down the corridor at full speed.

"W-Wait," Kieli gasped. Obviously he wasn't considering how much shorter her legs were than his as he pulled her along; she stumbled after him as best she could. They spotted the entrance to a sidestream in the wall ahead of them and plunged into it,

Harvey still dragging her. As they rounded the corner, her foot slipped on a puddle and her legs shot out from under her, tangling up in Harvey's and sending them both crashing to the ground with a squeak (Kieli) and a surprised "oof" (Harvey).

"I'm sorry!"

"...No, it's my fault." Harvey finally seemed to register that she was having trouble. He stood up and then reached down to her and lifted her to her feet. Arm still around her, he leaned one shoulder against the wall, silenced his breathing, and turned a wary eye to the waterway behind her. She could feel the heartbeat that had been so composed when they'd discovered the Church Soldiers earlier now pounding wildly, erratically against her.

They waited for a little while, but *it* showed no signs of chasing them. What sounded like a sigh of relief washed over Kieli from above, ruffling her bangs.

She tilted her neck back to look up at his jaw and whispered, "What was that? Have you ever seen it before, Harvey...?"

Harvey shook his head, eyes never leaving the stream's entrance. His face was still whiter than usual. "I don't know. I didn't see anything," he said, but the answer didn't seem to quite mesh with her question. Rivulets of water streamed from his soaking-wet copper hair and slid down Kieli's cheeks.

"Harvey, you're acting funny. Are you okay?"

"...It's nothing. I'm fine."

When she tried to press him further, he assumed a calm expression, though it looked forced. "That thing was probably what killed the guard. We should get out of here fast. Let's go." Speaking quickly, he pushed her away from him, and then his face suddenly stiffened.

"...Kieli." His voice lowered. "When I give you the signal, you run straight that way, and you don't turn around no matter what."

"Why—" she started to ask, lifting her head to look at him, and then she dropped her gaze, a sudden unease pulling her chin downward. Above her, Harvey gave a short sigh that seemed to say *You idiot.*

A greenish human arm was sticking out of Harvey's side — at exactly the spot where she had been squeezed up against him just a few seconds ago.

Five sharp-taloned fingers closed around ripe flesh and pulled it smoothly out through Harvey's back. Harvey's body listed to the side a little. She instinctively reached out to support him, her gaze shooting upward. She'd never sensed *it* circling around them at all, yet somehow there it was, standing behind Harvey.

That face that was smooth and featureless like that of a drowned corpse. Those bare eyeballs that looked as if they might fall out of the sockets any second, staring fixedly down at the meat caught in those fingers. The thing tilted its head, and then with a throaty growl, it stuck out its red tongue and it licked — it licked the flesh — *Harvey's* flesh.

Kieli's heart turned to ice.

"Kieli. Go." Harvey's voice in her ear penetrated the fog around her brain from what seemed like a great distance. Eyes riveted on *it,* she jerkily shook her head.

"I said *go!*" A hand on her shoulder shoved her violently away. Not a moment later, *its* hand unceremoniously swept straight to the side, grabbed Harvey's neck, and slammed him into the water without slowing down. Kieli stumbled toward him and fell, turning even as she did so to see that *it* was following him, too, about to jump in after him. Harvey didn't surface. Could he have drowned?

She whipped out the flashlight and pointed it right into the *thing*'s bulging eyes. The beam wasn't strong enough to blind *it*, but *it* did respond to the light, stopping right on the edge of the bank and ambling around toward her.

"This..." She gulped, flinching. "This way!"

At her shout, *it* charged fiercely toward her. Kieli spun around at the same time and took off running down the tunnel.

Her footsteps echoed as she splashed through the puddles, running along the dank waterway.

She didn't have a grip on the lay of the land, so she had no clue in which direction the exit lay. She just operated on instinct, picking the direction she thought the tunnel continued in. The one thing she had to avoid was hitting a dead end.

At some point she realized that the second set of footsteps that had been echoing behind her, not too close but not too far, had faded. Still running, she turned her head to look, and immediately slipped on the wet concrete and tumbled to the ground with a stifled cry of pain.

She'd banged both of her knees pretty badly, and for a moment the wind was knocked out of her. Still, she quickly sat up. Her heart was pounding with exertion — and more importantly, with anxiety and fear.

Had she managed to draw *it* at least a little away from Harvey? It worried her that Harvey hadn't surfaced, but surely, just as he'd always told her, he could manage something if he only had to worry about himself.

Kieli didn't quite stand up, but she braced herself so that she could take off running again at a moment's notice. Looking ahead of her, she saw an arched tunnel gaping in the wall a little farther ahead that must be the entrance to a sidestream. That spot was just a tiny bit brighter than everywhere else. Maybe it led outside.

She looked behind her for any signs of living presence, but it didn't look as if *it* had followed her this far. *I wonder where it went...*

She held her breath and focused on the sounds around her. All she could hear were the sounds of rushing water that filled the passageway, the faint background noise that was always in the underground air, and her own heartbeat, which throbbed harder the more she tried to quiet it. Now that she wasn't moving anymore, the chill crept into her bones in no time, yet her clenched palms were soaked with sweat. *Where is it?*

She couldn't see anyone in the hallway behind her. But for some reason, her muscles refused to relax. Something was definitely nearby.

Slowly and methodically, she swept her eyes over the area. First she traced the path she'd run along, gradually moving her gaze over the waterway to right in front of her, and then looking down at her own feet — the tips of her boots were hanging off the brim of the bank, and the black surface of the water immediately beyond dully reflected the light as it rippled.

Kieli's heart jumped in her chest.

No sooner had she instinctively jerked her foot back than a

hand sloshed up out of the water and clutched the air right where it had been. Sharp nails scratched against the concrete with a horrible high-pitched screeching that pierced her eardrums.

She forgot to even scream. She just started running along the bank again, stumbling blindly. Behind her she could sense *it* leaping up onto the path and coming after her. She veered ninety degrees to the right into the tunnel where she'd seen the light. If it turned out to be a dead end, everything was over.

Ahead of her was an arched sliver of sandy illumination.

It's the outside!

Fortunately, there were no iron bars here like the ones at the bottom of the waterfall. Thanking her lucky stars, Kieli sped up and flexed her knees to jump —

— And then came to a shocked halt as the sudden gust of wind whooshed past her face.

Clinging to the stone exit at the last minute, she looked down and saw her toes brushing the air beyond an ancient wall that plunged several dozen meters straight down to a paved road below. Between her boots, the shallow water of the passageway soaked through a crack in the wall and trickled down.

She was at one of the exits halfway up the inner walls that divided the city.

Sprawling below her was the giant slum of downtown, covered in a thin morning mist. As they got farther away from the wall, the shadows of the buildings grew lower and sparser, swallowed up by the red-brown wilderness that stretched beyond the horizon. A dry gust of wind blew at her feet and sent the hem of her coat flapping.

After staring dumbly at the view for a while, she snapped back to herself and looked back into the waterway.

It appeared at the opening into the sidestream. At first it seemed about to walk by, but then it rolled its glaring eyes toward the tunnel, caught sight of her, and stiffly changed direction, long arms still dangling seemingly carelessly at its sides. Slowly it approached her with sucking footsteps that made a sickening *squelch* against the ground.

She turned back outside again and scanned the wall in all directions, but she couldn't find any cracks or ledges to which she could escape.

The footsteps were getting steadily faster, closing the gap between them. Kieli's heel faltered back a little, catching on the edge of the precipice and sending a tiny bit of stone flying. It bounced down the wall and was swallowed up by the city below before she could blink.

She gulped in fright, but at the same time an idea occurred to her.

I wonder if I can do it...

There was no time to flinch. She couldn't think of any other option.

The footsteps broke abruptly into a run, slurring together into a harsh noise like someone pounding quickly on a flat board. Kieli stood right at the brink and faced *it* as it charged headlong at her.

She forced her heartbeat to slow, licking her dry lips.

Please let this work, she prayed. Not to God, but to her own judgment and good luck.

Right before the long arm that rose up before her could close around her throat, she took half a step backward.

Her body dropped. *Its* arm wheeled through empty air, fingers taking a few strands of her hair with them, and its momentum sent it sailing over her head.

Several seconds later, she heard the sound of something hitting the ground far beneath her feet, which were dangling in the air.

Clinging to the wall with every ounce of her upper-body strength and just barely hanging on, Kieli craned her neck to look down at the street below. Beneath her swaying legs, the green corpse looked tiny. Pieces of it were scattered all over the block.

Kieli closed her eyes and turned her face away, using all her might to crawl back up into the waterway.

As she sat in the shallow water, panting, her legs began to shake uncontrollably in delayed reaction. If her timing had been even just a little off and she hadn't been able to grab on to the edge, she'd have been the one splattered on the pavement right now.

When she put her hands to her knees to stop the shaking, a sharp pain zinged through her, and she gasped. It looked as though she'd scraped them up pretty badly; reddish-purple bruises were forming, and blood oozed from a bunch of little cuts. When had she fallen? *Oh, right...*

Kieli forced the pain from her mind and pulled herself up with one hand on the wall. *I can walk.* So ignoring pain was something anybody could do to some degree — she probably wasn't managing it as perfectly as Harvey, but she thought she sort of understood now, a little.

"Harvey…"

She stared straight ahead at the tunnel before her, and started walking.

I have to get back to Harvey.

He wasn't sure how many minutes had passed since he'd sunk into the water, but even his lungs were starting to scream. He wouldn't die just because he couldn't breathe, but there must be some sort of time lag between the oxygen deprivation and when his core would start pumping blood again, because it was no better than dying, and it was literally as painful as death.

In the muddy, pitch-black water where not a glimmer of light reached, it was all he could do to keep some sense of direction based on the pressure of the current, but he thought he'd been washed pretty far downstream.

Bastard…Harvey kicked his legs to try to shake off the sensation of hands grabbing at his ankle and dragging him down, but he couldn't control his movements very well underwater. The dark form he caught fractured glimpses of was definitely the *thing* from before.

It hadn't sneaked around them. There had been two of the damn things all along.

Maybe they had meant to attack the Church Soldiers, but if so, they'd probably automatically shifted focus to him and Kieli when they showed up just as the soldiers were disappearing. Or maybe the creatures had just figured they'd be an easier meal than a bunch of big men covered in plate armor.

Harvey felt anxious. If the other one was still back there with Kieli, he didn't have a second to waste playing with this one, but not only was he missing an arm, the thing had captured one of his legs, *and* he was underwater. The deck was just too stacked against him.

Did these guys escape from that *place…?*

He'd never imagined he'd run into them in a place like this — but it did make sense if he assumed they'd been traveling along the waterways. This place would be connected to the capital underground. He didn't know how many of them had settled down here or how long ago they'd come, but they seemed to have adapted extremely well to the water. The bones of their jaws and the nails on their fingers and toes were abnormally overdeveloped — as weapons to hunt their prey with? — and they even had translucent webbing between their fingers.

Did he have a weapon, too?

Remembering, he felt around in his coat pocket with his left hand. His fingers touched the jackknife. He'd meant to throw it away after he'd finished sawing at the bars, but somehow he'd forgotten about it, and it had been sitting in his pocket ever since. It was duller than a butter knife now, but Harvey guessed it was better than nothing. He gripped the handle and flicked it open with his thumb.

Suddenly the hand disappeared from around his ankle.

The abrupt release from bondage left him at the mercy of the current, and he got completely disoriented. By the time he began to curse to himself, the form had risen to the same depth as him and started to wrap around him from behind.

This bastard is smarter than I thought! He slid free from the clutching arms by the skin of his teeth, sinking deeper into the water. The momentum sent him spinning upside down. Without righting himself, he plunged his knife into the center of the shadow.

A blossom of red sprang up out of the uniform blackness and spread like smoke. As he'd thought, the blade was too loose; it didn't feel as if he'd wounded the thing at all. Harvey forced it in with brute strength and yanked it sideways. The heavy sensation of gouging flesh resonated all the way along his arm, and he felt a wave of discomfort, like something foreign was forcing its way up from his stomach into his throat.

The knife caught against bone, or muscle, or something, and refused to pull free, so he let go of it. He kicked the thing in its chest, and the motion propelled him at last to the surface.

As soon as his face got above the water, he started gulping in great, ragged breaths of air, sucking oxygen back into his lungs. Looking around, he saw the side of one bank gleaming whitely past the waves. All the strength was already gone from his arm, but he somehow managed to swim there anyway. He grabbed the edge and hauled himself up until he was lying facedown on his stomach with his legs still in the river, and then his strength gave out, and he couldn't move anymore for a while.

All the feeling that had been numbed crashed back down on him at once. The roar of the churning river, the sound of his own irregular breathing, the twitching stab of pain in his side every time he inhaled, the weight of the clothes plastered to his skin, the water coursing down his cheeks from his soaked hair to form a spreading gray stain on the concrete below him.

He shifted his face slightly and looked up out of the corner of his eye. Far above him was a domed ceiling covered in luminous moss. He seemed to be at a dead end.

After an interval of catching his breath, Harvey pushed himself up with his left arm and was trying to drag his lower body up onto the bank when something suddenly caught his eye.

A radio...?

There was something like a small gray box lying on the floor in front of him. It was a portable radio. Slowly he slid his gaze even farther forward, and in the bleary light of the moss, he made out the outlines of various other things washed up on the bank.

Or maybe fished out of the water?

It was a pile of bloated corpses. Most likely of people who had gotten lost in the waterways and drowned — but the majority of them had been half-eaten, their remains scattered about the floor. Bits of human body parts littered the bank like toys a child had grown bored with and tossed away.

It's a nest...

He forced down the bile rising in his throat. They were lower than animals. Sometimes one animal attacked another so that it could survive, but Harvey thought these guys just attacked and ate any living thing they happened across, without even really knowing why they were doing it.

He heard a splash behind him.

Shit—! He recovered his wits and pulled up the leg that was still in the water, but the hand that had vaulted out of the river seized his ankle before it was clear, and he ended up pulling *it* onto the bank with him.

With an unpleasant wet slapping noise, *it* used its other hand to crawl up the side. A rush of dirty water poured down from it to form a muddy puddle on the floor. Harvey thought it might actually be overflowing from inside the thing's body.

Its chest gaped open where he'd dug out a chunk of it with the jackknife, and blackish organs peeped out of it; they must have lost most of their function from tissue death. And deep inside that chest, a little to the left of center, was buried exactly what Harvey had expected.

Surrounded by a mass of bio-cables was the warped black stone, steadily blinking with a dull amber light.

He shuddered.

"Let go!" Harvey tried to shake off the creature, but instead it slithered up his body. The feel of its sticky skin clinging to his thigh sent a chill up his spine.

Ephraim.

What?! He was jolted by the voice that abruptly sprang up in his own head. It had to be a hallucination.

Superimposed on the rotting, shapeless face hovering over his was another face, one he recognized. It was a man who hadn't left much of an impression; his blue-gray eyes were the only things vaguely unique about him. The creature reached out to Harvey as if begging for help, and its half-melted mouth twisted in its half-melted face.

Hey, Ephraim. It's me.

"Stay away!" he cried, shaking his head to clear it of the unreal voice. At the same time, he plunged the heel of his foot into the gaping tear in its chest with enough violence to kick in those exposed organs. This finally had an effect. *It* rolled to the edge of the bank with a whine like a puppy's.

What the hell are you doing in my head?! Harvey sank to the ground and panted so hard his shoulders heaved, staring aghast at the *thing* curled up on the floor and cursing his own hallucination. *What the hell do I care you betrayed me* again *you bastard I'd be on cloud nine if you died in the street somewhere and your body was eaten by bugs and broken down into harmless molecules never show your damn face in front of me again — no, more like, why the hell can't I learn my lesson?! How many times does this have to happen before I get it through my head that nothing good ever comes of getting involved with that damn —*

It let out a low groan.

It seemed to have recovered from the damage in no time. It shuffled up onto its hands and knees, moaning, so Harvey smothered the churning swirl of thoughts in his mind and focused his attention on the enemy before him.

Apparently it had abnormally high powers of recovery. He guessed that to kill it he'd have to get its heart —

The creature, crouched on all fours, unexpectedly kicked off against the ground. Harvey had been watching it like a hawk, but he hadn't sensed any motion of warning, and his response was delayed. It scurried fast toward him with movements that didn't resemble a four-legged animal so much as a giant crustacean. Horrified by the grotesque sight, he tried to dodge, but an arm darted out at him from an impossible angle and a hand fastened onto his left wrist. He reflexively shifted to raise his right arm, but of course it didn't move, and he collapsed to the ground, landing on one shoulder. The force of the impact threw his whole weight onto his side. He bit back a scream and shoved down the pain.

Harvey didn't know if *it* was addicted to the taste of human flesh or what, but it opened its cavernous mouth wide and lunged at his neck. His left arm was pinned; he couldn't move it.

I can't block him —!

There was a shrill noise, like two hard objects banging together.

For a second he doubted his own eyes. "What the...?" The right arm that should have been broken and useless had flung itself in front of his throat at the last possible moment and taken the impact of *its* teeth. The metal framework creaked between the unnaturally gaping jaws, but still it seemed to resist. Sparks flew from the exposed cables as its motor thrummed.

"Stop it, don't hurt yourself—" No sooner were the words out of his mouth than his forearm collapsed under the pressure and flattened. Yet it didn't stop. With a screeching noise Harvey's mind couldn't wrap itself around, it was cruelly crushed between the thing's teeth.

Everything went utterly blank. A split second later, almost without conscious thought, he plunged his left hand into the cleft in *its* breast. He slammed the rib cage in and wrapped his hand around the black stone at its heart. It was hotter than he expected; he felt the skin of his palm burning. Ignoring this, he planted his foot on *its* chest for leverage and began to tear the stone from the bio-cables that connected it to the rest of the *thing's* body.

It probably didn't understand what Harvey was doing to it. But maybe it instinctively sensed the danger. It started to resist, contorting its body wildly.

Stop it, Ephraim! Please —

The man's face hovered above the *thing's* again and reached out a pleading hand. It was as if someone who knew what made Harvey tick was manipulating the illusion, because now he saw another face. It was another one he recognized, with sandy hair and an unshaven face...

Ju —

He knew it wasn't real, but his fingers slackened slightly all the same. Pointed talons dug at his face and scratched off the gauze over his right cheek, taking a patch of skin with them. He let out a hiss of pain.

Harvey put all his energy into the fight again, and this time he didn't hesitate as he ripped the last of the bio-cables and yanked out the stone.

His arm slipped out from between the thing's organs. The impact sent his back slamming into the floor. The giant form of his enemy, all strength gone, slumped on top of him. Even though its power source had been removed, its nerves seemed to react just a little longer, and its limbs flailed. But like springs going slack, the movements gradually grew dull, and eventually it dropped into stillness.

Even tugging his body out from under the huge creature

was too much trouble. He lay with his cheek pressed to the slimy concrete for a while, listening to nothing but the gasping sounds of his own breath. The fiery-hot stone in his left hand steadily cooled in the outside air. He wasn't gripping it tightly anymore, but it was stuck fast to his burned palm and wouldn't come off.

He was smeared from elbow to fingertips with black blood like coal tar, and he had a feeling that even if he washed it off now, the sensation of someone else's flesh and blood would be with him for a long time.

"I'm sick of this...," he grumbled softly.

He never wanted to do that again. To — to kill something like one of his own kind.

He finally summoned up the energy to move a little. Using his elbow, he crawled groggily out from under the heavy corpse on top of him. He shifted his gaze to the right arm still trapped underneath it where it had been dashed to the ground, and called, "Hey…"

There was no response. Harvey peeled off the stone stuck to his hand, along with the skin attached to it. Then he used that hand to pull out the arm.

Its metal framework was crushed and unrecognizable. Weak sparks rose from where the cables had melted from the high heat. "Hey, come on, answer me. You moved just now, didn't you? Do it one more time…," he said, and noticed that his voice was gradually breaking and falling soft.

Maybe before he could've taken it to a good mechanic and had it fixed, but now it was probably beyond repair.

When he pressed his forehead to the pathetically warped heap of metal his forearm had become, he could still hear the feeble sound of a motor coming from somewhere near the elbow.

With one last, short rumble, that quickly disappeared, too.

Harvey knew he had to stand up, but his sopping-wet clothes were stuck to the ground, and he couldn't move. *I have to go back, fast,* he told himself impatiently, but he couldn't quite recall what it was he had to hurry back to.

Huh?

Mixed in with the sounds of water filling the passageway, he could hear a familiar noise coming from somewhere. It was so horribly garbled with static it was hard to make out, but it was the up-tempo sound of stringed instruments.

Spurred on by the somehow nostalgic sound, or more like by a slap on the ass and a voice hissing *What are you doing resting in a place like this, you bastard?* he abruptly remembered. He had to get back to Kieli.

When he opened his eye, a shadowy form leaning over him let out a yelp and jumped backward. Harvey didn't really get who the unfamiliar man was or what was going on, but the guy was holding a broom and a dustpan, so maybe he'd been cleaning. A portable radio hung from a belt on his waist. Harvey had a hard time believing that radio waves would reach them this far down, but the noise was undeniably coming from its speaker.

The man was peering at him fearfully from a short distance away, but soon his face relaxed and he smiled innocently at Harvey. "Hey, I thought that was you. I took you for a dead body again."

Huh? He looked up at the man suspiciously and thought for

a minute. A man with cleaning implements and a radio...
"Oh!" He hadn't been in the best mental state at the time, but
he retained a vague impression of what had happened. It had
been a long time since he'd heard that guerrilla radio station,
and he'd felt oddly comforted.

Harvey narrowed his eye. "Give me my money back."

The man waved his hands around, flustered. "Ah, see, I spent
that a long time ago."

"I'm kidding. It doesn't matter anymore." He quirked the
corner of his mouth up in a smile, and then dropped his
gaze, already tired of talking.

After a hesitant silence, he heard the man's voice above
him. It was a mixture of surprise, exasperation, and wry
laughter. "You look terrible again. Are you alive?"

"...Fortunately," he said with a nod, and sat up unsteadily.
First he wiped the blood from his right eye with a shrug of his
shoulder, and then he looked down at the hole in his side. He
figured he could still walk. Probably.

It struck him as kind of strange that he'd answered with
"fortunately." He was pretty sure he'd never had the ability to
think of being alive as "fortunate" before.

Fortunately, he could still go home to Kieli.

All of a sudden reports came to Julius of a commotion outside of town involving a (failed) attempt to capture an Undying and the discharge of a knockoff carbonization gun. He
was lost as to what it was all about, but he temporarily with-

drew from the waterways along with the soldiers in his search party and dashed to the entrance into downtown.

A tiny civilian truck was parked there, surrounded by the black trucks of Church Soldiers. One moment the mercantile-looking man in front of it was whining in exaggerated tones something along the lines of "It's because you jerks took so long to show up that it got away from me," and the next moment he was clutching his stomach and crying for a stretcher.

Julius seized one of the nearby soldiers and requested an explanation. He was told the Undying who'd gotten away was a woman.

A woman?

He cocked his head. Apparently it wasn't the man they were searching for.

Then he noticed the two children clutching each other and cowering at the sidelines — though in fairness, he supposed that two short years ago he hadn't looked any older than the girl did. She was about ten, and the other one was a younger boy. They looked like siblings.

At any rate, it wasn't the kids who had caught his eye so much as the old radio the little boy was clutching lovingly to his chest. He couldn't imagine there were *two* groups of travelers who would lovingly carry a beat-up old antique that was so rusted it looked like something from the junk pile.

"They say that girl fired the weapon, but it wasn't a fatal hit, and the Undying got away."

"Her?"

At the soldier's explanation, he studied the girl again in surprise. From a distance she had seemed meek enough. When he left the men and walked toward her, she caught sight of him and shrank back as if overwhelmed. She seemed just as meek up close as she had from a distance.

"Reverend."

Being surrounded by all those brawny soldiers must have been frightening. She gave him an imploring look, and he felt momentarily disconcerted. But there was no point in confusing her more when she was already scared, so he didn't correct the false impression. To the average citizen, there probably wasn't much difference between a seminarian and a full-fledged priest. "Do you live in town?"

"Yes, at our relatives' house…"

"Okay, I'll have someone bring you there. I might have to ask you about all this again later, but go on home for today," he said, striving for his most adult tone so that he would sound like a priest. The girl bowed deeply and looked relieved enough to cry. In his mind, Julius laughed ruefully at the awkward position he was now in. He actually had no authority to release them without permission. In fact, he didn't particularly have the authority to be here at all; he was just butting his nose in. However, even if he didn't have authority, he did have power.

Julius dropped his eyes to the object in the boy's arms and changed the subject. "By the way, where did you get that radio?"

"This is the lady's," said the boy. He slightly emphasized the words "the lady's," as if proud. Unlike his sister, he didn't seem the least bit unnerved. Maybe he didn't understand the situation.

"Would you mind if I held on to it?"

"No, of course not," answered the girl for him, poking him

sharply with her elbow. The boy looked as though he hated to part with it, but in the end he reluctantly handed it over.

It was switched off. When he took it and inspected it more closely, he got the feeling it really was *that* radio after all. It seemed more than likely that this escaped Undying had something to do with Kieli and Harvey.

As he stared at it, turning it over in his hands, he heard the girl's thin voice say, "Reverend..." This time he started to tell her he was still just a seminary student, but after one look at her he shut his mouth.

She was standing there with her hands clasped in front of her breasts, lips trembling, and she went on speaking in a rush of words, almost more to herself than to him. "Reverend, I thought what I'd done was right. The Church teaches us that those people are abominable creatures cut off from God. And I always thought that was true." She paused. "But...maybe it's a sin to say this, but...are you sure I wasn't wrong?"

Julius wasn't able to answer right away. He met her expectant gaze in silence. He was sure the girl would be relieved if he told her, "What you did was right, so there's nothing for you to worry about."

But the only words that eventually came out of his mouth were, "I'm not a priest."

He had no authority to preach to her. He was bitterly disappointed with himself for running away like a coward only at the worst times like this. Perhaps the girl's face showed her own disappointment, but he turned around and left before he could see her reaction.

He ordered a nearby soldier to take them home and then

headed back to the truck he'd come in, saying, "I'm going back to the waterways. The search is still ongoing." As he was about to climb into the passenger's seat, there was a ring from the communicator on the driver's side.

The soldier standing by to drive him took the call. It looked as though the other trucks were all getting the same message; commotion suddenly broke out all around him. Julius swept his eyes over the scene, frowning. "What happened?" he asked his driver.

The other man looked as if he didn't understand it himself. "They say a corpse fell out of the waterway," he said.

She could hear a radio playing.

Guided by the faint static coming from somewhere past the section of tunnel she could see in the muted light of the moss, Kieli automatically picked up her pace. She sloshed along through the film of water covering the passageway, gritting her teeth against the pain in her knees.

She saw someone ahead of her in the waterway. He was leaning his slightly sagging right shoulder lightly against the wall to prop himself up as he dragged his tall, waterlogged body toward her. When Kieli stopped walking, he caught sight of her and stopped, too. He glanced back over his shoulder and murmured something. The sound of the radio faded quietly away, as if relieved to have done its duty.

Then he turned back to face her, and his expressionless mask faltered just a tiny bit. "... Are you okay?"

It was obvious *he* was the one who wasn't okay. Kieli scowled at him, a little annoyed. "I should ask you that."

They started walking again. The gap between them steadily closed until just as they were about to meet in the middle, Harvey slipped on a patch of slime. She reached out a hand to hold him up, and they went stumbling to their knees together.

"Heh, you fell for it," said a voice near her ear. It was scratchy, but Kieli could hear the mischief in it. The arm Harvey had wound around her shoulders didn't budge. It took a few stunned moments for her to catch on that he'd been faking, but when she figured it out, it rankled a little.

When she pressed her face to his chest and wound her arms around his back, she could feel the sharp angle of his shoulder blades even through the coat. "... You've lost some weight."

"Eh, it can't be that much."

"Yes, it is. I remember exactly how you felt before." The feel of the bony hand hugging her shoulder, its warmth, the voice that rumbled a bit in his throat, the way he talked, the rhythm of his breathing, everything — right now, she could remember all of it.

Kieli raised her face slightly and looked up at his closed right eye and the scar on his cheek. She bit her lip. "How come every single time I let you out of my sight, you end up looking like you're going to die? You're so dumb ...!" she spat accusingly, looking down again.

"Oh. Yeah ...," came the uncomfortable reply.

"You just left all of a sudden and didn't write me for so long! Do you get how completely selfish that was?"

"Yeah ..."

"And do you get how I felt this whole time?"

"Yeah."

"Liar. I know you didn't even think about it."

"...Yeah."

"The Corporal and Beatrix were worried, too, you know. Are you sorry?"

"Yeah."

"Say something that's not 'yeah'!"

"Yeah." And then, a second later: "Sorry."

It was a really short and clumsy apology, but it was straight from the heart. Kieli kept right on glaring at his collarbone for a while, anyway, lips pressed tightly together, but eventually she couldn't hold back the tears welling up in her eyes. She started to sob violently. It was like a dam breaking, and then she couldn't stop. She buried herself in the chest of the man in front of her and blubbered like a little kid.

"You're such a crybaby," said a discomfited-sounding voice above her head after a while. "I thought you'd grown up some, but on the inside you haven't changed at all."

"Shut up, I *didn't* cry!"

As a comeback, it didn't sound very convincing, but it was true. She *hadn't* cried all this time.

After all, she'd decided not to cry until she'd made him apologize.

A hand ruffled her hair, and a voice somewhere behind her left shoulder repeated, "Sorry." Then she heard it whisper one more thing, almost to itself.

...I'm home.

"This place is like a circus…"

When Julius arrived at the scene, there were a lot more onlookers than he would have expected. He eyed the crowd dubiously and then looked up at the wall beyond. Far up the cracked wall gaped the black mouths of a row of tunnels. Thin streams of water dripped down from them. He shoved his way through the throng of people (most of them residents of downtown), seeing a ring of soldiers huddled around the dried-up track of an open conduit running parallel to the wall.

The prone figure they surrounded must be the fallen corpse.

Even the highly trained Church Soldiers were grimacing and giving it a wide berth. The instant Julius saw it from the other side of the crowd, his eyes widened, and a second and a half later he looked away.

True, he'd have to be a messy corpse just from falling all the way from those tunnels up there (and I really don't want to see that, even), but doesn't it look like he was dead before *he fell…? He looks like a bloated-up drowned man, and like a burnt corpse with its skin melting off—*

"What is that thing…?"

Julius gulped, fought off the urge to throw up, and turned to question the soldier who'd come with him, but the man was already facing the other way and throwing up for real.

The orders were to carry away the corpse and to avoid the onlookers while they did it. While the troops prepared to transport him, reluctant though they were to approach him, the sounds of a heavy fossil-fuel truck engine roared up close to them.

Julius furrowed his brow at the truck as it drove over the embankment and entered the ruined conduit. It was definitely one of the black Church trucks, but its excessively thick armor gave it an overwhelming air of intimidation.

The soldiers shrank back, clearing space. The men who came out of the truck were clothed in pure white that contrasted starkly with its black paint. They were fortified with full-body armor and helmets that covered their faces; it all far and away outclassed anything the lowly city troops wore.

Undying Hunters.

As Julius gaped, they shoved the city soldiers aside as if it was their God-given right and started preparing to carry the corpse to their own vehicle. "Hey! What makes you think you can show up here out of nowhere and just —"

He was about to storm up to them and tell them off when another soldier stopped him with a whispered, "Master Julius, you shouldn't." He bit his lower lip in frustration. The Undying Hunters reported directly to the Council of Elders. This was the one unit he couldn't interfere with, even with all his father's influence to back him up.

The masked men whisked away the revolting corpse with supreme indifference and without any explanation. Julius watched it all with a glare, unable to hide his displeasure. The other troops seemed to share his feelings.

From all appearances, the Hunters couldn't care less. As soon as they finished collecting the awful body, they began forming a search team, as if they meant to take the next step in walking all over Julius and go investigate the waterways on their own.

"Has our escapee been found yet?" he asked the soldier next to him in a low voice.

"Not yet. We had to stop because of all this fuss...It doesn't look like we'll get the chance to investigate any further, either."

"Give me that," he said, and borrowed — or more accurately, snatched — the man's bayonet gun before turning on his heel and walking away.

"Er, uh, where are you going, sir?"

Julius didn't turn at the sound of the flustered voice behind him. "I just remembered something I have to take care of. No need for you to come with me." He forced his way through the bystanders and back to the truck he'd come in.

Kieli tried several times to get down. "I can walk by myself."

"It's fine. I want to carry you."

So as they made their way to the exit out of the sewers, she gratefully accepted the ride on Harvey's back, resting her cheek on the shoulder of his coat.

Afterward, she'd cried for a time, apologizing to him through her sobs. Harvey hadn't seemed to understand at first what she was apologizing for. When she explained, "For the thing about the guard who was killed," he looked just a little miffed before mumbling, "...Whatever. It doesn't matter what a bunch of people I don't care about think of me. But you—"

And then he broke off. Kieli felt as if he'd stopped right in the middle of something important, but he didn't continue.

Kieli fiercely told herself again that even if the whole world turned against Harvey, she would never, ever betray him.

And then they started walking along the waterway again. On their way, Kieli told him, from her perch on his back, all kinds of things about the last year and a half: life in the towns of East South-hairo, her live-in job, the time Beatrix had packed up the Corporal and sent him to a charity, and the time she and Beatrix had dressed up in disguise and crashed a cruising party at a port town.

While she told him her memories bit by bit, whatever came into her head, he just kept silently walking straight ahead without even responding; but whenever she thought, *Maybe I'll stop because I don't think he's listening anyway,* he'd choose that moment to prompt her with a little "Huh. Then what?" So it was really hard to tell whether he was listening or not.

Beatrix's name inevitably came up a lot, and it brought home to Kieli all over again that between one thing and another, they really had been together for a whole year and a half. "Beatrix is funny, huh? She's selfish and stuck-up and she does whatever she wants, but sometimes she surprises you by acting really nice or having this weirdly strong sense of responsibility…" She thought about that golden hair and sulky expression, and gave a pained smile.

"Didn't I tell you you could trust Beatrix?" answered Harvey, in this tone of *What, you just now figured that out?* And come to think of it, Kieli did remember that. At the time, they'd been in a pretty desperate situation, and it'd seemed as though he was just saying it on impulse to make her feel better, but now she guessed he must have just been telling the truth.

She was a little jealous of Beatrix, that Harvey talked about her that way, but now she kind of looked forward to seeing her again, wondering if from now on they could be normal friends, without reservations like they'd had before. It would be nice if they could be close the way she and Becca used to be.

Though she had the feeling she'd be getting a serious tongue-lashing about this whole thing first...

When we get back, I'll tell her I'm sorry.

Kieli closed her eyes lightly and inhaled. She could smell the faint aroma of tobacco as she leaned into his neck. He'd been in that cell, so he couldn't have smoked for a long time. Had the smoke seeped so deeply into his body that it was part of his natural odor now? It was the old familiar scent of him, the one she hadn't smelled in so long.

Mist-fine beads of water were falling down on them from the ceiling, filling her ears with the enjoyable sound of rain. The droplets felt strangely warm, like light raining down from the ceiling moss, comfortably caressing her cheeks.

Harvey was supporting her rear end with only his left hand, so she adjusted her grip around his neck so that she wouldn't slide off. While she was at it, she cast a look ahead of them. Far down the long stretch of passageway, a thin beam of sandy light was coming into view. A ladder along the wall led up to a square, cavernous opening in the ceiling. It was the drain on the edge of the uptown district that Kieli had climbed down from when she'd first entered the waterways.

Harvey suddenly stopped walking.

A wariness permeated the air, one that was quiet like a still pool of water, yet alert to the tiniest thing.

"I thought I'd find you here," said a voice that ricocheted off the walls of the passageway. A young male voice: not a child, yet not quite an adult.

Someone began making his way down from the patch of light in front of them. When he jumped off the ladder halfway down, the hem of his long robe billowed up in the wind, and then fluttered back down around his legs again as his feet touched the floor.

He wore black priest's garb; the gentle sand-colored light lit him from behind and cast his face into shadow. Kieli squinted. Then she saw who it was and sagged with relief.

"When I heard you'd gone down into the waterways, too, I figured you must have come through this drain."

"I'm sorry, Juli…" She ducked her head a little and hid behind Harvey's back, then noticed something was wrong. The wariness radiating from that back hadn't eased even the tiniest bit. Just as her mind started to question this, she heard a soft metallic click.

When she looked forward again, Julius was silently pointing a bayonet gun at them.

"Juli…?!"

Kieli slipped hastily down from Harvey's back. Pain flared up in her knees the moment her feet hit the ground. Ignoring it, she tried to run up to her friend, but Harvey's arm shot out to hold her back, and she was herded behind him. When she peeked up at him over his shoulder, his gaze was cold and unsurprised, trained on Julius. "You know you can't kill me with that thing."

Julius was silent for a moment. He pressed his lips together, looking as if *he* was the one cornered, and then solemnly opened his mouth, gun still not wavering. "I'll ask you one question. Are you the one who killed the guard?"

"No, Juli, he —"

He cut her off apologetically but firmly. "I'm sorry, Kieli, but you're not the one I'm asking." And he looked steadily at Harvey, waiting for his answer. Kieli bit her lip and almost cried, but Harvey was just his usual indifferent self, as though he really didn't care one way or the other.

"If that's what you want to think, be my guest."

"Was it you or not?" Julius repeated. His face was dead serious. Harvey sighed tiredly, but in the end he answered readily enough.

"No."

"...Fair enough." Julius breathed out and nodded lightly — did he believe them now? — but his hard expression didn't relax. "What did, then?"

"It sounds like you have an idea," Harvey answered, and she realized that Julius hadn't asked *who* did; he'd asked *what* did.

After a breath, he continued in the manner of someone telling important news, and Kieli thought this must have been the main issue all along. "We found a corpse downtown. It fell from the waterway. It was like a monster..."

"That was —" Kieli began unthinkingly, then swallowed the rest of the sentence and gripped the sleeve of Harvey's coat. *That was the thing I sent over the edge.*

"You stay quiet," Harvey whispered to her without taking his eye off Julius. Still staring fixedly at them, face harsh, Julius asked another question: "Undying Hunters from the capital carried it off. What . . . *was* that thing?"

"Undying Hunters?" Kieli said, surprised. She looked up at Harvey's profile, but he seemed to have expected this. His expression didn't change.

"There are a lot of taboo things in this world that you don't know about."

"Give me a straight answer."

Harvey thought silently for a minute, and then jammed his left hand into his coat pocket. Kieli saw Julius's whole body stiffen at the sudden movement, and her heart did a somersault in her chest, but Harvey, supremely unconcerned, just drew out something from the pocket and casually tossed it to Julius. "Here."

"Ack!"

Harvey seemed to be far better than Julius at situations like this. After Julius took one hand off his gun to catch the flying object, he realized he'd lost his offensive stance and made a bitter face. Then he frowned and looked down at it.

A black stone just about the size and roughness of Harvey's fist — seeing it even from this distance, Kieli's eyes widened. She looked back and forth between their faces.

"What is this?"

"Did you know there's a fossil energy lab in the capital?"

". . . I know it exists. What about it?"

"Try asking your dad about it," Harvey said, breaking off the conversation rudely. Then, with a whispered "Let's go" to Kieli, he started walking toward the exit Julius stood in front of as if he didn't have a care in the world.

It looked as though Julius didn't feel like pointing the gun at him again either way. He was obviously unsatisfied, but he just stuck the stone into his own coat pocket, reached underneath the coat, and produced a very familiar little radio.

Her own shriek was no surprise, but Harvey's voice joined her at equal volume before they both snapped their mouths shut in confusion. Then she was running up to Julius and practically snatching it out of his hand, crying, "Where did you get this?!"

Julius gave her a look that said *I knew it.* "Apparently an Undying woman was carrying it. So you two know her."

Beatrix! "Where is she?"

"She got away. We don't know where she went, either."

"What happened?!"

"They say she was headed to Gate Town in a traveling salesman's truck, but she was shot by another passenger, a civilian. That's all I know."

"*Shot*...?" Kieli murmured, stunned. She looked up at Harvey. He started to say something, too, stopped, blinked hard, and turned his back to them. He stilled and glared into the waterway as if searching for a presence there. A few seconds later, Kieli's ears picked up a faint metallic sound.

"The Undying Hunters have started searching the waterways. If you're going to run, do it fast. I won't help you," Julius said, scowling. He stepped away from the ladder. Kieli didn't think letting them go was much different from helping them — but when she stared blankly back at him, he glared not at her but at Harvey, and said in an unnaturally low tone, "*This* time, got it? We might be enemies the next time we meet. Be ready."

Harvey mumbled a curt affirmative and pushed at Kieli's shoulder. She let him urge her up onto the ladder, turning back to look at Julius one more time from across Harvey's arm. "Thank you so much for everything. I'm sorry things got so crazy again…"

"We'll see each other again, won't we?"

"Yeah. I think we will." And even though she didn't have any grounds for thinking so, she really did. When they'd parted the first time she hadn't thought she'd ever see him again, but here they were, so she was sure she'd get a third chance.

He smiled and nodded, youth and just a little bit of maturity mixing together in his dark green eyes. "Okay, that's a promise. And I'm going to be bigger than he is by then."

"In your dreams, moron," Harvey said maliciously, sweeping aside their reluctant good-byes. He gave the ladder a sharp kick for good measure, as if to tell her to get a move on. Kieli ducked her head and scrambled up.

When she stuck her head out of the drain in the ceiling, she was greeted by the sight of the back roads of uptown and the sandy skies above the rooftops of the houses. The dry city wind stirred her damp hair. It seemed like forever since she'd felt it.

She clambered up the asphalt onto the shoulder of the road, then crouched on her knees and peered down over the edge of the drain and saw that Harvey, the one who'd hurried her along in the first place, had come to a stop halfway up the ladder as if he'd abruptly remembered something.

"Julius." He cocked his head to the side and regarded the boy seeing them off from below. "The Undying Hunters will probably find him soon enough, but at a dead end on the east side, there's a corpse with a radio. Have your guys bury him if you can, okay?"

"Uh, sure…?" Julius obviously didn't understand, but he

nodded anyway, and Kieli saw Harvey breathe a sigh of relief. Then he shot up the ladder to where she waited, taking it two rungs at a time.

Harvey's scars looked so awful now that she saw them in the light. He didn't seem the least bit troubled about it, though. He just stood there shaking himself off like a dog, sending droplets of water flying out of his hair, and then looked up to the sky overhead with his left hand shielding his eye, as if the sky was a little too bright for him. Now that Kieli thought about it, with all the time he'd spent locked up in that underground cell, it must have been a long while since he'd stepped out into the sunlight.

"I hope Beatrix is okay. I wonder what happened to her…"

"We'll ask the Corporal about it later. Right now we have to hurry. Can you run?"

"Yeah." Before she let him push her into a run through the streets, she stopped for a moment and looked up into his face. He chose that second to glance down at her, as if he'd had the same thought she had. They exchanged meek looks, and then Kieli dropped her gaze to the radio hanging from her hand.

"I'd rather let him be for a month or so."

"Yeah…"

There was no doubt in her mind that the instant they turned the power on, a month-long lecture would begin.

Harvey sighed resignedly. "Oh, well. Guess we'll let him get it out of his system."

Kieli laughed and nodded. "We'll kneel humbly on our knees and listen together," she said, and then she slipped the radio's cord around her neck just as she always had.

THE STORY OF A CERTAIN UNDYING, GIRL,
AND RADIO ON AN AUTUMN AFTERNOON

He'd spent so long staring at ceilings that the sheer height of the sky made him dizzy.

Even on this planet blanketed with low clouds of fine dust, the sky was so high, so far away. It might look close enough to touch, yet he knew that he could never reach it, no matter how far up he stretched his hand. Legend had it that people had been able to see an unbroken view of the universe in the skies of the blue planet that had once existed at the end of the world, but Harvey couldn't quite imagine what a "clear sky" would look like.

As he stared up, hood pulled back off his forehead slightly, the thread of white smoke rising from the tip of his cigarette was sucked up into the sand-colored autumn sky.

"Anyway, your stupid face looks disgusting."

"Heh. You could call it a badge of honor."

"Like that even makes any sense. Take better care of your body, dammit," grumbled the radio perched next to him on the staircase. And even he didn't know himself what he'd meant, so nothing more was said about his injuries.

"Well? Are you 'ready' now? You're looking strangely cheerful."

Harvey let his gaze wander a little. "Uh, the thing is ... I had some unfinished business, so I hadn't felt like coming home yet, so I hadn't really gotten around to thinking much about, well, that."

"You jerk, you always put off dealing with anything troublesome!"

"No, no. I'm ready now," he amended hastily. Even if that was less thanks to his actively thinking about the situation, and more thanks to Kieli.

If Kieli hadn't come to visit him yesterday, maybe, just maybe, he would have run away by himself and never seen her again. A part of him had thought that if he was going to make her cry before long either way, maybe it'd be best to just leave things the way they were. "...But she came to get me, and seeing her made me feel relieved somehow, and I felt really guilty; so, I think as long as Kieli wants to be with me, I'll take that responsibility...I kind of think that's why the world gave me some more time."

"What do you mean 'some' more?...Hey, you'd better not be thinking you might not have much time left. You did tell me that the next time you got a deadly injury, you'd probably die, didn't you...?"

The radio's voice was suddenly meek, and Harvey couldn't help himself: it startled an unbidden laugh out of him. "What's with the funereal voice there?"

"What's so funny?! That was not the time to laugh!" the radio spat glumly, spewing static from its speaker.

Harvey answered in his normal voice, as if he felt bad for laughing when the Corporal was worrying about him. "But that's normal, right? Normal people die after deadly injuries."

"Forget dying, normal people can't move *after deadly injuries. You're the only one dumb enough to walk around with a hole in his stomach, making himself worse,"* retorted the radio snidely. Harvey couldn't argue with that, so he just hunched his shoulders and stayed silent.

Just when he'd finished his business in town and come back to their meeting point, his legs had failed him, and he'd collapsed on his rear end on the staircase. So now he was taking a break as he waited, and having a smoke while he was at it. During that time, he'd privately told the radio about the crack in his core.

"Now you listen to me — try not to block out your pain if you can help it. Pain is your body's way of telling you you're about to be in trouble. Actually recognize normal feelings. Be more thankful that you're alive!"

"Yeah, yeah, I got it." Harvey was grateful for the warning, but this was starting to get annoying. He wished he'd never said anything.

"Hey, you bastard, you're not listening to me, are you?! I'm worrying about —"

"I know, Corporal. Thanks."

"— You —" Caught off-guard by the frank thanks, the radio broke off mid-rant.

"I am properly grateful, you know. That I'm here."

He gazed up at the sky past the thin column of tobacco smoke.

He couldn't see a starry sky, but the sky he had was more than high enough for him.

Despite the Church Soldiers' information control, some sort of rumor — another body being discovered at the east end of the waterways — had leaked out, and all the onlookers had started drifting that way. Kieli slipped through the gaps in the one-way flow of townspeople, going the opposite direction as the crowd. It wasn't that she wasn't interested in the strange corpse, but the important thing right now was to take advantage of this confusion and get out of town.

The sports bag slung over her shoulder bounced off of her back. She'd briefly gone back to Julius's nursemaid's house to pick up her things and say thank you, for Harvey as well as herself. Harvey had told her to do it. When the lady had taken in Kieli's appearance, stoically trying to bear her soaking-wet clothes and the giant scrapes on both knees, she had almost tearfully pleaded that Kieli take a bath, get warmed up, and bandage her wounds before she left, so Kieli had lost a whole half hour she hadn't planned on.

Now she was belatedly beginning to worry that maybe Harvey had deliberately sent her to the lady so that he could disappear again. The closer she got to the train station, the faster her jogging steps got, until before she knew it she was running full tilt.

She came to a halt after plunging into the traffic circle in front of the station. She squinted past the line of parked three-wheeled taxis, but she couldn't see any heads of copper hair at the foot of the staircase where they were supposed to meet.

He's not there…

People running in the same direction as the rubberneckers and babbling in loud, excited voices; people running toward the train station, more worried about being on time for their departures — she looked around as well as she could over the heads of the churning crowd, but she couldn't find the one head she was looking for.

He's not there…!

She was automatically gathering herself up to run again when someone suddenly grabbed her arm from behind.

Whirling around with a shriek, she saw a tall figure in a dark gray coat standing there, hood pulled low over his face. One eye peeked out to look down at her, blinking. "How come you look like you're about to cry?"

"Wh-Why aren't you where you said you'd be ... ?!"

"I just figured I should stay out of sight. It was getting crowded," Harvey answered easily, completely oblivious to her feelings. Sure, that was the way he always was, but she couldn't help her morose expression. One corner of his mouth twitched up a little in amusement. "Sheesh. I'm not going anywhere."

So saying, he started walking toward the train station, pushing her along by the shoulder. "Let's get on board fast. They'll probably set up roadblocks pretty soon."

"...Okay." After she'd let him lead her a few steps, Kieli suddenly snapped back to attention. She stared intently up at his profile. *Maybe he pretended not to be there on purpose because he knew it would scare me. He's so warped.*

Harvey just nonchalantly averted his eye, so she couldn't tell whether it was true or not.

"What did you find out about Beatrix?" she whispered as they weaved quickly through the throng of people. Harvey and the Corporal were supposed to try to follow Beatrix's trail together while Kieli was getting her things. But now Harvey just shook his head lightly. Apparently they hadn't found anything.

"Oh," she said glumly.

"I left a message with the information peddler. I asked him to pass it along to the people on the parish border, too, so I'm sure we'll be able to get in touch through one of them eventually. Don't worry."

Harvey sounded casual about it, but when Kieli thought about how her own selfish actions had gotten Beatrix into this mess, she couldn't stop the flood of regret. She'd thought she'd be able to talk to the woman a lot more. She hadn't thanked her yet, or apologized yet, either, and her next birthday was still coming up...

"It's not your fault, you know," he said lightly, as if this kind of thing happened all the time. But maybe he was being a little bit considerate about her feelings, because he added, "As long as you're both alive, you'll be able to see each other again. She can take care of herself just fine."

"Although the same can't be said for you," jibed the radio.

Harvey twisted his lips. "Yeah, yeah." Maybe he seemed coldhearted, but Kieli was sure that wasn't it. He must really trust Beatrix that much.

...I hope someone thinks of me as special like that, too, even just a little. I want to be special to Harvey, and the Corporal — and Beatrix, too, if I can.

"Anyway, you two had better be ready," said the radio out of nowhere. They both looked down at him, blinking.

"For what?"

A highly bitter voice, accompanied by a highly displeased burst of static, announced from the speaker, *"As soon as we're on the train, I'm chewing you out until your ears bleed. I'll have you know, I've built up a TON of frustration — I mean, a ton of things I want to say to you for your own good."*

"...Okay," answered Kieli meekly. When she stole a glance at Harvey, however, he was muttering sore-loser things like "I knew I should have left him turned off for a while," and point-

edly looking away. Then his gaze abruptly froze on something, and he stopped walking.

In the distance, beyond the milky-white walls she could see from the station, stood the far-northern mountain range veiled in sandy gas. Sprawling in its center was a dark gray mechanical city, ponderous and quiet like a cluster of giant tombstones —

"Harvey…"

Under the shadow of his hood, the look in his coppery left eye instantly sharpened to a harsh glare. She could see the city reflected in it.

"…Do you want to go back there?"

"Hmm? Nah." Harvey blinked once and tore his gaze away from the city. With a wry little laugh, he answered, "For now, we're making a temporary retreat."

Whoo-oo-oo!

The muffled sound of the train whistle began to echo from the top of the station's staircase, and the flow of people grew more frantic. Urged on by the radio's hiss of *"Crap, we're going to miss it!"* they joined the wave of people rushing toward the platform and ran up the stairs.

Halfway up, Harvey turned back to Kieli, who was lagging a little behind him and to the side. "Kieli, hurry." He reached his one and only working hand out to her and knitted his brow just for a moment as if thinking about his next words, before giving her a lighthearted look as though he'd finally freed himself of something. "Do you still want to come with me?" he said.

Kieli prayed to the God who, if He actually existed, was probably watching them from somewhere in the sky but would almost certainly never reach a hand out to her. She didn't really expect much, but that didn't make her wish any less heartfelt. *Please, let me keep the feeling of this left hand wrapping around my right hand and pulling, and the sounds of our breath and footsteps as we run up the stairs, and the echo of our three voices talking, for as long as possible.*

Let's ride the train together, the three of us, like we haven't done in a while.

They could sit in those facing seats that brought back so many memories, talking or staring into space, while they watched the boring wilderness scenery.

Fortunately, after all that had happened to them, they wouldn't run out of things to talk about for a long while.

AFTERWORD

After a six-month break, I've finally managed to put out another paperback. In addition to the fact that my writing is naturally slow, I was moving to a new home and taking care of a dog and submitting a manuscript that got rejected and writing the script for a comic and making curry.

Hello, I'm Yukako Kabei. Thank you all so much for buying this book, whether you've been following the series or have just gotten interested now.

It's been almost exactly six months since I moved, but just as I predicted in the previous volume's afterword, I still have piles of cardboard boxes left unpacked — not that fulfilling that prediction is anything to boast about. I wonder when I'll ever be able to break free of this "I'm just living here temporarily" feeling... By the way, my new apartment is right near a horrendously complicated five-way intersection, and there's a lot of uproar. Even in the middle of the night, I often hear the sudden squeal of brakes outside my window, or the sirens of passing ambulances and patrol cars (strangely, there aren't really any accidents at the intersection itself; I think this is because the little Jizo shrine there absorbs all the disaster). It has a whole different feel to it than the old apartment three buildings from the train tracks, and in atmosphere it's like another face of a run-down city, so I actually like it more than you might expect.

This book, *Kieli IV: Long Night Beside a Deep Pool,* takes place a year and a half after *Kieli III: Prisoners Bound for Another Planet*. It's a little different from the previous volumes, which have been set in bone-dry backdrops. This time the story has a high water content, with plenty of steamy — no, that's not right — with plenty of *soggy* scenes. Once again, it's a story about a girl with a complicated personality and a man with a tiresome personality, getting together and being separated, and about a man who's tired of living finding meaning in life again...I think.

There are people with frustrated desires, or who are unaccounted for, or who don't feel like talking about what's happened to them, and there are plenty of things left unresolved; so I plan to continue *Kieli* a little longer. Though I have this anxious feeling that the moment I talk big like that, something will suddenly happen that makes it impossible to continue...

I hope you'll be kind enough to follow my characters' story for a while longer.

And my afterwords are starting to get totally repetitive, so this time I'd like to write something a little different...I'd *like* to, but my mind's all clouded up with this cold I've caught, so I can't think of anything...

Oh! I'll use this space to make a little advertisement. There is now a *Kieli* comic featuring Taue-san's wonderful artwork. It's being serialized in *Dengeki hp* Issue No. 26 (released October 2003) through next year's Issue No. 3. It's a side story that's not included in the novels, so it would make me very happy if you would enjoy it as a complement to these stories.

Now then, I know I say this every volume, but I received support from my editor and many other people in the production and publishing of this book. I hope I'm starting to cause you trouble less frequently…I *hope*…

To Taue-san, who once again graciously took on the job of providing a part of this book, drawing a sixteen-year-old Kieli that exactly matched my image of her, and a Harvey even more gloriously dilapidated than before. Thank you for always responding so amiably when I spam you with e-mails bragging about my dog.

To my family, friends, and acquaintances. Lately it seems as though the people around me are having a much harder time than I am, so I worry. I mean, I'm just bumbling through life reaping what I sow…I pray you'll all have good fortune in 2004.

And, of course, I give my greatest thanks and wishes for good fortune to you who are holding this book in your hands. I hope we get a chance to meet again.

Yukako Kabei